I0690298

DOGS IN DAFT OUTFITS

RAY HOBBS

Wingspan Press

Copyright © 2024 by Ray Hobbs
All rights reserved.

This book is a work of fiction. Names, characters, settings and
incidents are either the product of the author's imagination or used
fictitiously. Any resemblance to actual events, settings or persons,
living or dead, is entirely coincidental.

No part of this book may be reproduced or transmitted in any form or by
any means, electronic or mechanical, including photocopying, recording or
by any information storage and retrieval system, without written permission
from the author, except for the inclusion of brief quotations in reviews.

Published in the United States and the United Kingdom
by WingSpan Press, Livermore, CA

The WingSpan name, logo and colophon are the trademarks
of WingSpan Publishing.

ISBN 978-1-63683-060-5 (pbk.)
ISBN 978-1-63683-952-3 (ebook)

Printed in the United States of America

www.wingspanpress.com

Also by Ray Hobbs and Published by Wingspan Press

An Act of Kindness	2014
Following On	2016
A Year From Now	2017
A Rural Diversion	2019
A Chance Sighting	2020
Roses and Red Herrings	2020
Happy Even After	2020
The Right Direction	2020
An Ideal World	2020
Mischief and Masquerade	2021
Big Ideas	2021
First Appearances	2021
New Directions	2021
A Deserving Case	2021
Unknown Warrior	2021
Daffs in December	2022
A Worthy Scoundrel	2022
Fatal Shock	2022
Last Wicket Pair	2022
Knights Errant	2022
A Baker's Round	2023
Confusion to Zeus	2023
Ways of Gentleness	2023
An Eye to the Future	2023
Stage Direction	2023

Published Elsewhere

Second Wind (Spiderwize)	2011
Lovingly Restored (New Generation P ublishing)	2018

I wish to acknowledge the assistance of my brother Chris, who acted, as ever, as a sounding board for my ideas, and who helped fuel my enthusiasm throughout the writing of this story.

RH

A Yorkshire Dales Town

February 1973

1

The Trivial Round

The large kitchen clock was showing two minutes to seven when the doorbell rang. The joiner had arrived on time, thereby defying a popular stereotype.

Rhona opened the door to a powerfully-built young man with neatly-trimmed, medium-brown hair and friendly blue eyes. At least, they seemed friendly. Time would tell, but it was better to be positive.

'Miss Loveday? I'm Matt Brocklehurst. I've come about the hole in your wall.' As he spoke, his eyes strayed to the jagged aperture that revealed the interior of the adjoining outhouse.

'Thank you for coming, Mr Brocklehurst. Come inside, and then you can see it in all its chaos and devastation.' She stood aside to let him in. 'The previous owner was a keen do-it-yourselfer, but he never finished anything off. Between you and me, I think he realised he was being a shade ambitious with this project, and that's why he sold the cottage.'

He nodded sagely, as if that kind of thing were all too common, and asked, 'What do you want to use the outhouse for?'

'You can see how tiny the kitchen is. I want to extend it into the outhouse. I believe it was a wash kitchen, years ago, but it's time now for it to join the twentieth century, don't you think?'

He opened the door again and examined the stonework at ground level. 'Has the cottage had a damp-proof course added at some stage?'

'I had a chemical treatment done just after I bought it, a year ago. It

1

included the outhouse, and I had the floor of the cottage damp-proofed at the same time.' She closed her eyes tightly, recalling the expense.

'Good. The only problem is the stone-flagged floor. I recommend concrete over a damp-proof membrane. It wouldn't be very expensive.' He went outside again and peered up at the lead flashing, where the roof of the outhouse met the cottage wall. 'That's okay,' he said. 'If you like, I'll give you three estimates: one for putting a lintel over the opening and tidying the masonry round it, and another for that plus damp-proofing the floor, and adding an inner, block wall. The third estimate is for what I've mentioned so far, plus a ceiling, electric light and, if you like, an extension to the ring main.'

It sounded like an awful lot, and Rhona had to admit to herself that she hadn't considered the project in so much detail. She asked, 'Will you have to bring in an electrician to do that?'

'No, I'm a registered Electrical Installation Contractor.'

'And I thought I was just getting a joiner.'

'I'm a jobbing builder, really.' He added, 'I also do the plastering.' As he stood by the open door, a woman walked past with a dog that looked understandably embarrassed in a pink, quilted coat. 'Just look at that,' he said. 'What a way to rob an animal of its dignity as well as overheating it.' Belatedly, he asked, 'Have you got a dog?'

'No. Why?'

He smiled guiltily. 'I say these things and I usually live to regret it.'

'Rest assured that if I had a dog, I wouldn't dress it in pink or any other colour.'

'Just as long as I haven't offended you.' He turned towards the door and hesitated. 'Which part of the north-east are you from?'

'You noticed. I'm from Northumberland. My family live in Amble.'

'Lovely.' He grasped the door handle. 'Okay, I'll send you those estimates or drop them in.'

'Thank you.'

He'd been gone maybe twenty minutes when the phone rang, and it was no surprise when the caller turned out to be Gary.

'Hello, Goldilocks.'

'Well, if it isn't Gary Oldfield, Barnsley's very own Lothario, or so the gossip goes.'

'Who's this fella you're on about?'

'A Spaniard who kept his brain in his boxers.' She was sure boxer shorts hadn't been invented in Cervantes's day, but Gary wouldn't have heard of him, either.

'Oh, right. I expect he'd always know where to find it.'

'You should know. What do you want?'

'I wondered if you'd like me to come over and brighten up your evening. I thought I'd catch you at school, but you'd disappeared.'

'I had a builder coming to give me an estimate. As for tonight, I have a pile of marking, and when I've done that, I'll be ready for bed – alone.'

'Are you avoiding me?' He sounded like a plaintive child.

'No more than usual.'

'But I've got an empty evening ahead of me, Goldilocks.'

'Search your bookshelves, Gary. I'm sure you'll find one you haven't coloured in.'

'You're a hard woman.'

''Bye, Gary.'

'You'll break my heart one of these days.'

''Bye, Gary.' She put the phone down gratefully.

The next day, she ran out of excuses and had to agree to Gary picking her up and taking her for a drink. The remainder of the evening followed the usual formula, which meant that they went to the noisiest pub he knew, where they inevitably found several of his rugby mates; conversation became a series of references to sport and sex, and she felt like an observer at a pagan rite. Eventually, they returned to her house, where she offered to make coffee, and Gary lived up to expectations by suggesting an alternative agenda.

He grunted, giving a final, convulsive lurch before dismounting and subsiding unceremoniously beside her. After less than a minute, he asked, 'What's your family like, Goldilocks?'

She knew he intended his favourite form of address as a compliment, a reference to her reddish-blonde hair, but she'd disliked it from the beginning. Laying on the Geordie accent, she said, 'Me mam's a wicked woman, a bit too handy with the spells and potions, if you know what I mean, and me dad has no control over her at all. Me brother's a bit of a caveman, much like you, except he's quite intelligent.'

'You always put that accent on when you talk about home,' he observed.

'That's right, pet, Ah'm harkin' back to me roots.'

'Anyway,' he said, clearly nettled, 'being a PE specialist doesn't make me an idiot. Don't forget I teach geography an' all.'

'You don't need a brain for geography, just a map and a tin of pencil crayons.' She wondered how they'd strayed on to the subject, and remembered his question about her family. 'Why do you want to know about my folks?'

'I just want to know what to expect. I mean, is your mum like you, or what?'

'Yes, both physically and in character. I inherited my hair colouring from her, as well as these things, although, to be honest, I'm a bit better endowed than she is. Me mam's as flat as a plank.'

'I'm glad you got them, Goldilocks, wherever they came from.' As if to ensure they were talking about the same part of her anatomy, he demonstrated his appreciation with an enthusiastic squeeze, causing her to wince with discomfort.

'Gan canny, you'll make 'em disappear,' she warned, adding cryptically, 'me an' all, if you're not careful.'

'What's your dad like?'

'Fearsome, and deadly with a shotgun.'

'You're not playing fair. I want to know what to expect when I finally meet 'em.'

She sighed like a parent obliged to make the best of a disappointing child, and said, '*If* you ever meet them, you'll find out soon enough what they're like, while they're still getting over the shock of meeting you.'

He lay beside her, no doubt searching her last sentence for hidden nuances, until his thoughts gave way to a more basic need. 'Goldilocks...' he said.

'I know, I can feel it. Just hang on while I talk myself into it again.'

At Fifth Form Assembly the next morning, Rhona sat at the piano, obliged to lend her services because neither the Head of Music nor her assistant was a first-study pianist. She was watching her tutor group, who were supposed to be listening to their Year Head, Carol Merry, talk about the workhouse system. The subject was interesting enough, but Carol wasn't the most engaging of speakers, and Rhona wondered what the Fifth Form were really thinking about. So far, her own thoughts had covered the previous evening and, more particularly, Gary's total unfamiliarity with the concept of foreplay. She consoled herself as far as she could by reflecting that, at least, he didn't start things with a blast on his whistle as he did on the rugby field. She had to be thankful for that.

Carol asked the question, 'Why do you think they did that?'

Now jerked into guilty wakefulness, the Fifth Form exchanged questioning looks, as if each expected his or her neighbour to have been paying attention. They were all disappointed.

'I'll repeat the question. I asked you why the workhouse staff deliberately made life harsh for the paupers. Anybody?' She waited. 'No? It was to dispel any idea that the workhouse was a soft option. It was basically to save expense by keeping the numbers down. Now, do concentrate, all of you. I'm not reading this for the good of my health.'

Rhona's thoughts returned to sex with Gary, not because the memory was at all compelling. Quite the reverse: if nature had intended the process to be so irresistible as to ensure the procreation of the species, why had she found his regular, shuttle-like motion so soporific? She'd been tired, it was true, after a particularly demanding day, but she almost dozed off during his second onslaught. That should have told him something, but he'd been too offended at the time to learn anything from it.

'And now, I want you to turn to hymn number one-hundred-and-twenty, "New every morning is the love".'

Rhona swung round on the piano stool and played the first two phrases for introduction. It was time to think of loftier matters. She had the Lower Sixth for German after assembly, and that was lofty enough. As she played, though, the words of the hymn were a reminder of her current preoccupation.

> *The trivial round, the common task,*
> *Should furnish all we ought to ask.*

They were pious words, but Rhona wanted more from life than it currently offered. Some extra purpose would be welcome.

She arrived home to find a large envelope sticking out of the letterbox. It was headed: *Matthew Brocklehurst, Joiner and Builder*. She took it with her into the kitchen, where she filled the kettle and switched it on before opening it.

As he'd promised, there were three estimates, all of which looked quite reasonable at a first glance. She put them on one side for the time being. More than anything, she needed tea, and when it was brewed, she would be able to consider the estimates properly.

Sitting down with a mug of tea, she looked at them in detail. She'd had two other estimates, both on the high side and involving other contractors, so Mr Brocklehurst looked like being the winner. One question remained, and that was whether she could afford to have everything done at once, or whether it might be better to do it in stages, a possibility Mr Brocklehurst must have foreseen when he offered her three estimates.

After a second mug of tea, she elected to have the whole job done.

It would hopefully be completed by Easter, and if she ran short of money before then, there was always her dad, bless him. He'd just had another book published, so he was bound to be in funds. She dialled Mr Brocklehurst's number and found herself speaking to a recorded voice. She left a message, and was rewarded within thirty minutes or so, when he called her back.

'Miss Loveday, it's Matt Brocklehurst. I was in the shower when you phoned.'

'I'm sorry, I should have thought.'

'No, you weren't to know. How may I help you?'

Interestingly, he was one of the few people in the English-speaking world who said, 'may', rather than 'can', and that made him a very unusual builder. 'I'd like to go ahead with the third option, please. When could you start?'

'Let me see.' There was the sound of pages being turned. 'Ah, I can start the week after next, on the nineteenth.'

It couldn't be better. It was half-term. She would visit her mam and dad at the end of the week. 'The nineteenth? That's fine.'

'That's when we'll lay the concrete, but then we'll have to give it forty-eight hours before building on it.'

'Oh, I'm sure I can work round that, even if I have to leave a key with you while I'm away or at work.'

'Excellent. I'm being nosey, Miss Loveday, but where do you work?'

'I'm a teacher at Banfield High School.'

'That's nice and handy. Right, we'll be with you at about eight o' clock on the nineteenth.'

'How many of you are there?'

'Just me and Bev, my apprentice.'

'Thank you, Mr Brocklehurst. I'll see you then.' As she put the phone down, it seemed odd that a boy should be called 'Bev'. Presumably, it was short for 'Beverley', because she couldn't think of any other possibilities. Still, children were being given the strangest names, the *TV Times* being a common source, and Rhona welcomed almost any departure from the normal routine.

2

A Challenge

Mr Brocklehurst was only a few minutes late. It didn't matter, but he apologised all the same.

'I had to wait for Bev to get her little brother off to school,' he said. 'Her mum's evidently incapable of organising the job herself.'

Rhona looked more closely at the overall-attired apprentice, having recognised her almost immediately. 'Hello, Beverley,' she said in surprise. 'How are you?'

'I'm all right, Miss.'

'*Thank you*,' prompted her employer good-naturedly.

'Fanks, Miss.'

'You're welcome. It's good to see you again. What can I get you both? Tea or coffee?'

'Tea for both of us, please,' said Mr Brocklehurst. 'It's very kind of you.' Turning to Beverley, he said, 'Right, Bev, let's get this floor levelled.'

Rhona set about brewing tea, scarcely able to believe that the shy girl, who'd struggled to read and write, was now apprenticed to a builder.

She put two mugs of tea on the end of the worktop nearest them, and was about to draw their attention to the fact, when she heard the builder ask Beverley if she'd had any breakfast that morning. His question suggested that she might have previous form for going to work without.

'No, I didn't have time.'

'Silly girl. It's more important that getting Troy to school on time. I can't have you fainting away.' Softening the reproach, he said, 'You might fall into the concrete and disappear, and then I'd have to find a new apprentice as well as having to smooth the surface again.'

Rhona said, 'Give me a few minutes, Mr Brocklehurst, and I'll make her something.' She put the frying pan on the hob and opened a pack of bacon. 'I don't suppose you'd be averse to a bacon sandwich, either.'

'It would be hard to resist, Miss Loveday.'

Rhona put two more rashers into the pan.

After a few minutes, she put the bacon sandwiches on two plates and placed them on the kitchen counter with the ketchup and brown sauce beside them. 'Help your selves to sauce,' she said. She didn't use it herself, but kept it for the rare occasions when her brother came visiting. She pushed one of the plates towards Beverley, saying, 'Here y' are, bonny lass. Get that inside you.' Turning to her employer, she asked, 'It's all right her taking five minutes for breakfast, isn't it?'

'Of course it is. It's very kind of you, Miss Loveday. Thank you. What do you say, Bev?'

'Fanks, Miss.'

'It's no trouble, Beverley. It's the most important meal of the day. I should maybe had given you something a bit healthier than that, but I'm clean out of respectable cereals until I go to the supermarket.'

She went about her housework, stopping occasionally as her attention was drawn to the two workers and the relationship between them. The realisation that Beverley had found a sympathetic and encouraging employer made the day special all on its own. She watched them manoeuvre the cement mixer on to the tailboard of the pick-up, and then Beverley operated the hoist that lowered it to the ground.

By and by, Rhona received a discreet request. 'Bev's too shy to ask you herself, but she'd rather like to use your loo.'

'Of course, Mr Brocklehurst. Beverley, it's upstairs and straight ahead.'

'I've got a request as well. Will you please call me "Matt". Mr Brocklehurst was my dad.'

'Only if you call me "Rhona". I've been meaning to ask you if you're related to Brocklehurst Funeral Services.'

'I was, until about ten years ago. My dad died when I was at university, so I had to come home and take care of things. We sold off the funeral side, and I took on the joinery. I'd always enjoyed working there when I was a lad, and it was a seamless transition.' Then, as one thought led to another, he said, 'I had to work hard to rescue it from my ex-wife's clutches, but it was worth it.'

9

'I see.' She didn't, really, but she was sure he wouldn't want to talk about his failed marriage. She asked tactfully, 'What did you do at university?'

'Two-thirds of a BA in English. I loved it, but I enjoy this as well.' His attention seemed suddenly elsewhere.

'Is something wrong, Matt?'

'No, not at all. My eye just fell on the bookshelves through there, and I noticed the Oxford Book of English Verse. Which edition is it?'

'The Quiller-Couch. It's an old copy I found in Durham when I was a student there.'

'It's my favourite edition. I've also connected your name with that of Ivor Loveday. I see you have some of his novels up there as well.'

'He's my dad.'

'Is he really?' Beverley had returned, and he ruffled her hair absent-mindedly. 'I love his characterisation and the way he describes relationships.'

'I'll tell him when I see him. I'm going up there on Friday.'

'Thank you. I'd like him to know that.' He gestured towards the rumbling cement mixer and said, 'We'd better get back to work. It's lucky we came at half-term.'

When Rhona dispensed tea and biscuits that afternoon, Matt said, 'We enjoyed the piano earlier on. Schumann, wasn't it?'

'Yes,' she said, surprised, 'one of the *Noveletten*.'

'Lovely. Do you teach music?'

'No, I don't. One of my teachers gave me an excellent piece of advice when I was thinking of going into teaching, which was never to teach the subject that gave me the most pleasure. He said the kids would be sure to ruin it for me. I teach French and German, and now RoSLA's imposed a third language on me.'

'Who has?'

She laughed. 'I know. It sounds like someone from Central Europe, doesn't it?'

'Either that or a firm that makes cigarette papers.'

'It stands for the Raising of the School Leaving Age. We have to keep them until they're sixteen, now.'

'Of course.'

'I do a lot of playing at school, though. Both the Head of Music and her assistant are grudging pianists. Her first instrument's the clarinet, and her assistant, who's more what you might call academic, plays the violin rather badly, so I get lumbered with various things, concerts and so on, but I don't mind.'

'They're lucky to have you around.' He peered into the outhouse, where Beverley was patiently smoothing the surface of the concrete with a plasterer's float. 'It was kind of you to fix Bev up this morning,' he said. 'Both of us, really, but Bev was the one who needed it. She leads the most chaotic existence, but I try and persuade her to eat before she comes to work. No kidding, I could swing for that mother of hers.'

'Don't worry, Matt. I can always find something for her. I'm just happy to know that she's found the right job and the right boss, one that cares about her.'

'Oh well, it's up to us all to do what we can.' He was about to join Beverley again, when Rhona noticed a cassette recorder among the tools. She asked, 'Do you usually have music playing when you're working?'

'Yes, but we were quite happy listening to your playing, and we didn't want to make a noise and disturb you.'

'Feel free to play music at any time. You won't upset me.'

During the week, Rhona learned more about Matt's unusual background, including his fondness for literature and music, that seemed at odds with the artisan world of the builder.

'It's just possible I inherited my unworldly, romantic nature from my grandmother,' he said, 'although how she produced my dad I'll never know. He was as prosaic as anyone can be, and not remotely romantic.'

Rhona's interest was well alight by now. 'But your granny was, I take it?'

'I think she must have been. She was resident pianist at the New Electric Theatre until the end of the nineteen-twenties, when talking pictures made her redundant.'

'What a rotten shame. Where was that?'

'The picture house? It was in Market Street. It still is, but it became the Picture Palace and then the Savoy Cinema, and now it's derelict.'

'I know the building you mean. It's sort of easy to miss, isn't it?' To Rhona's idealistic way of thinking, it was too sad for words. First, Matt's granny lost her job, and then the cinema stopped functioning, probably becoming a bingo hall or something equally naff, and now the building had fallen into disuse. She asked, 'Who owns it?'

'Akengarth Amateur Operatic and Dramatic Society hold the deeds. They bought it for a song, so to speak, some years ago, with the intention of converting it into a theatre. They currently put their productions on at Banfield High School, as you probably know.'

'I should. They sometimes rope me in to accompany rehearsals, and I've played in the orchestra once or twice. Tell me, though, what happened then? Did they change their minds about converting it?'

'In a word, yes. They got Planning and Change of Use Permission, but then, when they saw the likely cost of the conversion, they rather lost heart.'

'Why-yer-bugger, man,' she said slowly and thoughtfully. It seemed all wrong.

'What?'

She smiled indulgently. 'It's something my grandad says when he hears something similar to what you've just told me.'

'It was a lot of money to find, Rhona.' It was obviously a source of sadness for him, too.

'I'm not disputing that, Matt, but it's still a bloody shame.'

'I can't help noticing, if you don't mind my mentioning it, that your accent has suddenly become more pronounced.'

'It's not surprising. I'm thinkin' of somethin' my dad told me years ago, something that happened when he lived in Yorkshire, before he moved to Tynemouth and became civilised.'

'I'll let that one go,' said Matt, smiling gamely. 'What was this thing that happened?'

'The local Congregationalists needed a new chapel because the old one was fallin' to bits. My dad's family weren't Congregationalists, you understand. His dad was manager of the labour exchange, so they were posh enough to be Church of England. Anyway, the members set about raising the money to rebuild their chapel. It took a good few years, but they succeeded in the end, and my dad says the building's still standing, except it'll be called something different now. Didn't they change their name last year?'

'The United Reformed Church,' he confirmed, completely bemused by her enthusiasm. 'Are you actually suggesting that Akengarth Amateurs could do the same?'

'Why not? If a crowd of people in Bradford can raise the money to rebuild a chapel, why can't Akengarth Amateurs rebuild a theatre? The only difference, as I see it, is that the Amateurs can have a drink at the end of the day without gettin' out the sackcloth and ashes the next morning, and if they roll their sleeves up and get on with the job instead of cavin' in, it seems to me they'll be ready for a drink now and again.'

'I suppose you could put the suggestion to them. Are you a member?'

'Aye, I pay me subs, so I've a right to be heard.'

That evening, Rhona received a phone call from Gary.

'All right, Goldilocks?'

'Fine, Baby Bear. How about you?'

He ignored her riposte and said, 'Are you busy tonight?'

'Very. I'm surrounded by wet concrete.'

'Can't you get out?'

'No, it's already set round me feet. I cannot move.'

'I meant, can't you come out to play?'

'No, I'm busy.'

'So you're not free.'

'Not even going cheap,' she confirmed, wondering if she really had to explain to him the meaning of 'busy'.

'I've got matches on Saturday and Sunday.'

'I'm going up home for the weekend, anyway.'

There was a pause while he thought. Then, he asked, 'What about next week?'

'Just a word of caution, Gary. Next week, nature is poised to say "no" to what you usually have in mind.'

'What?'

'Do I have to spell it out for you?'

'Oh, that. Can't you—'

'No.'

Audibly disgruntled, he said, 'In that case, I'll see you the week after next.'

She'd held her patience long enough. Suddenly bridling, she said, 'You may well see me then. As we work in the same school, I'm afraid it's inevitable, but as for spending time with me, forget it.'

'What?'

'You've taken me for granted once too often, Gary. We're finished.' She replaced the receiver and breathed an angry sigh. She really needed something more rewarding in her life, and she wondered if the derelict cinema might provide the answer.

3

PUTTING THE CASE

The journey to Amble was easy enough, lightened further by the stop in Newcastle to see her granny and grandad, and that was no hardship. She loved to see them, and they were just as pleased to see her. Also, the reunion with her parents at the end of the journey made it more than worthwhile.

She'd last been home at Christmas, but her mother hugged her as if she'd not seen her for months on end. Rhona had possibly been a little less than generous in her description of her to Gary, because, in spite of her fifty-two years, she still had a trim figure, and she was still very attractive.

'Come and see who's here, Ivor,' her mother called, and her father appeared in the doorway, as delighted as her mother, who said excitedly, 'Our Steve called in this morning. You just missed him.'

'Yes, that was a shame. What's he doing, now?'

'He's still working for that removals firm,' said her mother, as if it were an achievement, which, in a sense, it was. Rhona's brother was a bird of passage where employment was concerned.

'He's talking about forming something he calls a band,' said her father, whose appreciation of popular music had given up the struggle partway through the nineteen-fifties.

'But he can't play anything.'

'He says that's no problem. He'll buy a guitar and teach himself to play it.' He raised his eyebrows at the thought.

'Don't be unkind,' said his wife. 'He has to find things out the hard way. That's how Steve learns.' Reflecting soberly, she said, 'There's not a lot he can do with the one thing he's really good at.'

It was possibly true. Steve was a gifted artist, but opportunities were limited.

When they were settled, Rhona's mother asked, quite predictably,

'How's your love life, hinny? Are you still seein' that lad that plays rugby? We haven't had a chance to meet him yet.'

'You're not going to, either, Mam. It's all over.'

'Already?' When something surprised Rhona's mother, everyone remotely within earshot had to know about it. 'They don't last two minutes with you. What went wrong this time?'

'It was tedious. He was only ever interested in one thing, and I like to think I've more to offer than that.'

'I hope you haven't been misbehaving,' said her father with genuine, old-fashioned concern.

'You have to realise your dad never misbehaved, Rhona,' said her mother seriously. 'He was like a monk, as pure as the driven snow. Nothing like that ever crossed his mind, an' take no notice of my nose growing longer and longer as I speak.'

'Oh, good heavens,' said Rhona's father. 'Is nothing sacred?' In spite of his protestation, it was evident that he wasn't as upset as he made out.

Rhona laughed. 'I'm nearly twenty-six, dad, and I know what I'm doing.'

'Well, be careful.'

'Don't worry, Dad. As of last week, there's no man in my life. Let me change the subject, though, to one that you'll find much more welcome. I was talking with somebody yesterday, who's read some of your books and enjoyed them. He says he's particularly impressed with the way you model your characters.'

'It's very kind of him to say so. Are you likely to see him again?'

'Why aye, he's doin' some work for me on the cottage.'

Using his walking stick to lever himself up, he said, 'I'd a new one published two weeks ago. I'll give you a copy and I'll sign one for your friend.' He disappeared into his den and re-emerged with two copies of the book. 'What's his name?' He opened a copy and took out his fountain pen.

'Matt.'

'Is that "Matthew"?'

'Yes, but he prefers the abbreviated form. He's creating my new kitchen area. That's how I know him, although one of my ex-pupils works for him, as well.' A pleasing picture returned to her of Beverley in overalls, completely absorbed in her work.

'There,' said her father, blotting his signature.

'Thanks, Dad.' She took the two copies, opening one to read the outline on the flyleaf. 'This one's set in the First World War,' she remarked.

'I had to do a lot of research,' he said.

'Yes, because you just missed that war, didn't you?'

His look was sufficient reaction to her jibe.

Her mother asked, 'What else have you been up to?'

'I've been brushing up my Spanish so that we can give the kids something new, exciting and useful to do, now that they have to stay another year at school.'

'It beats me why they have to do that.' Her mother was always fazed by new developments in education. 'If they're not very bright and they wouldn't normally stay on to sixteen or eighteen, why don't they let them leave and get a job?'

'I reckon it's because there aren't all that many jobs for them, and keeping them on at school for another year is going to make a big difference to the unemployment figures, Mam.'

She sighed and said, 'Some things never change.'

After dinner, or 'tea', as her mother still called it, Rhona helped with the washing-up. It was unofficially the time for 'women's talk', and the prime topic, as far as Rhona's mother was concerned, was the unexpected ending of her daughter's relationship.

She placed the last of the dishes on the drainer and asked quietly, 'Was it just… you know… what you said?'

'No, but that was a part of it. He's as superficial as they come, it's impossible to have an intelligent conversation with him, and his idea of a night out was to take me for a drink with his marrers and then go back to my place to indulge in his favourite pastime, and he wasn't very good at that.'

Her mother leaned towards her and said even more quietly, 'Be careful what you say about that when your dad's around. He's always been protective of you, a bit old-fashioned, like.'

'I've noticed.' Reverting to the main subject, she said, 'Gary was getting rather too keen, as well. He was expecting to meet you and me dad and Steve. He asked me if I was like you.'

'What did you tell him?'

'I said we were very similar. I told him I'd inherited your strawberry blonde hair.'

'I cannot think you got it anywhere else,' agreed her mother, 'unlike your bust. I used to tell people that I'd put my share on one side for you, in case you had the same problem.' With a nod in the direction of Rhona's curves, she said, 'As things turned out, I needn't have worried, because you collared the family allocation.'

They put the dishes and cutlery away and joined Rhona's father in the sitting room.

As they sat down, he asked, 'Have you two set the world to rights?'

'We've done our best,' Rhona's mother told him.

'I've always said women's talk is best kept private.'

'You're probably right at that,' said Rhona.

'Anyway,' he said, 'apart from sending your boyfriend on his way, what else have you been up to?'

'It's funny you should ask that question. There's an old cinema in Akengarth that's fallen into disuse, and I want to persuade the local amateur dramatic society to rebuild it and convert it into a theatre.'

Back in Akengarth, she found that Matt and Beverley had been hard at work in her absence. The inner skin of lightweight blocks was complete, and the ceiling joists were in place.

'Hello, Rhona,' said Matt. 'Did you have a good trip?'

'Lovely, thanks.'

'Be careful what you touch. It's mucky in here.'

Conscious that she was holding him up, she came to the point and said, 'I've spoken to the chairman of Akengarth Amateurs, and he's not wildly hopeful. In fact, he was quite dismissive until he realised how determined I was. I'm going to speak to the committee on Thursday week, and unless they scupper the idea out of hand, I'll get a chance to speak to the multitude.'

' "Scupper" is an interesting word,' he observed.

'It always happens when I've been with me dad. I come back speaking fluent Long John Silver.' As the thought occurred to her, she said, 'He walks with a stick an' all, 'cause he was wounded in the war, but I don't think he's keen on parrots. At least, if he is, he's never let on.' Talking about her father jogged her memory, and she handed Matt a copy of the book. 'It's his latest,' she explained. 'He signed it for you.'

'How very kind.' He read the signature inside and asked, 'Will you give me his address so that I can thank him properly?'

'Of course I will.' She found a notepad and a pencil. 'This could be the start of a beautiful pen-friendship,' she said, writing her father's name and address for him.

With the return to school came the task of reminding Gary that their relationship was still over, that her rejection of him during half-term hadn't been a careless slip of the tongue, and that she had no intention of changing her mind. He tried persistent cajolery, and when that had no effect, being a man of little imagination, he demanded feedback.

'Would you say I was boring, Goldilocks?'

'Not in front of witnesses.'

'You wouldn't call me tight-fisted, would you? I mean, I gave you a good time, didn't I?'

'You always stood your round, I have to admit.'

'And you can't fault me for the other thing.'

Unimpressed though she'd been, Rhona knew better than to criticise a man's efforts in the bedroom, so she prevaricated. 'There's more to a relationship than that, Gary.'

'In that case, where did I go wrong?'

Rhona looked up at the staffroom clock. It was almost five o' clock and time to go to the supermarket so that she could go home and start cooking. She decided to be as honest as she could be without being unnecessarily hurtful. 'You went wrong,' she said, 'by treating it as if it were all about sex, by assuming that I shared your obsession, by expecting me to drop everything – no pun intended – when you called me, and by showing absolutely no imagination in choosing places to go and things to do. There's more, but I'll spare your blushes. Does that help?'

'So there's no possibility of another chance, then?'

'Right in one, Gary. The show's over.'

'Oh well,' he said, getting to his feet, 'at least you'd no complaints about the other.' His continued disappointment was evident, despite his casual manner.

'Goodbye, Gary.'

The show really was over, but another was about to begin; at least, preparation was imminent. The Music and Drama departments had emerged from their meeting earlier that day with the decision that the production that November would be *Oklahoma!* Although she hadn't been consulted, Rhona would be required once again to accompany rehearsals and impersonate the instruments missing from the pit orchestra. Life was taking on a familiar look once again, the trivial round and the common task. She was looking forward to her meeting with the Akengarth Amateurs' Committee, simply because it would be different.

A phone call, two days later, from David Warburton, Chairman of Akengarth Amateurs, advised her of a change in the arrangements.

'I've spoken to the other committee members,' he said, 'and there's some interest, but they feel that they'd like to hear what the members have to say. Would you be prepared to put your ideas before them next Thursday at an extraordinary general meeting? We'll hold it at the school, as usual.'

'Yes, I'd be only too pleased.' Large gatherings posed no threat to Rhona; in fact, she welcomed the opportunity, as it made more sense than addressing two meetings. Consequently, when the time came, she was confident and well-prepared.

She told them about the Congregational church and its members' fund-raising activities. 'It was a long time ago,' she said, 'and there are different ways of raising funds nowadays, but nothing else has changed.'

One of the members said, 'The costs aren't the same.'

'Neither are incomes. I shudder to think what I'd be earning in the nineteen-twenties.'

'What about tradesmen, then?' It was the same member. 'They don't come cheap.'

'No, they don't,' she agreed, but they often come with a wealth of goodwill.' Raising her voice, she asked, 'Is there an electrician in the house?'

A hand went up, and Rhona acknowledged its owner. 'Have we got a plumber?'

Another hand responded.

'I think there's probably a lot of expertise and enthusiasm among the membership,' she said.

Another member asked, 'What about running costs? Have you thought about that?'

'How many societies are there in the dale?' Counting on her fingers, she said, 'As well as us, there's the Light Opera, the Catholic Amateurs, the Baptist Amateurs, the Gilbert and Sullivan Society, the Male Voice Choir, the Thespians, and Wharfedale Players. If they all use the theatre, and I'm sure they would, that would defray expenses, wouldn't it? Also, if the theatre had a bar, it could be a regular meeting place for amateurs of all persuasions, as well as a lucrative side line.'

Yet another member asked, 'What sort of activities do you have in mind for fund raising?'

'I'm sure we're open to suggestions. There are raffles and events of various kinds. There could possibly be a regular monthly draw... I've no doubt you can think of many more.'

The member who'd brought up the subject of tradesmen asked, 'And where will you be while all this is going on, Miss Loveday?'

Rhona recognised the member as the father of one of her sixth form pupils. 'It's Mr Whitley, isn't it? I'll be with you, helping to raise the sum we need. I'm a member of this society just as you are, and this means a great deal to me.'

Eventually, the questions dried up, and the Chairman signalled that it was time to ask for a vote. 'You know, Rhona,' he said quietly, 'you've impressed me tonight. You should go into politics.'

'What a horrifying prospect.' She took her seat and tried not to think about it.

'Now,' said David Warburton, 'first of all, can we have a motion?'

A member raised her hand and said, 'I move that we act on Rhona's suggestion and refurbish the theatre.'

'The motion was put down by Ella Thorpe,' said Mr Warburton for the Secretary's benefit. 'Do we have a seconder?'

'Seconded,' replied another member, identifying himself. 'Brian Goodman.'

'Right,' said the Chairman, 'we have a proposal that we convert the cinema into a theatre, it's been seconded, and now we must take a vote. All those in favour of the motion, please raise your hands.' He looked around the hall. 'Straight up,' he said, 'so that we can count you.'

The counting was carried out by three members of the committee, who agreed on the total.

'All those against.' He waited, but no one voted against the motion. 'In that case, Rhona,' he said, 'it looks as if you've got yourself a job.'

4

PHILISTINES

Rhona thought it only right to report back to Matt after the meeting, firstly, because she knew he was interested to hear about her progress, and secondly, because she hoped to enlist his numerous skills for the project at a later date. She caught him when he was taking a break from the plastering.

'Something that's quite remarkable about committees,' she told him, 'is their facility for reproducing their own kind. In the beginning was the Committee, and it begat the Theatre Committee, and the Theatre Committee begat the Planning Committee, and the Planning Committee is in the process of begetting yet more committees. Before long, we'll need a family tree to keep us in order and avoid demarcation disputes.'

'But you got what you wanted,' he reminded her. 'I'm very impressed, considering I thought the theatre was a dead duck.'

'It has to happen, Matt. It's written in the stars. Art and communication are vitally important if we're to maintain a civilised society. I said as much at our last full staff meeting, and there was some agreement.'

'*Some* agreement?'

'I'll admit that the Maths, Physics, Chemistry, Biology, Geography, Business Studies, PE, Home Economics, Technical Drawing, Woodwork and Metalwork were less than enthusiastic, but they can't be expected to subscribe to grown-up thinking.'

Matt laughed good-naturedly. 'I do admire someone who doesn't know when she's beaten,' he said.

'Who's beaten? With English, Needlework, History, Art, Music and Drama as our allies, we'll be a thorn in the side of philistinism for as long as it takes to civilise the world.'

Matt picked up an envelope and took a poster from it. 'This came this morning,' he said. 'It's destined for my window, but I thought you'd like to see it. I know you're a devotee of Schumann.'

'Yes, I am, but how did you know?'

'Nothing obvious, but you played one of the *Noveletten* last week, quite beautifully, I have to say, and if that weren't enough, you're certainly at one with him on the subject of philistinism.'

Having conceded that the evidence had been somewhat obvious, Rhona studied the poster, which advertised an orchestral concert the following month at Metcalfe Hall by the National Sinfonia. 'Damien Franklin,' she read.

'Joint-First Prizewinner in the Leningrad Piano Competition.'

'I remember. He's playing Schumann's *Konzertstück in G*.' She thought about it a moment longer and said, 'Much as I love the Concerto, it's good to trot out something different once in a while. Will you be going to this concert?'

'If I can find someone to go with. I always think these things are better shared.'

Rhona agreed with him. Her restrictive and unstimulating relationship with Gary had starved her of culture, to the extent that she was experiencing what she suspected were withdrawal symptoms. 'If you want company,' she offered, 'I'll go with you.' She was confident that Matt was unlikely to read anything into her offer other than her wish to share the enjoyment of the music.

'Will you really? That would be excellent.'

'I'll get the tickets. I'm going to Shuttleworth's this afternoon for some music, and they'll have them on sale, I expect. They usually do.'

'That's good of you. I'm a little tight for time, as it happens.'

'In that case, I'd better leave you to get on with your work,' she said. 'By the way, the tickets are on me as a "thank you" for being so obliging.'

'I appreciate that. Thank you.'

'That's all right. You can get the chips on the way home.' His blank expression prompted her to explain, 'It's something my dad says when he buys the last round of drinks. It doesn't really mean anything.'

He blinked several times and asked, 'Does that mean we won't have chips on the way home?'

Realising she was dealing with an alert mind, she said, 'That's up to you, Matt. You're paying. Anyway, I'll leave you to get on.'

'Give your jeans a dusting-off,' he said.

'Oh heck.' She realised they'd come into contact with plaster. 'I'll let you know when I've got the tickets.'

'That's fifty-five new pence, Miss Loveday.' The assistant slipped the music into a paper bag bearing Shuttleworth's name and logo, a letter 'S' superimposed on a treble clef. 'Prices are going up all the time.' Decimalisation was two years old, but people were still talking about 'new' pence, possibly out of nostalgia for the currency they'd known for so long.

'In that case, Christine, I'll pay for it now while it's still only fifty-five pence.' She handed the exact money to the bemused girl, an ex-pupil, who was no doubt wondering whether to assure her former teacher that prices were not escalating quite as quickly as that, or simply to leave her in her regrettable ignorance. 'Oh, I've just remembered,' said Rhona. 'Are you selling tickets for the National Sinfonia concert at Metcalfe Hall? I think it's on the ninth of March.'

'Yes, you like that kind of thing, don't you? I remember now.'

'That's why I'm here, Christine.' She thought that might have been obvious.

'You're not the only one who does, because they're going ever so quickly.' Christine took out a plan of the auditorium and consulted it. 'All the seats in the stalls have gone,' she reported. 'How many tickets do you want?'

'Just two.'

'There's two here,' she said, pointing to a couple of adjacent squares at the front of the dress circle.

'Fine, I'll take those two, please.'

'Right, Miss Loveday.' Christine located the appropriate tickets and marked an 'x' with her ballpoint in each square. 'They're forty-five new pence each, so that's ninety new pence, please. I hope you enjoy it, but I can't see the point, myself.'

'In that case, why do you work in a music shop?' It seemed a fair question.

'It's a job, isn't it?'

'There's no denying that. Thank you, Christine.' Rhona paid for the tickets. 'Thanks for your help. Have a good weekend when you get one.' She often felt sorry for weekend workers such as shop assistants. As she saw it, it was no kind of life, even for someone who couldn't see the point in orchestral concerts.

'Thanks, Miss Loveday. You too.'

Rhona left the shop and stepped out into the High Street, retreating immediately into Shuttleworth's entrance when she saw Gary. He appeared not to have seen her, and she pretended to study a stack of records while he walked past the shop, oblivious to her presence. Unfortunately, it turned out to be a frying pan and fire manoeuvre, because when she stepped out again, she did so into the path of one of her least favourite parents. In fact, in that split second, Rhona promoted her into uncontested first place. 'Hello, Mrs Caukwell.'

'Oh, Miss Loveday, I'm glad I've met you. I hear the school's putting another musical on.' Her tone was at odds with her greeting, and she made the observation in a way that seemed to suggest that she blamed Rhona for the whole business.

'Doesn't news travel fast?'

'What is it this time?'

'What's what?'

'What musical have they decided on?'

'*Oklahoma!* That's with an exclamation mark.' Rhona wished she would go away and blight someone else's Saturday afternoon. She must surely have things to do. Incantations over bubbling cauldrons didn't mutter themselves. She might even have some innocent shopping to do, in which case Rhona pitied the hapless shop assistants.

'A waste of time, I call it. I suppose you're in favour of it.'

'I have to be. I help to make it happen.' Rhona actually had reservations about the choice of musical on this occasion, but that was a purely a matter of personal taste. She wasn't a devotee of Rogers and Hammerstein, but she was strongly in favour of the annual production.

'I think you'd do the kids more good if you taught them spelling and grammar instead of having them dress up and prance around, playin' silly beggars on stage.'

'Oh, but I do, in French, German, and now Spanish.'

With a look that was capable of souring milk at a hundred paces, the disapproving parent said firmly, 'I mean in English.'

'That's the preserve of the English Department,' Rhona told her, 'and we don't want a demarcation dispute, do we?'

'No, we don't,' said Mrs Caukwell, becoming increasingly nasal in her condemnation. 'It never takes a right lot to bring schoolteachers out on strike.'

'Wildcats, all of us,' agreed Rhona.

Reverting to her original grievance, Mrs Caukwell said, 'I don't know what's to be done about this annual play nonsense. The Headmaster's evidently given it his blessing, so there's nothing to be gained by complaining to him.'

'You need to go higher than the Headmaster,' said Rhona, scenting fun for the first time.

'The Chairman of the Governors?'

'No, higher than him.'

'The Chief Education Officer?' Mrs Caukwell's excitement increased with each possibility.

No, higher still. Think big.'

'Our Member of Parliament?'

'No,' said Rhona dismissively, 'she's a mere pawn in the political process. Go higher.'

'The Education Secretary?'

Rhona winced. 'Margaret Thatcher would no doubt agree with you, but I think you should aim higher still.'

'Not the Prime Minister?' Mrs Caukwell was almost bursting with enthusiasm, a rare occurrence.

Rhona nodded confidently. 'Address your letter to the Right Honourable Edward Heath, MP, and ask him if he agrees with you that musical and theatrical performances are a waste of time.'

'Do you think it'll get something done?'

'Not for one minute, but you'll feel better for getting it off your chest, and you might give him a chuckle as well.' Rhona could visualise the grinning Prime Minister's shoulders heaving the way they did in lighter moments.

Enthusiasm gave way to a snort of derision. 'I might have known I couldn't have a sensible conversation with you. You were just the same when our Paul were doin' German.'

'Some things never change, Mrs Caukwell. Have a good weekend.' Rhona walked on, thankful that Paul Caukwell had given up German at the end of the third year. Being in a public place, she tried not to laugh as she remembered hearing how he'd told his parents he'd been learning about the genital case. Maybe 'genitive' and 'genital' really did mean the same to him, but Mrs Caukwell hadn't been impressed.

She headed back towards the carpark, where a kind of string quartet had gathered. It was only a 'kind' because it included a double bass instead of a cello. In any case, it was playing Mozart's Serenade for Strings, *Eine Kleine Nachtmusik*, which was orchestral when everyone had their own, but the buskers were making a cheerful sound, and a small audience had gathered to listen to them. Some of them were dropping coins into the double bass case provided somewhat optimistically for the purpose, and Rhona added her offering. It pleased her that people were performing music in the open air, as they'd done for centuries, only taking a break when forced to do so by a puritanical dictatorship that had taken philistinism to its furthest extreme.

The musicians came to the end of the first movement, and there was a flurry of applause. Some people possibly thought the entertainment was over, or maybe they had more pressing matters to attend to, because they began to drift away.

As the second movement, the *Romanza*, began, a young woman said quite audibly, 'I wish they'd play summat we know, for a change.'

Maybe that was the answer to the decline in popularity of classical music. People wanted what they knew. One day, someone might start up a radio station specialising in well-known repertoire, so that no one ever felt threatened by the unfamiliar. It would always have an important part to play, like the annual school production or the theatre conversion, just as long as the likes of Mrs Caukwell never gained the upper hand.

5

A Word of Caution

With or without funding, there was early enthusiasm for the theatre conversion, to the extent that the Planning Committee was faced with a squad of eager housewives all keen to clean up the interior before any work could begin. It was fortunate that one of the members present was Terry Cooper, the plumber who'd identified himself at the EGM.

'You're putting the cart before the horse,' he told them. 'The first thing we need is a project manager.'

One of the mop-and-bucket party asked, 'What's one o' them when he's at home?'

'Somebody who knows the building trade, who can organise the job step by step, so that things get done in the right order. Otherwise, you'll find yourselves doing jobs and then undoing them because you've forgotten something. With the right project manager, that doesn't happen.'

The same woman asked, 'An' where are we goin' to find this clever fella?'

'I don't know,' admitted Terry. 'The ones I know would be too busy to take on something like this, and they certainly wouldn't be prepared to do it buckshee.'

There was a general consultation, which seemed unlikely to yield a positive result, and Rhona was about to call the meeting to order, when someone said in a loud voice, 'How about Dennis Fisher?'

'Someone else said, ' "Lovey" Fisher?'

'Yes, he's in the building trade.'

Terry said, 'He's an architect, really.'

Rhona tapped the desk with her pen and asked, 'Will someone please tell me about this Dennis Fisher?'

'He produced some shows for us,' said Terry. 'He did *The Sound of Music* and *South Pacific*.' He smiled broadly at the memory.

Rhona asked, 'What's the joke, Terry?'

'It's just that he always gets carried away with whatever show he's working on. When we were rehearsing *The Sound of Music*, he spoke all the time like a German *Oberleutnant*, or whatever they're called, and then, when we did *South Pacific*, he came over all American. Otherwise, he calls everybody "darlings", "loves" and "sweeties". He's as camp as a pink Primus.'

'Camp or not, would it be a good idea to approach him about managing this project?'

Terry became serious again. 'He could do the job,' he said, 'and it won't cost you anything to ask him.'

The following morning, Rhona gave an individual task to each member of 5C, who were to role-play a shopping experience in Spain.

'Martina, what's your task?'

'I'm the assistant in a clothes shop, Miss.'

'Good. Are you clued up?'

'I think so, Miss.'

'Right. Who's the first customer? Christine? Show us how it's done, Christine.'

The nervous shopper walked up to the imaginary counter.

Martina asked, '*Buenos dias. ¿Puedo ayudaria, Señora?*'

'Excellent, Martina. Okay, Christine.'

'Right, Miss. *¿Dónde puedo probarme esto?*'

Rhona asked, 'Did everyone follow that? Michael, what did they say?'

'Martina asked what Christine wanted, Miss, and Christine asked her where she could try something on.'

'Good.' Responding to a snigger from one of the usual suspects, she said, 'If you ever visit Spain, Lee, you'll spend your whole holiday at the airport, trying to find someone who speaks English. That's before the Spanish police realise what a nuisance you are and lock you up.'

Turning back to the two girls, she said, 'Okay, Martina, where can she try it on?'

'She can try it on with me anywhere, Miss.'

'Thank you, Lee. Don't call us, we'll call you, but don't hold your breath.'

Undeterred, Martina said, '*El vestuario está aqui a la derecha, Señora.*'

'Excellent,' said Rhona. 'James, what did she say?'

'The waiting room's on the right, Miss.'

'Good lad.'

5C went on to enact several more transactions before the class buffoon halted the proceedings once more.

'Miss?' Unusually, Lee's hand was in the air. He didn't usually bother with that courtesy.

'Yes, Lee?' She hoped it was going to be a sensible question, although there was little chance of that.

'How do you say, "Where can I buy a packet of three?" ' His question prompted sneering laughter from those closest to him.

'You certainly wouldn't find them in a clothes shop. Even you should know that, and if you're trying to embarrass me, you have a short memory, because you've tried it several times and failed each time.'

'It's a serious question, Miss.' A snigger in the direction of one of his cronies contradicted that assertion, not that Rhona was at all surprised.

'Do you really mean to say you'd fly to Spain and leave it until possibly the last minute to buy the necessary equipment?'

'Well,' he said, still sniggering, 'supposing I did?'

'Your best bet, Lee, is to get one of the bigger boys to buy you some in England, the way you usually do, and then take them with you, but don't carry them in your suitcase, whatever you do.'

'Why not, Miss?'

'Because, if I know your mam, she'll smack you from one end of Benidorm to the other when she finds them.' Her advice earned the laughter of everyone except Lee. 'What's your next lesson, Lee?'

With a curled lip, he answered, 'Games, Miss.'

'Rugby, eh?'

'Yes, Miss.'

She nodded. He and Gary would have a meeting of minds. Meanwhile, Rhona's next class was 2A for German. She waited until they were settled, and then said, 'Look carefully at the picture, and then somebody tell me what it says underneath.' She looked at the show of hands and said, 'Andrew.'

'*Den Hund der Gärtner jägt*, Miss.'

'Good. Remember that "*der*" is pronounced "dare". What does it mean?'

'The dog is chasing the gardener, Miss.'

The rest of the class erupted into laughter, and Rhona smiled at the image his interpretation created. 'Everyone, look at the picture again, and then someone else can have a go,' she suggested. 'Yes, Tamara?'

'The gardener's chasing the dog, Miss.'

'That's right. Now, even allowing for topsy-turvy German sentence construction, how can that sentence possibly tell us that?' Not surprisingly, not one hand went up. 'All right, I'll tell you. First of all, though, which is the object of the sentence? The dog or the gardener? Andrew, this is your chance to redeem yourself.'

'The dog, Miss.'

'Correct, but what gender is "the dog"?'

'I can't see, Miss. Its hind leg's in the way.'

Rhona sighed impatiently and asked, 'What gender is "*Hund*"?'

'*Neuter*, Miss.'

'That's right. Well done, Andrew. You'd normally expect it to say, "*Das Hund*", wouldn't you?' There was general agreement, so she said, 'But, you see, when a masculine or a *neuter* noun is the object, the article, the "the" word, becomes *den*. Right, so masculine and *neuter* object nouns take on *den* instead of *der* or *das*, but feminine object nouns are not affected.' Seeing a hand raised, she asked, 'Yes, Melanie?'

'Why aren't they, Miss?'

'It's the usual story, Melanie. As ever, we girls just get left out in the cold.'

Her explanation triggered an amused reaction from both sexes, and when the noise died down, she said, 'Seriously, no one knows why the feminine noun isn't affected. It's just the way the – here's a new word for you – *accusative* case works in German.' She wrote it on the board. 'Now, we'll work a few exercises, and then I'll set you some for homework.'

A meeting had been called for those members of staff who had been co-opted to take part in the school trip to Brittany at Easter. Being a member of the Modern Languages Department, Rhona had no choice, as it was one of her contractual duties.

She found Nigel Ellis, the head of department, in his classroom. So far, no one else had shown up.

'Ah, Rhona,' he said, 'keen as ever.' For his part, he looked as silly as ever, with his straggly beard and clean-shaven upper lip. Those who'd seen *Moby Dick* usually referred to him as 'Captain Ahab'.

'No.'

'No?'

'No,' she confirmed. Clearly, someone had to move the conversation forward, so she explained. 'I indulge in various activities by choice. I play the piano because it gives me a great deal of enjoyment, I enjoy cooking and baking, and I drink red wine because I like it. On the other hand, I accompany children on trips abroad because I have to. It's as simple as that.'

He seemed genuinely surprised. 'But don't you feel that you're making a difference to their lives?'

'By being on hand to keep them from fighting and fornicating in foreign parts, yes, but I'd rather do something positive.'

Nigel was saved further argument, when two more of his department arrived, followed by a further two keen helpers from Maths and History. Rhona greeted them, feeling particularly sorry for Sue Womersley, who was new to the department and unaware, as yet, that she was a lamb poised to enter the abattoir.

'Good afternoon, everyone,' said Nigel in his self-important way. 'This meeting is simply to keep you all informed, so it shouldn't take long. As you know, the party will be divided into two, one half being accommodated in Dinard, and the other in Paramé. This is purely because of numbers, but it will be an opportunity to separate any warring factions.'

Rhona was unconvinced. In the testosterone-enriched world of adolescent boyhood, there would always be the risk of friction, at the very least.

Nigel continued. 'I've made a list of the visits we'll be making during the course of the week. The first will be an afternoon in St Malo, an ancient town with many attractions. We shall also visit Mont St Michel, famous for its *crêpes* and for being at the mercy of the tide; we shall see Carnac, the site of a civilisation that predates Stonehenge, and finally, we shall take a boat trip to the Isle de Cezembre, which was the last stronghold of the Nazis in Europe. There will naturally be opportunities for our party to enjoy, also, the beaches of Dinard and Paramé.' He looked up and asked, 'Are there any questions so far?'

'Yes.' Janice Watts from the Maths department raised her hand quite unnecessarily.

'Yes, Miss Watts?'

'If the children are going to be allowed on the beaches, I hope someone will insist on appropriate behaviour. Nowadays, it's quite common to see girls walking along the streets of tourist resorts in their swimming costumes. That's when they're not kissing, semi-clad, on the beach.'

'Perhaps you would like to brief them about that, Miss Watts.'

'Very well. I think it's highly necessary.'

'I agree with you. Correct behaviour in bathing apparel will be mandatory.'

Rhona bit her lip to keep herself from laughing. The chaste Miss Watts talking dirty was one thing, but only Nigel would use words like 'bathing apparel' and 'mandatory'.

Ronald Harwood was next to speak. 'Smoking,' he said. 'What are the rules about buying cigarettes?'

'They'll be allowed to buy duty-free cigarettes for their parents and other adult relations, but smoking on the trip will not be tolerated, and any packets of cigarettes we find with a broken seal will be confiscated.'

There were no dissenting voices, so John Fieldman raised his hand. 'I've beed wodering about school udiforb,' he said. It was unfortunate that a member of the Modern Languages Department should suffer so frequently from colds.

'Yes,' said Nigel, 'I've been thinking about that, too. I think we should insist on it so that we can keep an eye on them at all times.' Again, no one dissented, so Nigel closed the meeting.

As they walked along the corridor, Sue Womersley asked Rhona, 'Why were you smiling when John spoke? The poor man has alopecia, and with no hairs in his nostrils, he's bound to catch colds more frequently than the rest of us.'

'He has my sympathy, Sue, but when he calls me "Rhoda", it always reminds me of the limerick.'

'Which one?' Sue was very naïve.

'The one about the man-hating harlot called Rhoda. It's not fit for your innocent ears, Sue,' she assured her.

'Oh dear.' Changing the subject, she said, 'I'm really looking forward to the trip. I've never been to that part of France.'

Rhona refrained from comment. It was possible to be too cynical.

6

MARCH

ECSTASY AND CHIPS

Matt helped Rhona out of her coat, provoking an expression of surprise.

'Thank you, Matt. That's very kind of you.'

'It's one of life's normal courtesies,' he said, handing the coat to her.

'Not in the circles I frequent.' She draped it over the back of her seat.

'I'm sorry to hear that. By the way, I like your dress. I hope you don't mind my saying so, but it looks perfect on you.' It was lime-green, and Rhona was quite keen on it, too.

'Matt, you're a total surprise, gentlemanly conduct, compliments and appreciation, all in one package. Thank you.' As if she were sharing a secret, she said, 'Actually, this is my going-to-concerts-and-functions dress.' It had quite a short skirt, and that possibly appealed to him as well. He was only human, after all.

'The perfect choice.' He studied the programme.

'I'm glad they're playing the Sullivan,' she said. 'It makes a change from the usual repertoire.' The *Overture di Ballo* was the first item on the programme.

'Me too.'

The musicians were taking their seats on the platform, and the usual pre-tuning cacophony began. Eventually, the leader raised his bow and the orchestra tuned to the oboe's 'A'.

'We're doing *Oklahoma* at school,' she told him with little enthusiasm.

'Bad luck.'

'If they wanted to play cowboys, *Annie, Get Your Gun* would have been a better choice.'

'Infinitely better. Give me Irvine Berlin any day.'

It pleased her that they were in agreement, but that was where their conversation had to end, at least for the time being, because the conductor was making his way to the rostrum amid eager applause.

The inclusion of Sullivan's *Overture di Ballo* was an unusual and encouraging initiative. Even in the nineteen-seventies, most people associated Sullivan with the Savoy Operettas written in collaboration with W S Gilbert, and the rest of his output was largely neglected. A glance at the programme notes told Rhona that the overture was first performed in 1870. More than a hundred years later, someone had blown the dust from its cover and given it a much-deserved and overdue airing. Looking discreetly around the dress circle and noting the delighted expressions of many of the audience members, she wondered how many of them were hearing it for the first time, at a loss to understand why such a masterpiece was so seldom played.

The music ended with its exciting *galop* sequence, and the audience demonstrated its appreciation with enthusiastic applause, which seemed to confirm Rhona's suspicion. She said, 'That was wonderful.'

'Superb,' he agreed.

The conductor re-emerged for Tchaikovsky's *Orchestral Suite Number Four*, also known also as *Mozartiana*. Neither of them knew it at all well, but they enjoyed it nonetheless.

The next item was the Schumann *Konzertstück in G*, the piece that had attracted Rhona's interest when Matt showed her the poster. They waited as the piano was pushed into place and the lid opened. The conductor and the guest soloist came on to the platform, acknowledged the applause and took their places. Matt glanced at Rhona, possibly sensing her excitement. She'd told him she loved Schumann, and she was anticipating it eagerly.

The music began gently with one of Schumann's trademark, riding-through-woodland motifs, gradually building up to a dramatic interlude, relaxing again into a tender, romantic passage that led in turn to more drama. Rhona closed her eyes in concentration and self-indulgence, living every note, totally involved in the performance.

As the music reached its intense conclusion, she blinked, and a tear escaped one eyelid. She was surprised to feel a handkerchief being placed in her hand, and realised that Matt had anticipated her need.

'Thank you,' she said, making a hasty repair. 'I'll let you have it back when I've washed it.'

The applause for the pianist and the orchestra was deservedly whole-hearted, but it eventually abated, and Matt said, 'I'll find our drinks while you powder your nose.'

Rhona shook her head in wonder and patted his hand before seeking the powder room.

When she returned, she found him and their drinks at a small table. He pulled out a chair for her.

'Thanks, Matt, you're treating me like royalty, tonight.'

'Not at all.'

'Oh, that was wonderful,' she said, pouring tonic water into her glass. Then, to avoid misunderstanding, she said, 'Not that, just then, although it was highly necessary. I meant the Schumann. Wasn't it brilliant?'

'It's a masterpiece, and he played it superbly well,' agreed Matt.

'Wasn't Schumann just the ultimate Romantic? At least, I reckon it's between him and Chopin, but I haven't formed a definite conclusion yet. It depends on the day of the week and which way the wind's blowing.'

'I gather it's blowing Schumann's way, tonight.'

'I reckon so.' Looking around her, she said, 'Something I've thought for a long time is that concertgoers belong to one category or another. I'm possibly wrong to classify people this way, but it's difficult to ignore that there are people like me, who can't exist without music; there are those whose knowledge of it is maybe sketchy, but who simply love, as Sir Thomas Beecham said, "the noise it makes", and then, there are the posers, who talk loudly about musicians, singers or dancers and claim a knowledge of the arts that's downright spurious.'

'But,' said Matt, 'their money's as good as anyone's, and they're helping to keep music in the public domain.'

'You're right, of course.' Harking back to the programme, Rhona said, 'It's hearts on sleeves next.'

'Is that how you see Cesar Franck?'

'Yes. I still enjoy his music, but I always get the impression that he would leave dear Félicité in absolutely no doubt as to where she stood.'

'Isn't that a good thing?'

'Oh yes. Some men are emotionally mute, so you never find out how they feel, but I don't suppose Franck ever told her simply that he loved her. I reckon he'd spend half an hour telling her he did, and why he did, and about the depth of his feelings, and then he'd compare them with every wonder in his vocabulary.'

The bell rang, marking the end of the interval.

Matt laughed. 'I'll bear those thoughts in mind while we listen to his symphony,' he said.

Despite Rhona's assessment of Franck's character, they both enjoyed the symphony.

'That concert was enjoyment from beginning to end,' said Rhona as she took Matt's arm outside the hall.

'It was,' he agreed, 'and I still think the enjoyment is greater when it's shared.'

'After tonight, I'm convinced of it.'

They chatted as they walked to the carpark, where Rhona unlocked the passenger door to let him in. He waited until she was safely in her seat before taking his.

He asked, 'Are we going via the Central Fisheries or the Happy Haddock?'

'Why do you ask?'

'If you remember, I'm getting the chips on the way home.'

'Of course.' She remembered that conversation. 'Which do you prefer?'

'My preference is for the Happy Haddock. They have a special way with Haddock.'

'I expect they keep them happy.'

'Okay, let's head for the Happy Haddock. You know where it is, don't you?'

'Yes, and I can smell it from here.' She drove on for a mile or so and pulled into the side of the road beside the brightly-lit shop.

'What would you like, Rhona?'

'Just haddock and chips, please.'

'Not mushies?'

'I don't think so. I make an effort to be sociable on Bonfire Night, but I don't care for them all that much.'

'Okay.' He got out and walked into the shop, leaving Rhona to enjoy the concert again in retrospect.

She was surprised to see Matt leave the shop, at one point, and go to a nearby telephone box. However, he was only in there for maybe a couple of minutes before he returned to the shop for his order, which he brought back to the car.

'It's come to something,' he said, taking his seat again in the car, 'when fish and chips come to more than a ticket in the dress circle, but I don't really mind.'

'You have to look further than lop-sided values,' said Rhona. 'Musicians are paid peanuts, but fish have to be caught, potatoes have to be grown, picked and made into chips, and peas have to be... mushed.'

'That's too grown-up for me,' said Matt.

'But you were very quick.'

'There was no one else in the shop. Leeds United and Wolves are playing tonight, apparently, and they'd just started playing injury time when I arrived.'

'Do you like football?'

'No, cricket's my game.'

She re-joined the main road. 'I'm being nosey,' she said, 'but I was surprised when you went into the phone box.'

He laughed. 'I phoned Bev to ask her to put three plates in the oven to warm.'

'I didn't realise she was at your place. Still, it's none of my business.'

'It's nothing like that,' he assured her. 'Every now and then, she fancies a spell of peace and quiet. Actually, she can't stand the chap who's moved in with her mum, so she uses my spare room.'

'Poor girl.'

She drove into Akengarth and pulled up outside Matt's yard.

'It'll be safer inside the yard, round the back,' advised Matt. 'Right, right again and right into the yard.'

'I didn't know there were car thieves in Akengarth,' said Rhona, following his directions.

'I'm not aware of any, but there are careless drivers, and they can be as big a nuisance.'

'I thought it was such a law-abiding place.' She parked the car behind Matt's pick-up, and they went into the house, where they found that Beverley had laid the table in readiness.

'Leeds one, Wolves nil,' she told them.

Matt asked, 'Did you see the match?'

'Yeah. Norman Hunter got sent off, Mick Jones passed the ball to Jack Charlton, and he scored the winning goal with a header.'

'Much the same as usual, then.' He handed the parcel to her, leaving her to serve up.

Rhona asked, 'Do you need a hand, Beverley?'

'No, I'm all right, Miss.' She added hastily, 'Thanks.' She was much more at ease with Rhona than she ever had been, but she was still learning good manners.

In a very little time, she returned with two plates, followed by another, which she set on the table.

'You're a good girl, Bev,' said Matt.

Beverley sat down, smiling at the compliment, and said, 'It's getting late, Matt.'

'Stay here, if you like. The spare bed's made up.'

'Thanks.'

Impressed by the easy way they made the arrangement, Rhona asked, 'Does it happen often?'

'Bev spent her eighteenth birthday here,' said Matt. 'Rather than go home late at night, she stays here. Her mum doesn't mind.'

'She don't give a f… don't care, neiver,' said Beverley, lacing her chips with ketchup.

Matt added diplomatically, 'It means she's not going home in the dark.'

Rhona asked innocently, 'Is it dangerous hereabouts?'

'The only danger round here's farmers' lads, Miss. When they've been on t' lotion, anybody's fair game.' For a girl with learning problems, Beverley could be old beyond her years. Dismissing the subject, she asked, 'Where did you go tonight?'

'We went to a concert,' Matt told her.

'What sort of concert?'

'There was an orchestra, and a man played the piano.'

'Was it nice?'

'It was ecstasy,' said Rhona, 'and that's the nicest anything can ever be.'

7

THE VEXING, THE VILE AND THE VULNERABLE

For all her idealism, Rhona had to admit that wishes seldom came true, so she was all the more surprised by Helen Porter's announcement during Any Other Business at the Curriculum Meeting.

'Following consultation between the Music and Drama Departments,' said the Head of Drama, 'it's been decided that we shan't, after all, be performing *Oklahoma!*'

'Oh, my beating heart,' said Rhona. 'Thank you, Santa, all your little elf and fairy helpers and all the children, their dolls and their teddies, who wrote pleading letters to you.'

'We feel,' said Mrs Porter, ignoring Rhona's response, 'that, with so many pupils keen to take part, we couldn't involve as many as we would like, so the production will now be *Annie Get Your Gun*. It offers much more in the way of chorus work.'

'A welcome change, however sudden,' said Rhona. 'If you change it again, you will tell me before the first rehearsal, won't you, just so that I don't turn up with the wrong score?'

'I'm sorry, Rhona,' said Helen. 'It was a last-minute decision, and we didn't have time to tell you.'

'Poor little Cinders, that's me. Always the last to be told.'

'Let's move on,' said Ian Crawley, Deputy Head responsible for Curricular Matters. 'The change has been minuted, and I've told you before about sarcasm, Rhona.'

'What have you told me, Mr Crawley? You know what my memory's like.'

'I've told you,' he said with dwindling patience, 'that sarcasm has no place at a professional meeting.'

'Only twice, Mr Crawley, now I think about it. Be fair. Even the Bellman had to say things three times to make them official.'

'All right, I'm telling you for the third time. Let's have no more sarcasm at meetings. It's not helpful.' In a belated double-take, he asked, 'Who's this Bellman, anyway?'

'One of the hunting party,' John Pitcher, Head of English, told him with a mischievous smile. Crawley was universally unpopular and fair game for most members of staff.

'I'd rather you didn't refer to hunting, John. I'm violently opposed to it.' 'Don't worry, Ian. The quarry pulled off a clever stunt at the last minute and got clean away.'

Stifling a smile, Rhona asked, 'What about irony?'

'What about it?'

'Now that we no longer have total freedom of speech, am I allowed to use irony? It's a literary device,' she explained. The Deputy was, after all, a mathematician, who might easily be excused for wondering if 'Irony' were next to 'Bronzey' on the Ford colour chart.

'If it's an extension of your wit, no, you're not.' He addressed the meeting again. 'Has anyone any other business?'

'There's something I think I should mention,' said Sally Gunn, the shy and hesitant member of the Needlework Department.

'Well, do tell us before we die of suspense,' said Ian.

'And we all heard you say,' said Rhona, 'that sarcasm has no place at a professional meeting.'

The chairman's withering look rivalled Bill and Ben, the Flowerpot Men in speaking more eloquently than he ever could.

Helen caught her after the meeting. 'I really am sorry, Rhona,' she said. 'We couldn't tell you before the meeting.'

'Well, Helen, you know me, always one for a challenge.'

'Do you want a library copy of the vocal score, or will you use your own again?'

'I'd better stick to my own. I pencil all kinds of notes in them, warnings to myself, reminders, expletives, rude remarks and that sort of thing. The library wouldn't appreciate it.' As an afterthought, she said, 'I haven't written in my copy of *Oklahoma!* I'll see if Shuttleworth's will let me swap it for *Annie Get Your Gun*.'

'That's a good idea.'

'I know. 'Bye.' She had to go home and eat fairly quickly. The Planning Committee had asked Dennis Fisher to join them. It would be interesting, at least.

Dennis was a large man, both in height and girth, with a fancy for brightly-coloured clothes, it seemed. His shirt was bright orange, and his tie a depiction of dense forestry. He also wore a number of rings that seemed to compete with each other in gaudiness. Rhona, who was trying not to form preconceived ideas about the guest, had asked David Warburton to chair the meeting. She'd been conscious almost from the beginning that he was reluctant to delegate responsibility for long.

He said, 'I expect you've heard about the old cinema, Dennis.'

'Not for quite a while, love. Has there been a development?'

'Yes, there has. We've decided, as a society, to go ahead with the conversion and refurbishment, as originally planned.'

Dennis was shaking his head hopelessly. 'You must be stark, raving bonkers, all of you. I don't enjoy being a wet blanket, sweeties, but there's so much to be done. What it really needs is pulling down.'

David shuffled uncomfortably. 'I'm sorry to hear you say that, Dennis, because we were going to ask you if you'd consider taking on the role of project manager.'

Dennis's ample frame began to shake with undisguised merriment. When he was able to speak again, he said, 'I'd be as daft as you lot if I considered it, even for a minute, love.' He grasped the chair arms and levered himself to his feet, causing the chair's joints to protest loudly. 'Let's not waste each other's time, love. If you want a producer, I'm your man, but do yourselves a favour and forget about the cinema.'

David also rose to his feet. 'Thank you for coming to talk to us, Dennis,' he said. 'I'm sorry we couldn't reach agreement.'

'You've just got to be realistic, love. 'Bye.'

'Goodbye, Dennis.' When the guest was gone, David turned to the committee. 'Back to square one,' he said wearily. 'Maybe he's right.'

'Just a minute.' Rhona was no less disappointed, but neither was she disheartened. 'Dennis's opinion is a personal one, based on what? I wonder how long ago he last looked at the cinema.'

'Whenever it was,' said David solemnly, 'it can't have improved an awful lot since then.'

'Of course not, but what I'm saying is, he made his decision based on what he remembered of it, and memory can do strange things, as you all know.'

'That doesn't solve our immediate problem,' said Terry Cooper, 'which is to find a project manager.' He added apologetically, 'I'd do it myself, but I've got too much on. I'll help with the plumbing and heating, but that's as much as I can offer.'

'And it's greatly appreciated, Terry,' David assured him.

Rhona had been thinking. 'There's someone I could try,' she said.

David looked up with new interest. 'Who's that?'

'Matt Brocklehurst. He's extending my kitchen, and he's doing an excellent job.'

'He's a good joiner,' said Terry, 'and he knows the building trade. Do you think he'll do it?'

'There's only one way to find out.'

Purely by luck, Rhona arrived home from work the next day as Matt and Beverley were loading the tools, mixing board, buckets and other equipment, on to the pick-up.

'Come and have a look at your extension,' said Matt.

'All done?'

'In the last half-hour,' he confirmed.

She went in through the kitchen and stared. 'It's amazing,' she said. 'You've done a wonderful job, both of you. Thank you ever so much.'

'You're welcome.'

'Let me have your bill and I'll settle it straight away.'

'That's my kind of customer.'

She filled the kettle and asked, 'Would you both like a brew?'

'I think we could manage that.'

She took some biscuits from a cake tin and put them on a plate.

'You like chocolate wholemeal biscuits, don't you, Beverley? They're plain chocolate, but I don't suppose you'll mind that.'

'Yes, please, Miss.' Awkwardly, she added, 'Thank you, Miss.'

'Help yourself.' Turning to Matt, she said, 'I was singing your praises to the Planning Committee last night.'

'Oh, yes?'

'They'd asked a chap who'd done some productions for them in the past if he'd consider taking on the job of project manager.'

'Dennis Fisher?'

'That's right.'

He laughed. 'I hope he turned them down.'

'He did. As a matter of fact, he poured scorn on the idea.' She put teabags into the three mugs and poured water on to them. 'Why did you say that?'

'Dennis Fisher's no builder. He's an architect of sorts, all theory and design concepts.'

'So it was a lucky escape.'

'You could say that,' he said, accepting a mug of tea. 'Thank you.' He turned to Beverley and said, 'You'll ruin your figure with those things, Bev.'

'Leave the poor girl alone. She's worked hard for them.'

'I bet you don't eat chocolate biscuits, Rhona.'

'Not usually, but sometimes I'm tempted.' Rhona could delay the moment no longer. She had to ask him. 'Matt, would you consider being project manager?'

'And see the job through to the end?'

'Yes.'

'Free, gratis and for nothing?'

'I'm afraid so.'

He hesitated, eventually saying, 'It depends.'

'On what?'

'It depends on who asks me.'

'I'm asking you, Matt. Don't make me beg.'

He tried his tea, which was evidently too hot. 'All right,' he said. 'I'll do it.'

With undisguised relief, she said, 'You lovely man. Thank you.'

'Mind you, I'll expect chocolate digestives, and so will Bev when she's working on it, although I don't know what it'll do to her figure.'

Rhona took in Beverley's tiny waistline and said, 'It'll take some spoiling, Matt.'

It was only after she'd eaten that Rhona found the envelope. It was pinned to the message board beside the worktop. When she opened it, she found the bill. Everything apart from the extra window was itemised, and the total was exactly the same as the estimate.

After she'd eaten, she wrote a cheque and put it in the envelope with the bill. Then, after a moment's thought, she put her coat on and drove to Matt's yard. Not surprisingly, the office was closed, so she walked to the house, and was about to push the envelope through the letterbox, when the door opened.

'Hello,' said Matt. 'I've heard whispers of immediate payment and other exciting stories, but here it is in reality. Thank you, Rhona. Will you come in and have a drink? Say you will, because I'm all alone this evening.'

'How can I refuse?' She followed him into the small sitting room.

'I hope you like red wine, because it's all I've got.'

'You're speaking my language, Matt.'

'Let me take your coat.' He helped her off with it and hung it in the hallway. 'Take a seat. I'll be with you in a minute.'

Left alone in the room, Rhona was drawn immediately to the books that filled both sides of the chimney breast and extended beyond it. Matt's taste in literature seemed to embrace five centuries, although the twentieth was probably best represented.

'I haven't read them all,' he said as he entered the room. 'They're only there for show.'

'I don't believe you. Do you treat all your customers like this?'

'Only when they pay my bills while the ink's still wet on them.' He handed her a glass of wine.

'Thank you.' She waited for him to sit down, and said, 'I noticed the kitchen window wasn't on the bill.'

'Oh well, it was one I'd had in the yard for some time, so I threw it in as a bonus.'

'You're too generous, Matt, but thank you.' While it was on her mind, she said, changing the subject, 'I've been meaning to ask you something.'

'Ask away. I've no secrets. No embarrassing ones, anyway, more's the pity.'

'I just wondered how you came to take Beverley on as your apprentice.'

He took a sip and gave the wine a look of approval. 'It was one of those chance things,' he said. 'Your school asked me to give her a fortnight's work experience. The man who contacted me told me she wasn't very bright, but if I could let her sweep up and make the tea, it might give her a sense of purpose.'

'That would be Richard Harrison.'

'That was his name.' He laughed. 'I get the idea from the way you spoke his name that you're not his biggest fan.'

'Not really. I keep wondering what chance the poor little buggers have when people like him expect so little of them.'

'Well, I found that Bev had more going for her than I'd been told, and when I realised things were tight at home, I gave her a Saturday job. Make no mistake, though, I gave her the apprenticeship because I recognised potential in those delicate hands.'

'You're a lovely fella, Matt, and I can't tell you how pleased I am that Beverley's doing so well. She was in my tutor group. That was for registration and administration, but I never taught her. All I knew was that she was having extra help with the basics.'

'She still is.' He smiled at the thought. 'Now that she can see a reason for measuring up and allowing for various things that get in the way, she's a lot better with numbers.'

They chatted easily for a while, and then Matt said, 'We've talked about me and about Bev, but I know very little about you. I'm being nosey, I know, but you're used to it by now.'

'There's not a lot to know. I did Modern Languages at Durham and got the job I do now at Banfield High. I couldn't be more boring if I made it my life's work.'

'You're not in the least boring. You even have an exciting name. "Loveday" sounds like a great occasion.'

She was happy to enlighten him. 'In Medieval times,' she told him, 'it was a day for reconciliation and for cementing relationships. According to my dad, it was also a time for self-healing. You had to be able to forgive yourself as well as others. Me mam says he made that up, but she's a hard-headed Geordie, so she would say that.'

He eyed her speculatively and asked, 'Are you like her?'

'In most respects.' She kept quiet about the minor difference in their bust measurements. There were some things you didn't share with a man you hardly knew. 'She's fifty now, but she's a very attractive woman for her age.'

'So are you, Rhona, even though I don't know your age.'

'Thank you. Usually, if a man says something like that, I know he's after something, but you're genuine, and that's nice.'

'The genuine article,' he agreed, standing up again. 'I don't know why I left the bottle in the kitchen. I'll go and get it.'

He was only just out of the room when she heard the outside door open, and then the inner one opened, and Beverley burst into the room, clearly agitated. Strangely, she was still in her overalls.

'Beverley, what's the matter?'

For a moment, the girl stared, open-mouthed, and then Rhona opened her arms and drew her in. 'It's all right,' she said as Beverley began to sob, 'tell me when you're ready.'

Matt was standing behind her, holding the bottle of wine and only a little puzzled. He said, 'Something's happened at home, I'll bet.'

Eventually, the sobs grew fewer.

'Take your time,' Rhona told her.

'Can… can I… stay here?'

'Of course you can,' said Matt, 'for as long as you like. You know that.'

Rhona fumbled in her bag and took out a tissue. 'Here,' she said, 'dry your tears, but don't try to talk yet.'

Matt said, 'I'll get you some chocolate.'

Rhona wondered what kind of contribution chocolate would make, and then she realised he was probably talking about the liquid kind. If Bev was particularly fond of it, it was probably a good idea. 'Come and sit down with me,' she suggested. 'Now, has something happened at home that's upset you?'

Beverley nodded.

'Something to do with your mam or her fella?'

She nodded again. 'Scott.'

'What happened, Beverley?'

'He was... watching me run... the bath. He wanted... to know what I... had on under my... overalls, and he started unfastening... the buttons to find out.'

Rhona could see where one button had been ripped off completely.

'He put his... hand inside me... clothes.'

'Oh, you poor girl.' In the absence of anything more helpful, she held her closer.

'I got away from him... and came here.'

Matt put a mug of chocolate down on the table beside her, saying, 'You don't have to go back, Bev. We can pick up your things and you can move in here, if you like.'

She nodded gratefully.

8

ANOTHER WORLD

Matt handed Rhona a hard hat and watched her put it on. 'It suits you,' he said.

'Bright yellow plastic? Thanks a ton.'

'No, everything suits you, Rhona. You've got that special quality that makes you look *chic* in a bin liner.'

'Don't you believe it.' She left him to wonder about that in his own time, as he seemed more content to shine his torch into every corner of the building.

'It's creepy in here,' she said, watching the shifting shadows as the beam of torchlight switched from one neglected feature to the next.

'Maybe, but there's no evidence of damp, and it seems to be dry. That's more important than you'd think. It rained today, but none of it found its way in here, so we can stop worrying about the roof.'

'Was that going to be the first job?'

'It would have been. You need a sound roof before you can think about rewiring and the rest. It makes sense when you think about it.'

'It does,' she agreed. Her eye fell on the raked seating in the stalls and she asked, 'Are these seats likely to be any good? They look to be all in one piece.'

He considered that for a moment, and said, 'The cushions are detachable, which is just as well, because they'll need re-upholstering.' He touched one seat and said, 'They're dry, but dirty, and they may be home to rodents or other vermin.'

'Urrgh!'

'I was only answering your question.'

She recovered her composure and asked him, 'Would you mind answering another?'

'As long as you promise not to scream. You make me nervous when you do that.'

'I'll try.' More seriously, she asked, 'What happened at Beverley's house this morning?'

'We collected her things, of which she has pitifully few, wrapped them in a red spotted handkerchief, and told her mother she was off to seek her fortune.'

It was a start, she decided. It was possibly he would become more lucid later. 'Was Scott there?'

'Yes, he currently lives there, I'm told.' He examined a row of seats. 'Yes,' he confirmed, 'these'll need re-upholstering, but the frames are good. I need to look at the floor in a better light. I'll bring the generator next time, and then I'll be able to see everything.'

'Did he get stroppy or what?'

'He thought about it, but I talked him out of it. He's a simple soul and easily persuaded.'

She sighed heavily and said, 'I'm not going to get any sense out of you, am I?'

'Not until I've finished looking round this place.' Pointing his torch at the ceiling, he said, 'You'll have to forget the fancy plasterwork and chandeliers. We'll put a false, plasterboard ceiling up with basic house lights. It may be necessary to make the proscenium arch maybe six inches or so lower than we would like, but we can't have everything.'

'What was Beverley's mam's reaction?'

'She called me a few names and told Bev she could get lost if that was how she felt. Her temper was a bit muted by her usual standards, but she was worried that I might give her bad publicity by shopping Scott to the police. Having said that, though, she wasn't feeling too well-disposed towards him, either, judging by the language she was using.'

'Will you contact the police?'

'No.' He turned his torch on the projectionist's room. 'With some modern and sophisticated lighting equipment, that could be quite useful,' he said. Then turning to Rhona, he said, 'I know it was unpleasant enough for Bev, but as indecent assaults go, it wasn't serious enough to get the police excited, especially now she's over eighteen. If she'd still been a minor, it would have been different.'

'So he gets away with it Scot-free.' She added, 'The awful pun, by the way, was intentional.'

'I wouldn't say Scot-free, exactly. He wasn't feeling too happy when we left him.'

'Well, at least you showed you were taking the matter seriously. You do take it seriously, don't you?'

'You bet your life, I do, especially when Bev's the victim. The poor kid's suffered too much already.' He shone his torch on his watch and asked, 'Do you fancy a drink?'

'Go on, you've talked me into it.' They left the building and hurried through the rain to Matt's house to call for Beverley.

Matt had just brought the drinks to their table in The Pack Horse, when he suddenly chuckled.

Rhona asked, 'What's tickling you?'

'I'm a wally.'

'I know you are, but what's funny about that?'

He took a draught of Theakston's bitter and explained. 'I was surprised when I found the theatre dry, but now I think about it, I can remember the roof timbers being replaced and the slates turned. It was the first and the last thing they did when they bought it, because that was when the money ran out and they got cold feet.' Momentarily distracted, he inclined his head towards the bar and said quietly, 'Just look at that.'

Rhona followed his gaze and saw a woman standing at the bar in a yellow, hooded cape. Beside her, stood a cocker spaniel looking justifiably embarrassed in a matching, yellow PVC coat.

'I suppose, even if somebody told her that spaniels are bred to work outdoors, she'd prefer to treat it as a pampered child.'

'It's never too late for a sinner to be converted,' said Rhona. 'You could make her evening memorable with some interesting facts about gundogs and PVC coats.'

'No,' he said, 'I don't want to upset her when she's out for an evening of carefree enjoyment. I'm a gentle soul, really, one who prefers to make allowances and live and let live.'

Beverley had been quiet until then, but she evidently felt moved to say something. 'You weren't being gentle when you banjoed Scott this morning, Matt.'

'You weren't meant to see that, and anyway, he took a swing at me first.'

'Oh, Beverley,' said Rhona, 'now you've let the cat out of the bag. Fisticuffs indeed, not that I disapprove in this case. Is that why he wasn't feeling happy when you left him, Matt?'

'Very likely.'

'Well, he had it coming to him.' Surprisingly, Beverley, usually so quiet, had more to say, this time to Rhona. 'Nobody calls me "Beverley" nowadays, Miss, not since I left school.' Then, perhaps feeling that she was being a little forward, she said, 'I'm only telling you 'cause you're the only one that does, but it doesn't really matter what you call me.'

'I'm usually the last one to latch on to a trend, but it obviously is important to you, so I'll offer you a deal. I'll call you "Bev" if you'll consign "Miss" to the history book and call me "Rhona". Is that all right with you?'

Bev appeared to be struggling with the message, and then she said, 'Do you want me to call you... your first name?'

'That's the idea, Bev.' She lifted her glass. 'I mean, we're drinking partners now, so it seems only right.'

'Right, Miss... Rhona.'

'That's the spirit, Bev.' Speaking to Matt again, she said, 'I'll be missing for a week at Easter. I'd better let the Amateurs know, or they'll think the job's proved too much for me an' I've done a bunk.'

'Are you going somewhere nice?'

'A nice place. Shame about the circumstances. We're taking a school party on holiday to Brittany.'

'Where's that, Miss... Rhona?' The transition was still causing hiccups along the way.

'The most westerly part of France.' Meeting a blank stare, she translated. 'The left-hand side bit that sticks out more than the rest.'

'Do they talk foreign, there?'

'They speak a curious French dialect, Bev, yes.'

'What's that?'

'Dialect? It's the local way of speaking. You know how people in London speak differently from people round here, don't you?'

She nodded.

'They speak their dialect, and you speak yours. If it comes to that, my dialect is different from yours.' She surveyed the glasses and asked, '*Encore les boissons*?' Explaining for Bev's benefit, she said, 'That's French for "Same again?" '

'Matt said, 'You can't get these, Rhona.'

'Of course I can,' she said, picking up the empties. 'I'm halfway to the bar and I'm a determined woman. Don't trifle with me.'

She paid the barmaid and brought a pint of Theakston's, a half of lager and a glass of red wine back to the table.

'Thank you, Rhona,' said Matt, taking the beer from her and giving the lager to Bev. 'I'm still trying to come to terms with a woman buying a round.'

'You quaint, old-fashioned thing.'

Changing the subject, he asked, 'What's so daunting about a school holiday? I've never been on one, so I ask the question purely out of ignorance.'

'A dangerous mixture is formed when free-range teenagers go on a residential trip. Mother Nature tends to be over-generous and indiscriminate with the testosterone and oestrogens during pubescence, and when we're not keeping the warring factions apart, we're keeping watch outside the girls' rooms to keep the lads out.'

'I see.'

'And I can't get out of it. Teaching languages means I'm obliged to go on these damned things. It's a shame, really, because Brittany's a lovely region.'

In a belated contribution, Bev said, 'I couldn't go on them holidays. They were too much money, and anyway, I never did Foreign at school. I were always in Remedial.'

'You're right about them being expensive, Bev,' said Rhona, 'but not all the children who are going on this one speak French particularly well. Some of them will have to rely on Mr Ellis, Mr Fieldman, Miss Womersley and me to do their talking for them.' As she spoke, she wondered how John Fieldman was going to communicate in a predominantly nasal language, hampered as he was by his chronic absence of nasal consonants. The children he taught had a perpetual struggle. Still, as Sue Womersley had pointed out so arbitrarily, she had to feel sorry for the poor man.

The woman who had come in earlier had doffed her yellow cape and was performing the same service for her dog.

'That's right,' said the landlord. 'That way, he'll feel t' benefit of it when you take him outside again.'

'She's a girl,' the woman told him shortly, clearly nettled by his amused observation.

The man who was with her said, 'Surely, it's our decision whether or not we protect our dog against the elements.' He had been sipping the same pint of bitter since their arrival.

'It could only be your decision,' agreed the landlord. 'I can't think of any bugger else who'd do such a thing.'

'Put your *pelisse* on, Fiona,' said the man. 'Clearly, we've come to the wrong pub.'

The landlord watched dispassionately as the woman fastened her cape and the dog's coat, and the two swept out of the pub with the dog in shamefaced attendance. 'It's always them as *sip* their ale,' he remarked. 'It's as if they don't trust it.'

There was general agreement.

'I always wanted a dog,' said Bev, and it was plain from the wistfulness of her tone that it really had been a long-standing cause for regret.

'Not to dress up, I hope,' said Matt. 'That's what dolls are for, isn't it?'

'I haven't never had a doll, neither.'

Not for the first time, Rhona felt desperately sorry for her. 'Didn't you have a teddy or anything like that?'

'No, I wanted one, but they were too much money.' In an abrupt change of subject, she said, 'My mum's fed up with Scott. He were too idle to get up and go to work. He kept phonin' in sick, an' now he's got the sack from his job.'

Matt emerged from an attitude of thoughtfulness, and said, 'It's no good. As hard as I try, I still can't feel sorry for him.'

'It'll be better for Troy when Scott goes.'

'Yes,' said Matt, 'I can give you a home, but I can't legally do the same for Troy. In any case, he needs his mum, at least, when she's not distracted.'

Now that the subject was out in the open, Bev became more forthcoming. 'When I had to get Troy off to school,' she said, 'that were when Scott were in bed wi' me mum an' he wouldn't let her get up to see to Troy, so I had to do it.'

Matt nodded solemnly. 'You're a good girl, Bev. Your heart's in the right place.'

So was Rhona's, and it was currently breaking for the unfortunate girl and her little brother. She hoped Scott would bugger off soon and let Troy have his mam back. As parents went, she was a poor excuse, but she was the only one he had.

9

MOTION SICKNESS AND THWARTED LUST

Because Easter was unusually late, with Good Friday occurring on the twentieth of April, school broke up for two weeks on the thirtieth of March, to close again for Easter weekend. The party for St Malo assembled outside the school at eight-thirty on Monday, the second of April. The coaches that were to take them to Sheffield Pond Street Station were due to leave at nine sharp. There was only one scare, the missing pupil arriving shortly after eight forty-five, with her mother loudly disclaiming responsibility.

'It said nine o'clock in t' letter,' she protested loudly to her daughter's great embarrassment. She was still protesting when the coaches pulled out. Seated across the aisle from the mortified child, Rhona spoke soothing words to her, whilst occasionally issuing warning looks at the grinning oafs who would otherwise have turned the situation into one of sadistic merriment.

When the subject had been finally laid to rest, David Eastwood, who occupied the seat behind Rhona's, said, 'I think I'm going to be all right. I didn't take a sickness tablet this morning, but I think I'll be okay.' From his tone, it was clear that he was trying to convince himself.

'Try to think about something else, David,' she suggested. 'You can make yourself ill just by thinking about it.'

'I don't need to think about it, Miss. I've only to go down t' road in a car and I start. It just shoots out all over t' place.'

'David, if you can't stop thinking about it, at least stop talking about it, will you?'

'Why, Miss?' It sounded like a genuine question.

'Because if you go on and on about it, you'll make everybody else feel sick, and that'll be an awful lot to have on your conscience.'

'But Miss—'

'Be quiet, David.'

'Miss?'

'I told you to be quiet.'

Another voice said urgently, 'He's going to be sick, Miss.'

Rhona pressed the button, and the coach came to a halt. 'Come on, David,' she said, 'quickly.' He left his seat, and she could see that his face was drip-white. 'Right, down to the front and on to the grass verge.' She propelled him, almost carrying him along the aisle and finally helping him down the steps and on to the grassy bank. He turned towards her, but she stopped him. 'No, the other way, an' then you'll do it on the grass and not me.' For added safety, she held his shoulders from behind.

'I feel horrible, Miss.'

'I know you do. What did you have for breakfast this morning? Bacon and egg? Sausages and beans?'

'No, Miss, Frosties.'

'Oh, lovely, lovely Frosties coated with sugar and soaked in rich, creamy milk and more sugar.'

That did the trick. He heaved several times, emptying his stomach on to the verge.

'There now, you won't be sick again, but for goodness' sake think about something else.' She pointed him up the steps of the coach and thanked the driver for his co-operation.

'Are you looking for a job, love? I can use somebody like you at getting 'em off t' bus in time.'

'No,' she told him, 'I'll stick to the job I've got.' School trips only happened once a year, thank goodness.

The train journey from Sheffield to Portsmouth was largely uneventful. Some of the party complained loudly about what Rhona thought was a passably good lunch, but the chief complaint was about the absence of chips, so she didn't take it at all seriously. Happily, no one else was sick, and the party boarded the *M V Rennes* at a little before six, that evening.

As a seasoned traveller, Rhona had reserved a cabin and, having eaten with the other members of staff, that was where she retired ahead of the heavy swell that was forecast for the crossing. Gratefully, she undressed and climbed into her bunk, satisfied that she'd made her contribution that day.

After a sound night's sleep, she went on deck the next morning to find a lot of miserable children and at least three wretched members of staff, all anxious to reach *terra firma* in St Malo. The heavy swell had been too much for them.

Rhona tracked down Nigel Ellis, who was also recovering from the crossing, and relieved him of the schedule and lists of pupils and staff, reasoning that she was in better shape than he was to take charge. Two motor coaches would take them to their hotels, one in Dinard and the other in Paramé, but before that could happen, everyone had to be rounded up.

Miraculously, she achieved that, and herded the party ashore and into the coach park, where she sent half of them on their way to Dinard and accompanied the remaining half to the Hôtel Des Bains in Paramé.

When the children were in their allotted rooms, girls on the first floor, boys on the second, Rhona said to Sue Womersley, 'You'd better get your head down until lunchtime. You'll feel better then.'

'How is it you're so bright and bouncy, Rhona?'

'I had a comfortable night in my cabin. It's worth remembering that you can't be seasick while you're lying on your back. It stabilises the fluid in the ear canals, apparently.'

'But how did you know that?'

'My dad told me. He was in the Navy during the war.'

Sue nodded slowly. 'I can see I've got a lot to learn about this business.'

'If you've realised that, you've learned something already. Go on, fill your room with zeds. I'll keep an eye on the girls.'

'What are zeds?'

'Multiple occurrences of the final letter of the alphabet. They're what you do when you sleep, something else I learned from my dad.'

Happily, Nigel recovered quickly, and Rhona was able to hand the reins of control back to him for the first day-trip, which was to the ancient settlement at Carnac. Rhona was unsure what the children would make of an arrangement of prehistoric monoliths, but her doubts were relieved when they learned that some of them had been altars for human sacrifice, complete with channels carved into the rock, so that the victims' blood could be drained away.

One of the boys said, 'Come on, Miss Loveday. Lie down on this one and we'll take your photo.'

'All right,' she said, arranging herself on the stone plinth, 'although I'm making a big enough sacrifice already by being on this trip.' She noticed that the girls were innocently photographing the features that had escaped the boys' attention. Growing up was something girls did while boys were still being boys, she decided.

The long drive back to Paramé featured a chorus of protest at the packed meal the hotel had provided, and hotel food generally. Being different from that to which they were accustomed, it was held, by popular definition, to be inferior. Otherwise, the journey was punctuated by relief stops where trees provided adequate concealment, and more impromptu pauses *pour permettre les vomissements*, as Rhona explained to the harassed French driver.

Back at the hotel, she wondered if she had time for a bath before dinner, so she collared a trusty pupil. 'Graham,' she asked, 'will you be really helpful and ask the Maître d' Hôtel what time dinner will be served?' He looked doubtful, so she prompted him. 'Say to him, "*Bon jour, monsieur. Dites-moi, sil vous plaît, on dine à quelle heure, ce soir?*" Have you got that?'

'Yes, Miss.'

'Good lad.' He went on his way, and she waited.

Eventually, he returned, but he appeared to be in a state of amusement.

'He says six-thirty, Miss.' He delivered the information whilst holding his laughter in check with some difficulty.

'Well done, Graham, but what's the joke?'

Scarcely able to contain himself, he managed to say, 'Mr Fieldman stopped me and asked who I was looking for, Miss. When I told him, he wanted to be sure I knew what to say. I said you'd told me, but that didn't stop him.'

Against her better instincts, she asked, 'What did he say?'

Graham snorted and then collected himself. 'I don't know, Miss. I couldn't make out what he was saying. I just did it your way, Miss, and the Maître d' Hôtel said, *"À dix-huit heures et demi"*.'

'Very loyal of you, but the poor man can't help having a cold, Graham.' All the same, she could understand the boy's amusement. 'Thank you for doing that, anyway.'

'That's all right, Miss.' He went on his way, but before Rhona reached the stairs, Sue Womersley said, 'That boy was making fun of John Fieldman. It's disgraceful.'

'He's thirteen years old, Sue. It's what children do, and you must have heard me correcting him.'

'I suppose so. By the way, I've been wondering what you meant when you mentioned a limerick.'

'It's a piece of humorous doggerel, usually five lines long and it follows the rhythm of the Irish jig, hence its name.'

'I know what a limerick is. You said John reminded you of one.'

'You really don't want to know, Sue. Now, I'm going to have a bath before dinner, so you'll have to excuse me.'

The bath was a much-needed oasis of peace and solitude, and dinner with her colleagues was almost civilised, but to fall into bed was sheer luxury, and she was soon asleep.

She had no idea what had roused her; in retrospect, it was most likely a creaking floorboard, but she was suddenly awake and conscious of movement outside her room. Pulling her dressing gown on over her pyjamas, she opened her door to see two boys making their furtive way along the passageway. She wasn't at all surprised when she recognised Lee Gregory, the boy who had tried to disrupt the Spanish lesson about clothes shopping.

'You lads, get back to your rooms, now. Go on.'

'We was looking for the toilet, Miss,' said Lee. 'It's hard to find it in the dark.'

'You know perfectly well you'll find it on your own floor. Now, get a move on.'

As they shuffled away, she noticed that the door of one of the rooms was ajar, and she heard a girl's voice whisper, 'You wouldn't think she was young once, the way she goes on, all prim and proper.' Rhona decided to ignore it and go back to bed. As an old woman of almost twenty-six, she needed her sleep.

In the morning, she rounded up the two girls and delivered a warning. 'How do you imagine your parents are going to react?'

Disbelief, fear and horror paraded across the girls' features. One of them said, 'Are you going to tell them, Miss?'

'Nothing actually happened, did it?'

'No, Miss, nothing. You stopped 'em before that.'

'All right, but if there's another incident, I shall tell them, make no mistake about it.'

Fear gave way to gushing relief. 'No, Miss, there won't be, Miss, honest.'

'Good. Off you go to breakfast.'

'Yes, Miss. Thanks, Miss.'

'For what it's worth, I was young once, a very long time ago by your standards, but I was never as daft as you two.' She went in search of Lee Gregory and found him in the dining room. His face paled when he saw her.

'Who was that lad you were hanging around with last night?'

'Keith Bentley, Miss.'

'Find him, Lee, and bring him to me.'

'Right, Miss.' He began his search, which took no more than two minutes.

She eyed the two who stood before her and asked, 'What do you think your parents will say when they hear about last night's episode?'

'We were looking for t' toilet in t' dark, Miss. That's all we were doin'.'

'Don't lie to me, Lee. Those girls were expecting you. I've already spoken to them, so the game's up.'

Keith, the other lad, said unsurely, 'Are you going to tell on us, Miss? My dad'll give me a right beltin'.'

'Mine will an' all,' said Lee.

'And richly deserved, I'd say.' Rhona disliked even the idea of physical punishment, but there was no need for them to know that. 'As nothing actually happened,' she said, 'I'll tell you what I've told the girls. I'll let it go this time, but if there's another incident, I'll make sure your parents know all about it, because I'll tell them myself. Right?'

'Right, Miss. Thanks, Miss.'

'Yeah, thanks, Miss.'

'Off you go to breakfast. That's if you've still got an appetite.' She doubted it. 'And try to keep your minds above your waistbands.'

When she took her place at the staff table, Nigel Ellis asked, 'What was all that about?'

'I caught them in our passageway last night, en route for fun and games with Julie Davies and Lyn Stewart, so I've given them all a suspended sentence.' She tore a croissant apart and buttered it. 'If there's another attempt, I'll tell their parents and leave it to them to sort out.'

Sue Womersley was staring at her, open-mouthed, so Rhona explained, 'Being the animals they are, they'd arranged a *rendezvous à quatre*, Sue.'

'I gathered that, but how did you know about it?'

'They woke me up. If you haven't already noticed it, this building is so old, all the stairs and floorboards creak like the doors in a gothic film.'

'I didn't hear anything.'

'In that case, it's just as well I did.'

John Fieldman leaned across the table to say, 'I dever heard theb leave their roob, Rhoda.'

Sue looked inquisitively at Rhona, who shook her head minutely. The innocent had to be protected, and Sue was virtue in human form.

As far as Rhona was aware, there were no more nocturnal excursions, and the party got through its visits to the Isle de Cezembre and Mont St Michel without incident.

On the coach to the harbour at St Malo, Sue asked Rhona again about the limerick. 'I'm not a child,' she insisted.

'No, but you're still too young for that kind of thing, and I wouldn't dream of offending your sensibilities.'

'Oh, all right if you say so.' She shook her head hopelessly. 'I don't get it, though.'

'No,' said Rhona, bored with the conversation, 'That doesn't surprise me.' She comforted herself with the knowledge that they would be back in England the next day, and that she would be free to resume normal life, which included visiting her parents and checking on progress at the theatre.

10

FAMILY, FUND-RAISING AND A CONFIDENCE SHARED

It was always a joy for Rhona to call on her granny and grandad in Newcastle, and they were just as delighted to see her.

When they'd greeted one another and Granny was putting the kettle on, Rhona asked, 'How are things goin', Grandad?'

'Canny, mind. I still got the allotment, and I get to see me old marrers down the pub. Them that's left, anyway, an' that's important. Anyway, what have you been up to, bonny lass? Your mam said you'd gone to France.'

'That's right. I've just got back.'

He was shaking his head in mock-bewilderment. 'What do you want to go to that place for? I couldn't get home fast enough when they sent us there.'

She laughed. 'That's because there was a war on, Grandad. Things have changed since nineteen-eighteen.'

'Nineteen-blood— Nineteen-twenty, I came home, an' not before time.'

'Bill Headley,' said Rhona's granny, bringing the teapot from the kitchen, 'I could hear you from the kitchen, swearin' like a drunk at closin' time.'

'I never said it, woman. I stopped mesel' before it was out of me mouth.'

'It wouldn't have mattered,' said Rhona. 'I hear worse than that every day.'

'Well, you shouldn't have to.' Her granny poured the tea and handed a cup to her. 'You'd better put your own milk in, hinny. I always get it wrong.'

'You don't get anything wrong, Granny, either of you. I'm just happy to see you both again.'

'And we're happy to see you,' said her grandad, 'now that you're home safe an' sound.'

'He won't leave it alone,' said Granny Headley, sounding like a parent who has long-since given up. 'He'll be lookin' out for Zeppelins next.'

'It's safe enough over there,' Rhona assured him.

'Anyway,' said Grandad, 'what sort o' things do the bairns get up to when they go on these holidays?'

'They go on day-trips. We went to places like Carnac, which is like Stonehenge, but even older, and its inhabitants were maybe more bloodthirsty than our forebears. Then we went to an island that the lads loved because it's full of old German guns and abandoned vehicles, and we visited Mont St Michel. It's very much like St Michael's Mount in Cornwall, except that it's famous for pancakes of various kinds, as well as getting a mention in *The Scarlet Pimpernel*. The girls loved that.' It seemed to her that they were owed it after the Isle de Cezembre.

'Why, it seems to me they could have found all that here in England. All except for the German guns, an' I cannot see what's so fascinating about them. We were happy enough to leave 'em behind.'

'It wasn't just those things, Grandad, it was an opportunity to speak French with the natives and experience a different way of life.' She thought of the children's reactions to French cuisine and wondered how successful the holiday had actually been.

'You know,' said Granny, 'your mam would have enjoyed that. I reckon she could have made herself useful with her French.'

'I'm sure she could,' said Rhona, 'and she'd have been more help than some of the staff we had with us. We could certainly have done with another pair of eyes and ears.'

They both looked at her in surprise, but it was her granny who asked, 'What do you mean, Rhona?'

'We had to keep the lads and the lasses apart after bedtime, and it seemed to me I was the only one guarding our floor. Maybe the others were heavy sleepers, but I was saddled with the job.'

'Do you mean the lads tried to…?'

'That's right, Granny. Boys will be boys, and some of the girls are happy to let them be as boyish as they like, but I caught them before they could get together.'

'The little devils,' said Granny, 'and at their age.'

Her husband grunted. 'You'd be surprised how young they start gettin' ideas these days. They know more at fourteen than I did when I was twenty—'

'That's enough of that, Bill,' said Granny mischievously, 'givin' secrets away, and to your granddaughter, too.'

Rhona wasn't offended. She was just happy to be with them again.

It was the same at home. Her presents of duty-free perfume and cognac were naturally well received, but it was her visit that gave her parents the greatest pleasure.

'Ah'm glad your holiday went all right, hinny, 'cause I know you weren't lookin' forward to it.'

'That's right, Mam. It wasn't too bad.' She smiled, remembering her conversation with Granny Headley. 'We should have taken you with us as extra help.'

'Well, you only had to ask.'

'I'll bear that in mind another time, Mam.'

Her mother picked up the bottle of perfume and looked at the label. 'It was good of you to bring me this,' she said. 'You must have known it was me favourite. You know, your dad once brought me perfume, make-up and stockings all the way from New York.'

'I had to do something to get into your good books,' he said.

'Haddaway,' she said good-naturedly. Then, reverting to the previous conversation, she said, 'I don't suppose French has changed much since I last used it.'

'Not a lot,' confirmed Rhona. 'They don't *écoutent la telegraphie sans fils* nowadays, they listen to *la radio*, like everyone else, but not much else has changed.'

Her father smiled and asked, 'How did you know about *la TSF*?'

'I found an old textbook in my storeroom. It was written in the thirties, and it was full of prehistoric vocabulary. When I looked at it, I thought about you two learning French all those years ago.' She reflected for a moment and said, 'Maybe quite a lot has changed, after all.'

'Not at this house,' her mother assured her. 'We still call it the "wireless".'

'Sometimes, we go to a magic lantern show,' said her father confidingly. 'At least, we did when the horse trams were running.'

'Careful, Dad. That's living dangerously.'

'Yes, and that reminds me. How are you getting on with the theatre?'

'It was at the planning stage when I left for France. One thing is bothering me, though.'

'What's that?'

'The seats. Apparently, the iron frames are okay, but the upholstery will need replacing, and I don't know where that's going to come from. As far as I know, theatre seats are usually covered in velour, and that sounds expensive.'

Her mother stroked the arm of her chair and said absently, 'I used to deal with the people who supply the manufacturers of bus and train seats. You could try them.'

Rhona put her mother's suggestion to Matt before a meeting of the Planning Committee, and he made a mental note of it.

The greater part of the meeting was about finance. So far, the only fund-raising initiatives were a general appeal and a regular raffle.

'Madam Chairman,' said Terry Cooper, 'Something we've not considered yet is a cricket match.'

'You've got me there, Terry. They don't play cricket where I come from. As far as I'm concerned, it's something my dad gets excited about, but I don't know the first thing about it.' By way of explanation, she said, 'My dad's a Yorkshireman, you see.'

If Terry were impressed by her half-Yorkshire credentials, he made no mention of it, but persisted with his idea. 'If we could put a team together, Madam Chairman, 'we could challenge Akengarth CBA to a charity match, but we've got to get off the mark now, before they complete their fixture list.'

Rhona was struggling. 'What does CBA stand for?'

'Cricket, Bowling and Athletics Club,' Terry told her patiently. 'Athletics died its death after the war, but Cricket and Bowling survived.'

'Aye,' said another member, 'cricketers keep on coming, and the geriatrics in the bowling club seem to get recycled somehow.'

'We should be able to put a team together, Madam Chairman,' said Matt, speaking for the first time. 'I remember playing in a fund-raising match against the Amateurs when I was in the Cricket Club, and it wasn't all that long ago.'

'Aye,' said Terry, by-passing the Chair, 'you did most of the damage, as I recall.'

'Very well,' said Rhona, 'who's going to organise it?'

'I don't mind doing that,' said Terry. 'That's unless somebody has an objection.'

The unnatural silence that followed his offer seemed to be an indication that no one else was eager to be saddled with the job.

She and Matt discussed it later in the Pack Horse.

Rhona asked, 'Where are all these players going to come from? Terry was keen, but the others were trying to make themselves invisible.'

'Playing in a match is one thing. We won't have much difficulty in getting eleven players together, but organising everything is a pain in the... neck... However, as well as being a good plumber and heating engineer, Terry's a natural organiser, and you may like to remember that for future reference.'

'Thanks for the tip.'

'You're welcome. I think you'll find that he's a more than adequate captain as well. He's a useful late-order batsman, not brilliant at bowling, but his tactics and team management are worth having.'

It was an aspect of Matt that was new to her. 'It sounds as if you're both keen,' she said.

'Terry and I were both in the Cricket Club at one time, but other things, mainly work, got in the way.'

'Of course, cricket is a way of life down here, isn't it?'

'No.' He shook his head emphatically. 'It's much more than that.'

She laughed. 'You're a funny lot.' Looking at his glass, which was almost empty, she asked, 'Are you ready for another?'

'I'll get 'em.'

It was an argument she was never going to win, so she waited for him to get the drinks.

When he returned, she asked, 'What's Bev doing tonight?'

'She went to her mother's to see Troy, but he'll be in bed by now.' He added, 'She's safe enough. Her mother gave Scott the order of the boot, and he moved out while you were in France.'

'Good. Let's hope she doesn't find herself another one like him.'

'We can only hope,' he agreed.

'On the subject of Bev and Troy,' she said, as they'd been very much on her mind, 'I went shopping after I got back from France, and I've got something for both of them.'

'Oh, well, Bev will be back by now. If you've got it with you, you can give it to her tonight.'

'Okay.' She looked at him questioningly.

'What's the matter?'

'Don't you want to know what it is?'

'Of course not. It's none of my business.'

'It's not a secret.' Eyeing him impatiently, she asked, 'What's the joke?'

He shook his head in amusement. 'Only a woman could make a mystery of something and then turn it into a guessing game.'

'Don't be silly.'

'Rhona?' He narrowed his eyes in appeal.

'What?'

'I know you can't wait to tell me, so I'll ask you. What have you bought Bev and Troy?'

'You're exasperating, Matt.'

'I know.'

Her expression softened, and she said, 'I've bought them each a teddy bear. Every child should have one, and it's the greatest shame they've had to wait so long.' Almost to herself, she said, 'They must have been among the first teddies to be sold with VAT on the price tag.'

'A milestone purchase, Rhona, and it was a kind thought, as well. Troy's only ten, but I'll admit, Bev's waited a long time for hers. Mind you, I'm sure she'll appreciate it.' He added wistfully, 'She appreciates most things, mainly because she's had so little.'

'You're never too old for a teddy, Matt. I've had mine for as long as I can remember.' Recalling some dramatic moments in his life, she said, 'I had to sew him up twice when he was falling apart.'

'What bear could ask for greater dedication than that?'

72

'Don't make fun, Matt. A girl's relationship with her teddy bear is a serious and sacred matter.'

'I don't doubt it. I'm no stranger to sentiment, you know.'

'You could have fooled me.'

'Well, that's where you're wrong.' He drank slowly, no doubt to keep her in suspense. She was beginning to get his measure.

'What are you sentimental about, Matt?' It would probably be daft, but she had to know.

'You mustn't mock.'

'That's good, coming from you.' She was nevertheless determined to hold the moral high ground. 'All right,' she said, 'some of us respect the feelings of others.'

'That's a relief.'

'I suppose it is. Are you going to tell me something, or does it have to remain a secret?' There was a limit to her patience.

'You won't tell anyone, will you?'

'Of course not.'

He hesitated, and then said, 'I once had something so precious that I could hardly bear to let it out of my sight. It was a present from my parents, who knew how much it meant to me. I was only twelve at the time.' He paused in fond recollection.

'Go on.'

'That Christmas night, by which I mean the end of Christmas Day, not Christmas Eve. It's important that I make that clear, because—'

'Get on with it, Matt.'

'All right. That night, I took it up to my room and placed it on my bedside table, so that it would be the first thing I'd see when I woke up on Boxing Day.'

'Don't keep me in suspense.'

Almost breathless in his excitement, he said, 'It was a point seven six, two-stroke glow-plug engine for my flying scale model of a Sopwith Camel.'

'Matt,' she said with studied calm, 'if my glass was still full, I'd empty it over your head for that.'

'But you need me to manage the theatre project, so you'll have to be nice to me instead.'

'Just now, it's the only reason I can think of.'

11

THINGS TO BE DONE

Part of the helter-skelter of the new term was the initial rehearsal for the show. There was little for Rhona to do, other than repeat the phrases Jane Baxendale was teaching the chorus; in fact, Jane could easily have done it herself, had she given it more thought. There was nothing difficult about repeating, 'Doin' what comes natur'ly,' as the chorus were currently demonstrating. The situation wasn't without its entertainment, however, as Jane, providing Annie's part for the time being, was singing it as she sang everything, like an operatic soprano, and anything further removed from Annie's hill-billy persona was impossible to imagine. Rhona's attention wandered, recalling Bev's initial bewilderment and then her delight at receiving the teddy bear. According to Matt, it now occupied a permanent place in Bev's bed. Troy was reportedly captivated with his during his more private moments, although it was no surprise to Rhona that she'd not yet received a message of thanks. Unlike Bev, Troy had no one to teach him about good manners.

The rehearsal eventually reached its end, with Jane remarkably cheerful. 'Don't worry,' she said, 'they'll get the idea.'

Rhona, who was not even slightly worried, agreed with her for the sake of good relations, and made her exit.

In doing so, she came across Gary, clad in his tracksuit after his evening devotions, or 'rugby practice', as he called it.

'Hello, Rhona,' he said. 'Fancy seeing you here at this time of the day.'

'So you've learned to tell the time, Gary. I always said you could do it.' As she spoke, she felt a touch of shame. After all, he'd stopped calling her 'Goldilocks', so she felt that an olive branch was called for. 'We've been rehearsing *Annie Get Your Gun*,' she explained. 'They need me to play the piano.'

'Oh.' Gary's musical appreciation extended as far as *Black Sabbath*, which explained his monosyllabic response, not to mention his limited vocabulary and prematurely-impaired hearing. Then, as his thoughts moved on, he said, 'I see Akengarth Amateur whatever-they-are are going to play the Cricket Club. Aren't you involved with that lot?'

'Yes, but I won't be playing. They've got all the big-hitters they need.'

'Do you play, Rhona?' He evidently found the idea amusing.

'No, and that's another reason I won't be taking part.'

He appeared to struggle with that, but gave up on it and said, 'They'll get hammered.' He made the prophesy with easy-going confidence.

'By "they", I imagine you mean Akengarth Amateurs.'

'Yes, they don't stand a chance.'

'That's not the point Gary.' She'd spent the afternoon teaching children of limited ability, and she needed a break from it, but she nevertheless made an effort to enlighten him. 'It's a friendly match, a fund-raising event for the refurbishment of the old cinema. It's not one of your bloodthirsty encounters.'

He shook his head mockingly. 'Forget it, Rhona. There's no such thing as a friendly match. The whole idea of playing sport is to win.'

'As long as the match brings in the money we need, it won't matter to me who wins.'

He gave her a pitying look and said, 'Come out with me for a drink, Rhona, just for old times' sake.'

'No, thank you, Gary.'

'Nothin' heavy, just a drink,' he coaxed.

'Not even that.'

'I won't try anythin'.'

'I think we've just established that, Gary. I need to go, now, and get to the supermarket before it closes, so that I can eat tonight.'

'I miss your cookin', Goldil— Rhona.'

'I only cooked for you once, and you sulked because you couldn't have chips.'

'They weren't the only thing I didn't get that night.'

'Nature's calendar can be very hard on someone as single-minded as you, Gary, but I must leave you to ponder your misfortune alone. I've no doubt I'll see you tomorrow.'

She was washing up after dinner when the phone rang. She dried her hands and answered it. 'Hello.'

'Rhona, it's Matt. I took my generator to the theatre so that I could see everything lit properly, and I've made a full inspection. I can tell you about it now, or you could come over for a drink. Otherwise, it'll keep.'

'What an array of choices! No, you can come over here. If Bev's at a loose end, you can bring her with you as well.'

'If you're happy with that, I'll see you in two shakes.'

'Lovely. 'Bye, Matt.' She put the phone down and set about tidying up the sitting room, reflecting as she did that the theatre was taking over her life. Still, she'd wanted a sense of purpose, and now she had one.

Matt and Bev arrived within ten minutes, he bearing a bottle of Bordeaux and she a tightly-folded note, which she put into Rhona's hand. 'It's from Troy,' she explained.

'Thank you, Bev.' She took the note and unfolded it to read it. It was written in brown crayon and the letters were ill-formed.

deR miss luvdaY thank you foR the Tedy baRe iT is veRy nice + iT was veRy cind of you luv from TRoy

'I told him what to write,' said Bev proudly.

'Thank you, Bev. He did well, and you did well to help him.'

Matt followed her into the kitchen to open the wine. 'She surprised me with the note,' he said.

'Poor little scrap. I mean Troy, not you. There are some bairns who just make you want to take 'em home and give 'em what they've been missing.'

'I just did, except I can't give Bev everything.'

'You give her plenty, Matt.' She picked up three glasses and said, 'Come on, let's take the wine in before we end up cryin' on each other's shoulder.'

Rhona set down the glasses and said, 'You can join us with the wine, Bev, or I've got some lager in the fridge, if you prefer that.'

'Can I have a lager, Rhona? She added a belated 'please' without being prompted.

'Of course you can. Just a minute.' She returned to the kitchen, took a can of lager from the fridge and poured half of it into a tumbler, stopping before the head foamed over the rim of the glass. She'd never learned to do it properly.

'Thanks, Rhona.'

'You're welcome, Bev.' Turning to Matt, she said, 'I've been told the Amateurs' cricket team doesn't stand a chance against the local side.'

'Who told you that? Neville Cardus or E. W. Swanton?'

'No, I don't think I know either of them. It was the Head of PE at school.'

'Gary Oldfield?' Matt seemed to find the information amusing.

'You know him, obviously.'

'Yes, I know him, all right.'

'Aren't you goin' out with Mr Oldfield, Rhona?'

'No, Bev. I went out with him briefly, and briefly is long enough for anyone. Too long for some.'

'Don't worry about the cricket match, Rhona,' said Matt.

'I'm not worried. I told Gary that as long as it's a financial success, I don't care who wins.'

Matt was shaking his head, presumably at the sacrilege he'd just heard. 'Let's talk about something else,' he suggested, 'the theatre floor, for example, as that's why we're here.'

'All right,' said Rhona, 'tell me about the theatre floor. I hope the news isn't too bad.'

'About a quarter of it's in a bad way with common furniture beetle.'

'With what? I don't want anything common in our theatre.'

'You're right not to want this, Rhona. It's even more commonly known as "woodworm". Still, it could be worse.'

She stared at him in mock horror. 'Don't tell me there's an even more vulgar insect at large.'

'The worst scenario would be dry rot, but there's no sign of that so far.'

'Phew. What's to be done about the ill-mannered beetle?'

'The floorboards that are badly affected will have to be taken out and discarded. The rest can be treated with a strong insecticide that has an unpleasant smell, but that will fade with ventilation.'

It was all strange and new for Rhona. 'Are the worms likely to come back and take up where they left off?'

'No, the insecticide will take care of that. Also, the new flooring will be in chipboard.'

'How will that help?'

'Woodworm can't cope with it. It makes them ill.'

'I hope they get on with it quietly.' She looked across at Bev, who seemed amused.

'Bev's seen it all before,' said Matt.

Bev nodded, and Rhona felt easier, knowing she was in the hands of experts.

'Another good thing—'

'I must have missed the first one.'

'The absence of dry rot and the fact that only twenty-five percent of the floor is affected.'

'Sorry, I'd forgotten about that. What's blessing number three?'

'In order to treat the floor, it'll be necessary to remove the seats. When that's done, they can be stripped of their upholstery and taken for sand-blasting and painting.'

Again, Rhona was struggling. 'Why do they need sand-blasting?'

'It's to clean them and de-rust them. Then they can be painted in hammer-finish paint and they'll be as good as new.'

Rhona shook her head in wonder. 'They say Rolls-Royce think of everything, but you can give them a run for their money.'

'Who says Rolls-Royce think of everything?'

'I don't know. It's a joke my dad once told when he thought I was out of earshot. Me mam overheard him and she called him a dirty-minded sod. I just thought it was funny. I was only about sixteen, then.'

Bev broke her silence by asking, 'Who's Rolls-Royce?'

'They make the poshest motor cars and aircraft engines,' Matt told her, 'and they do think of most things.' Looking at Rhona, he said, 'You'll have to tell me that joke some time, Rhona.'

'I'd die of embarrassment, honestly.'

'In that case, I'll tell you what else needs doing at the theatre.'

'You mean there's more?'

'Quite a lot more. The place needs rewiring, plumbing and heating, a false ceiling, a stage and an orchestra pit plus redecoration and a carpet in the foyer.'

'Won't it be necessary to carpet the auditorium as well?'

'That's dodgy as well as expensive. Maybe runners in the aisles would be ok, but too much in the way of textiles would soak up the sound from the stage and the pit.'

'I hadn't considered that.' In truth, she was learning a great deal.

'It's important, and you have to take into account, as well, the fact that an audience does the same thing. There's much more resonance in an empty theatre than a full one.'

Rhona hadn't realised there was so much involved. She picked up the bottle and asked, 'More wine, Matt?'

'Yes, please.'

She topped up his glass. 'What about you, Bev? Would you like to get yourself another can of lager from the fridge? I think there's one left.'

'Thanks, Rhona.' Bev went to the kitchen and returned with a can of Carlsberg, which she opened and poured deftly into her glass. Rhona resolved to let her pour her own in future. It would save further embarrassment.

'This theatre project is going so well,' she said, 'I could almost work up a an interest in the result of the cricket match.'

'We'll convert you,' said Matt confidently. 'You'll forget all about football, and you'll be discussing fielding positions and umpiring decisions before you can say so much as, "Howay the lads!" '

'For what it's worth, Matt, I'm not keen on football, either.' However, she was keen to see things start happening at the theatre.

12

A FOREIGN LANGUAGE

It was as well that the Amateurs had contacted the Cricket Club when they had, because most fixtures had already been made, but it turned out that Saturdays were usually free, and the 26th of May, the Saturday before Spring Bank Holiday, seemed to appeal, so it was agreed that the match would take place then. For Rhona, however, cricket posed a foreign language that was beyond her scope, so she was happy to give Terry Cooper total freedom with the team, while she liaised with the Cricket Club wives and girlfriends in organising tea.

It wasn't long before the subject of the forthcoming match was raised at school, although there was little Rhona could usefully add to the dialogue when Gary cornered her in the staffroom.

'Hey, Rhona,' he said, 'you didn't tell me Matt Brocklehurst was turning out for the Amateurs.' He sounded unusually peeved, even to Rhona, who was all too familiar with his childlike reaction to disappointment.

'I didn't know it was expected of me,' she said. 'Do you really need prior notice of who's playing? In any case, I leave that kind of thing to Terry Cooper.'

Gary's expression went unchanged. 'You might have warned me that Matt was playing.'

'Draw that lower lip in,' she told him with studied patience, 'and tell me why the fact that Matt is playing has come as such a devastating shock to you.'

'You don't know what he's like, Rhona.'

'I've a rough idea. Matt and I are good friends, as it happens, and the last time we spoke, he told me not to worry about the match, whatever you said.'

The bell sounded for the end of the lunchtime break, so they continued their conversation as they walked along the corridor.

'Oh, *you've* nothing to worry about,' said Gary pettishly.

Rhona shook her head. 'No,' she said, 'I'm still in the dark, Gary. Please enlighten me.'

'Matt Brocklehurst was the Cricket Club's secret weapon in every match we played.'

'How secret could he have been if he played in every match?'

'Women just don't understand.' It was Gary's parting shot as he turned to go down to the changing rooms. Rhona carried on to her teaching room, where foreign languages were infinitely more comprehensible than Gary Oldfield's resentful utterances.

She registered her tutor group for afternoon school and sent them on their way to make room for the Lower Sixth.

When her class was assembled, one of the boys, who was clearly unable to contain himself, said, 'You've upset Mr Oldfield, Miss.'

'Apparently, although I've only the vaguest idea of how I've managed it. Perhaps, before we get started, someone will explain the mystery to me.'

There was an audible groan from some of the girls as the boy who'd made the remark said, 'He learned from someone else in the Cricket Club that Matt Brocklehurst is turning out for Akengarth Amateurs, Miss.'

Like a Greek chorus, the girls struck a simultaneous pose of boredom. Rhona sympathised, but she had to know more. 'That much I've gathered, but what is the problem, Michael?'

'Well, Miss, Matt is a fairly ordinary batsman, a number seven or eight, but he bowls at... probably... well, certainly well over eighty miles an hour and he's both skilful and accurate as well.'

Eighty miles an hour sounded fast, but with Rhona's ignorance of cricket, she had to ask, 'Does that make him a man to be feared?'

'Very much so. That and his fielding, Miss. He used to field at first slip for the club. He was what, in the game, we call "a safe pair of hands", but that's a classic understatement. Basically, if it comes low off the bat, he'll catch it.'

She might have described Matt as a safe pair of hands, herself, although the cricket connection was beyond her. 'Thank you, Michael.

I now understand why Matt told me not to worry about the match.' She gave a theatrical sigh and announced to the class, '*Winterreise*, by Wilhelm Müller.' Opening the book in front of her, she said, 'Compared with cricket-speak, nineteenth-century German poetry will be child's play.'

Rhona had invited Matt and Bev to dinner that Saturday, and she'd been looking forward to it, but as soon as she stepped inside the theatre, she became aware of a nauseating stench that excluded all thoughts of food. 'You weren't joking about the insecticide, Matt,' she said.

'It'll fade, don't worry.' He led her to the other side of the auditorium and showed her the gaps where the infested floorboards had been removed.

'Where are they now?' She asked the question out of concern for the remaining floorboards.

'Terry and I had a bonfire. If the woodworm were still in residence when we lit it, you can be sure they no longer pose a threat to anyone.'

'I just hope the new floorboards have more luck.'

'We'll use flooring grade chipboard,' he told her confidently.

'Is that good?' She was finding builders' jargon almost as incomprehensible as cricket-speak.

'Is there an item of food that you'd refuse, even if you were starving and reduced almost to a skeleton?'

'Marrow,' she told him, grimacing as she spoke its name. 'Likewise aubergines, in fact, pulpy vegetables in general.'

'In that case, if I tell you that woodworm feel the same way about chipboard as you do about stuffed marrow, you should be reassured.'

'Are they really as choosey as that?'

'Just like you,' he confirmed. 'It's the glue in the chipboard as well as the sawdust that puts them off, although that's not the only thing they avoid. Very hard timbers are strictly off their menu as well. Oak blunts their teeth, and blunt teeth present a handicap they haven't yet learned to overcome.'

It was beginning to sound like the kind of thing that would excite a writer of children's stories, and it was too much for Rhona's active imagination. 'I'd better go,' she said, looking at her watch. 'I need to get dinner on, so I'll see you both later.'

Rhona put the chicken and ham pie she'd prepared into the oven and went upstairs to change. The potatoes and vegetables could go on when Matt and Bev arrived, and the starter was cold, anyway.

Looking into her wardrobe, she realised she had a choice of only three, or possibly four, things. Clothes were expensive, and she'd been spending her money on other things, notably the extension.

Eventually, she decided on the green dress she'd worn for the concert. All right, Matt had seen it, but she'd been brought up to wear what she liked and not to dress for anyone else's benefit. In any case, it wasn't like that with Matt. It was one relationship that was reassuringly platonic.

She put her face on, painted her nails, and then finished dressing before going downstairs.

The starter was ready, the potatoes and vegetables were prepared, and the ice cream was in the fridge, as was the white wine, should it be needed, although both she and Matt usually favoured red. Bev would doubtless have other ideas, but she was prepared for that. She opened a bottle of red Burgundy to let it breathe, smiling as she remembered her mam's account of her first date with her dad in Liverpool, eating at a posh restaurant for the first time in her life. 'I nearly died when I looked at the menu,' she'd said. 'It was full of things I'd never heard of, but your dad set me right, and I reckoned that somebody posh enough to be an officer and the son of a dole office manager must know what he was talkin' about.' Theirs must have been a strange relationship, at least to begin with, but it had been a good match. She had that to thank for her very existence.

The doorbell interrupted her thoughts, and she quickly turned on the hob under the potatoes and vegetables before going to the door.

'Hello, you two,' she said, accepting a kiss on the cheek from Matt.

Bev looked unsure, as she so often did, so Rhona kissed her on the cheek and said, 'It's lovely to see you as well, Bev. Howay inside, now.'

'Rhona,' said Matt, 'you look stunning.'

'Thank you, Matt.' She wondered if he recognised the dress, or if, like most men, it had passed him by that he'd seen it before.

As if he were reading her thoughts, he said, 'It looks perfect on you. I remember saying so at the concert, and I'm still impressed.'

'How not like a man, and thank you again, Matt.'

Bev was wearing jeans and a plain shirt, but that didn't matter. It was likely the poor kid didn't possess a dress or a skirt. 'What would you like to drink? We could start the wine, I suppose.'

'Good idea,' said Matt.

'What would you like, Bev?'

'Have you got any lager?'

'I got some in specially for you.' She took a can from the fridge and handed it to her with a tumbler. 'Red or white, Matt? If it influences your decision, we're having chicken and ham pie.' The aroma from the kitchen complemented her announcement.

'Oh, that's a tough one. Shall we defy tradition and have the red?'

'Yes, let's. We can always open the white later if we change our minds.' She poured two glasses of the Burgundy.

'I'm looking forward to this,' said Matt. 'I haven't tasted a home-made pie for ages.'

'Just reserve judgement until you've tried it.' She'd actually decided on the pie, partly because she was confident of the outcome, but also because it was unlikely to cause any awkwardness for Bev, unused as she was to eating in company.

'I'm sure it'll be superb.'

'You're too kind, Matt.' As they sat down, she said, 'You've also caused a stir at the Cricket Club.'

'I can't imagine why, but I'm sure you're going to tell me.'

'Well, I know nothing about cricket, as you're aware, but I gather you have a reputation as a bowler, and now they know you're playing, they're not so confident about winning.'

Bev grinned. 'They call him "Blaster" Brocklehurst.' She evidently found the title amusing.

'And I thought cricket was a gentle game,' said Rhona. 'Anyway, what's so funny about it, Bev?'

'Matt's gentle, all right,' she explained, 'unless you're a batsman.'

'It's all bar-room talk,' said Matt. 'I'm the very essence of mildness, just as Bev says.'

The memory of Bev's ordeal with Scott, and Matt's reaction to it came to mind. 'To most intents and purposes, Matt,' she said, 'I'm sure you are.'

'Anyway, who told you that about the Cricket Club?'

'Gary Oldfield.'

Matt smiled broadly. ' "Bunny" Oldfield?' Well, we'll have to wait and see.'

'Everywhere I go, people are communicating in code,' said Rhona. 'Why is he called "Bunny"?'

'It's not a general nickname for him,' explained Matt. 'I just call him that because, the few times I've played against him, he's been my personal bunny rabbit.'

'And I thought he was straight. I don't think I want to hear any more.'

'He always bowls Mr Oldfield out,' said Bev, 'so he's Matt's "bunny".'

'It's a slang term for an habitual victim,' explained Matt. 'Nothing to do with sexual orientation.'

Bev stared at him, open-mouthed, but she kept quiet.

Rhona, however, was shaking her head in bewilderment. 'And they say German irregular verbs are a mystery,' she said.

'Like any sport, cricket has its own language,' said Matt. 'Just be thankful the match is going to bring in most of the money we need, and leave the language to us.'

'*Most* of it?' Rhona wanted to believe it, but she still hesitated.

'We'll fill the ground, so the ticket money will be considerable. On top of that, there'll be raffle ticket sales and buckets everywhere for donations.'

It was too much to take in. Happily, the oven timer summoned Rhona to the kitchen with the comforting knowledge that, incomprehensible though its language was, the cricket match was going to make a huge contribution to the theatre.

13

A Ready Ear

Matt had long since realised that life had prepared him less than generously for the responsibility he'd assumed in taking Bev under his roof. As her employer, he'd been confident enough that he could meet his obligations, but the demands of that calling were almost insignificant beside those he was experiencing now. Her greatest need was, and always had been, the love and guidance of at least one parent. Instead, she'd never known her father, who had apparently disappeared on learning of her mother's dilemma. Troy's father, also, had followed his example, Bev's mother had shown herself to be pitifully equipped to care for her children, and the luckless girl's fortunes now lay in the hands of a bachelor with absolutely no experience of parenthood. The knowledge weighed heavily on his mind as he looked repeatedly at the time and waited for her return.

It was quite normal for an eighteen-year-old girl to go on a date; he couldn't argue with that, and he'd treated the news, at least outwardly, with kindly interest, realising that this was his first encounter with a dilemma most fathers experienced several times before accepting a state of affairs that was beyond their control. The difference was that Bev wasn't his daughter and, because of that, the whole thing had come as an unsettling and unnerving jolt.

It wasn't yet ten o' clock, and it might be midnight before she came home, so watching the time was a ridiculous way to spend the evening. Having decided that, he realised that he was incapable of concentrating on anything else and, after a moment's deliberation, he picked up the phone and dialled Rhona's number. The dialling tone purred only a few times before she answered.

'Hello?'

'Rhona, tell me if this is a bad time, and I'll leave you in peace.'

'What a negative way to start a conversation, Matt.' She was almost laughing. 'It's a perfectly good time. I've finished marking and I've just poured myself a glass of wine. What are you doing?'

'Behaving like an idiot. Bev's gone on a date, and I'm sitting here like a nervous parent, watching the clock and biting my nails.'

'Hasn't this happened before?' She sounded surprised.

'I imagine she led a pretty normal life up to a few weeks ago, but with all the upset of leaving home, the normal things have taken a back place.'

'Ah.'

Strangely, he found a hint of comfort in that one little word, or rather in her tone. ' "Ah" what, Rhona?'

'My dad used to react like that. Curiously, he never worried about my brother Steve, but he treated me as if I were the last innocent soul on the planet. That was until I went away to university, and he'd no idea what I was getting up to then.' She seemed to consider that briefly, and said, 'You know, just thinking about a recent conversation I had with him, I don't think an awful lot's changed in that respect.'

'It's ridiculous, Rhona. I feel more than ever responsible for her, now that she lives under my roof.'

'Do you think that's ridiculous? I think it's lovely. I mean, you're not legally responsible for her wellbeing, but you've made yourself morally responsible, and I admire you for it.'

'Do you really?' He was feeling better already.

'Aye, but make the most of it, because I'm feeling generous tonight. I'm not usually so free with my compliments.' Before he could speak, she said, 'I'll hold on, if you like, while you get yourself a drink. It seems to me you need a one.'

'Bless you, Rhona. I'll be back in a minute.' He put the phone down and went to the kitchen to open a bottle of wine. Then, having poured himself a glass, he returned to his chair and picked up the phone. 'Are you still there, Rhona?'

'Why aye. I'm not going to desert you in your hour of need. Not 'til my eyes start to close, an' then you'll be on your own, because I'll be no use to you or anybody else.'

'Don't let me keep you up.'

'I'll let you know, don't you worry. First things first, though. You've got to realise that no amount of worrying is going to going to make a scrap of difference to anything. Bev's gone out to enjoy herself, and one thing I've learned about her in the last few weeks is that she's not short of common sense. Just don't ask her to write about it. She'll demonstrate it in other ways, though.'

Now he felt much more relaxed. 'Thanks, Rhona.'

'It's no trouble, bonny lad. Put it down to my Geordie upbringin.'

'You said your mother was like you. Are the others the same?'

'Let me see.' After a fleeting silence, she said, 'Me mam, me granny, me grandad an' me are all birds of a feather. Me dad's maybe a bit more reserved, being a Yorkshireman, but he's a kindly soul. As for Steve, he's got a good heart, but he can't settle at anything.'

Smiling to himself, he said, 'Your accent's broadened again.'

'Aye, you know what they say. You can take the lass out of Newcastle....'

'I like it. What does your brother do?'

'Basically, anything, but not for long. He's working for a removals firm in Gateshead, but I don't know how long that's going to last.' Almost as an afterthought, she said, 'I wish he'd find something that'll allow him to use his real ability.'

'What's that?'

'He's quite a talented artist. He did try art college, but he dropped out of that.' Evidently musing again, she said, 'You know, what he really needs is the right kind of girl.'

'Do you mean responsibility?'

'Not immediately. He couldn't handle that. No, the trouble with Steve is that he doesn't respond well to being pushed into doing anything. He needs to be led, and you can't beat a woman's hand when it comes to that.'

Her last observation made him laugh. 'I'm sure you're right, Rhona. In my experience, the fair sex has nothing to learn about manipulation.'

'You make it sound underhand. Mind you, I have to admit, it can be.' Returning to the original subject, she asked, 'Are you feeling any happier, now?'

'Much happier, thanks, Rhona.' He looked at the time and said, 'I'd better let you get on with whatever you were doing.'

'Aye, I've got a busy day tomorrow, with some of my less-able kids and the younger end, so I'll get an early night. I suppose I'll see you at the cricket match.'

'I'm sure you will. Thanks, Rhona, and goodnight.'

'You're welcome, Matt. Goodnight.'

Now in a more settled mood, he took down one of Ivor Loveday's novels to read again, and he was well into it by the time Bev walked in. She seemed happy enough, and he reminded himself that it was only to be expected. He waited for her to hang up her anorak, and said, 'Hi, Bev. Did you have a good time?'

'Okay.' She thought quickly and added, 'Thanks.'

'What would you like? Chocolate?'

'I'll get it. Do you want anything?'

'No, thanks. I'll stick with the wine.'

When she returned from the kitchen, she asked, 'What have you been doing?'

'Reading.'

She nodded slowly, and then surprised him by saying, 'I wish I could do proper reading.'

'You don't do so badly, Bev.'

She was inclined to be dismissive. 'That's only work,' she said, 'not proper reading, like you do.'

'Well, you can't beat practice.' Almost without thinking, he said, 'Why don't you have a word with Rhona? Ask her if she can find some books that'll help you.'

Bev looked up in surprise. 'Does Rhona know how to do remedial?'

'I'm sure she does, and in several languages.' Suddenly, Rhona had become a source of expertise as well as reassurance. As if he hadn't noticed it already, her influence was growing.

'Food is vitally important wherever you go, but in France, it's a matter to be treated with great respect.'

'Why, Miss?'

'Because, Christine, that's how the French feel about it, and when they put their best efforts in front of you, they like to know they're appreciated.' Memories of Brittany returned momentarily, but Rhona quickly dispelled them. 'Incidentally, I'd far rather you put your hand up if you're going to ask a question.'

'Miss, do they talk English in their cafés?'

'A great many French people speak English,' Christine, 'and they will, quite often, but they don't like it to be taken for granted any more than I like calling out. Now,' she said, addressing the class again, 'you're all going to write down this list in your vocabulary books, because I want you to learn it for a test on Friday, but before that, you need to know how to pronounce these words.' A familiar raised arm caused her to break off again. 'I want the whole class to learn this, Christine, so please give them the opportunity by saving your questions for later.'

'You told me to put me 'and up.'

'I know, Christine, but save it for later. Now, everyone after me, *le repas.*'

'*Le repas.*'

'*Le petit déjeuner.*'

'*Le petit déjeuner.*'

'*Le déjeuner.*'

'*Le déjeuner.*'

'Miss?'

'I've asked you not to call out, Christine.'

'Can you get fish and chips in France?'

'Everyone, *le diner.*'

'*Le* dinner.'

'No, it's pronounced *dee-nay.*'

''Cause if you can't get fish and chips, there's no point in you going, is there?'

There was no point in punishing Christine Harrison with a detention or an imposition. Sanctions would do no good at all. As with all chronic attention-seekers, her case needed to be addressed by a common strategy, and that could only come from higher authority. For the moment, Rhona could only say, 'There are thirty-six children in this class, Christine, and each of them is entitled to an equal share of my time. How do you feel about taking more than your share?'

'I were only askin' a question.'

'So, answer mine, Christine. How do you feel about taking more than your share?'

The child's answer came in the form of a humph followed by, 'So, now I get done just for asking a question.' She underlined her frustration with another humph and stared out of the window.

'*Le beurre.*'

'*Le beurre.*'

'*Le pain.*'

'*Le pain.*'

...

So far, Nigel Ellis had not encountered Christine Harrison.

'You're lucky, Nigel.'

'Her name has occurred at HoD meetings, I have to say.'

He pronounced 'HoD' as an acronym. It stood for 'Heads of Department', but it always set Rhona in mind of a triangular receptacle for carrying bricks. 'In that case, why has nothing been done about her?'

'Someone is looking into the problem, Rhona, but the child has problems. She's one of a large family, and that possibly explains her attention-seeking behaviour.'

'I'm sorry for the poor kid, Nigel, but I'm also concerned for the other thirty-five in her class. While she's bending my ear, they're not getting the attention they need.'

'I'll speak to her year head and find out what's happening. Meanwhile, did you know that John Fieldman is leaving us in July?'

'You know me, Nigel, always the last to hear anything.' She wasn't disappointed to hear the news, albeit belatedly. John Fieldman's contribution to the department and the school generally had been barely noticeable. 'Where's he going?'

'He's got a job at the Education Office, in parental liaison.'

'Oh, glory.'

'What's the matter, Rhona?'

'I just had a mental picture of him answering the phone. "Good bordig. Johd Fielded speakid. How cad I be of assistads?" '

'I think you're being a trifle unkind, Rhona.'

'To be honest, I think so too, and I apologise for it. I should take a leaf out of Sue Womersley's book and feel sorry for the poor bugger, even when he calls me "Rhoda", like the girl in the limerick.'

'What?'

'Never mind.'

It seemed that Nigel had more news for her, a fact that he signalled, as usual, by shifting the papers on his desk. 'I don't know if you realise it, Rhona, but John has a Scale One.'

'I thought he only had alopecia.'

He ignored her reaction and went on. 'As such, he is second-in-command, as it were, of the department.'

Rhona tried to dispel the picture of Nigel and John parading in military uniform and planning major strategies. 'I never realised that,' she said, reflecting that her ignorance of the fact spoke volumes for the impact John Fieldman had made as second-in-command.

'When he leaves, that scale point will, of course, be made available to another member of staff, and I'm recommending you, as you're the senior member of the department, and because of your proven ability, both in the classroom and on foreign holidays.'

'Thank you, Nigel.' The money was minimal, but the scale point would be an acknowledgement of her worth, and it might even help her get a head of department job at some time.

'The decision, however, rests with the Senior Management Team, but I'll keep you posted.'

'Thanks, Nigel.' As two of the deputies were respectively of the Maths and Chemistry Departments, she was now less than excited, as the scale point would be awarded to someone who taught a useful subject, such as Maths, Physics or Chemistry. Now Rhona was also looking forward to the cricket match. It would be a welcome diversion from workaday frustration.

14

A Game of Surprises

There was a mysterious gathering on the pitch; at least, it was mysterious in Rhona's view, but then, that description applied to anything connected with cricket. This particular gathering consisted of the man in the straw hat and linen sports jacket, Terry Cooper and one other. The meeting dissolved quickly, and Terry walked over to the pavilion to speak to his team, which was so far incomplete, as Matt had not yet arrived. Rhona had been looking out for him, but without success, because neither he nor Bev were to be seen, not that Bev's attendance was essential, but it was rare that they were not seen together.

Not surprisingly, Terry shared Rhona's concern, because the first thing he said to his team was, 'I won the toss and I've decided to bat first. Has anybody seen Matt Brocklehurst?' On learning that no one had, he said, 'I've put him down to bat at number seven. I hope it's a while before we need him.'

At the due time, the Club side emerged, as Terry said, to take the field and, as they processed out of the pavilion, Gary Oldfield leaned over to say to Rhona with satisfaction that was unpleasantly obvious, 'Your danger man hasn't turned up. Your side might as well concede the match now.'

'Bugger off, Oldfield,' said Terry.

'What did you say?'

'What I should have told you some time ago,' said Rhona. 'He told you to bugger off, and I wish you would.'

Gary's captain was calling him, so he left them and joined his team mates in the middle. As soon as they'd gone to their fielding positions, the Amateurs' opening pair walked out to the wicket.

Rhona asked, 'What are they doing?'

'The opening batsman's taking guard,' Terry told her. 'The umpire's telling him where to put his bat,' he translated.

'It's a pity he doesn't tell Gary Oldfield where to put his.'

'He's not the most agreeable of characters,' agreed Terry, 'and it looks as if he's going to open the bowling.' Gary was throwing the ball into the air and catching it with theatrical nonchalance while the umpire held out a restraining arm. At the umpire's signal, he walked back to his mark and began his run-up. As he did so, Rhona became aware of voices behind her. One of them was Bev's, and she was helping Matt on to the bench. He looked awful; his face was covered in perspiration, and he sank gratefully on to the seat Bev had found for him.

'Matt,' said Rhona, 'what's the matter?'

'I'll be okay. I'm fine.' Clearly, he was neither.

'I wanted him to go back to bed,' said Bev, 'but he wouldn't.' With the tone of someone twice her age, she said, 'You know what he's like.'

'You should be in bed,' said Terry, 'much as we need you.'

'I'll be all right.'

'I'll get you a cold drink,' said Rhona, heading for the pavilion, where several women were drinking coffee prior to setting out tea for the interval. She asked them, 'Is there a fridge here?'

'Aye, there is,' said one of them. 'It's ancient, but it's all we've got.'

'I need to get some chilled water for Matt,' she said. 'He's got 'flu or something.'

'He looks like it,' one of them agreed, looking out of the opened window. 'He's in a shocking state.'

The first woman who'd spoken dropped a handful of ice cubes into a pint glass and filled it with water. 'There y' are, love,' she said. 'Tell him to get that down his neck.'

'Thank you very much.'

'That's all right, love. Listen, don't worry about helpin' us in here. We've done it a thousand times. Just look after Matt.'

'Thank you, I will.' She took the glass of water out to him. He was sitting with his head back and his eyes closed, so Bev took it from her. As Rhona watched, she ran one hand over the cold condensation on the glass and transferred it to Matt's forehead.

'Thanks, Bev,' he whispered.

'Listen, Matt,' said Terry, 'you're not in a fit state to play. Let the lass take you home.' Turning to Bev, he asked, 'Did you drive him here?'

'Yeah, he can't drive like this.'

'No,' said Matt, 'this match is important. I'll be okay.'

Two things were very evident to Rhona. One was Matt's stubborn single-mindedness, and the other was Bev's practical and capable devotion to the man who'd befriended her. The two impressed her so much that Terry's groan came as a jolt. 'What's the matter, Terry?'

'George Richards is out,' he said. 'We were relying on him to keep things steady.'

Polite applause accompanied George's return to the pavilion and Sam Fox's walk to the wicket.

'Six for one,' said Terry. 'What a start.' He nevertheless welcomed George back sympathetically. 'I've got you down at number seven, Matt,' he said, 'but you can go in further down if you find it easier.'

'Matt,' said Rhona, 'you should be in bed.'

'I'm not going to bed before I've sent Gary Oldfield back to the pavilion with his tail between his legs. I hear he was shooting his mouth off earlier, when I wasn't here.'

'That's a hell of a sacrifice you're making, Matt,' said Terry.' A moment later, he spoke again, this time in alarm. 'Bugger! Sam Fox is out.'

Matt asked, 'What's the score?'

'Ten for two.'

'Bugger,' agreed Matt. Then, remembering he was in mixed company, he apologised quickly. 'Sorry, ladies.'

'I'd say it myself,' said Rhona, 'but I'm more concerned about you, you daft bugger.'

Bev nodded in agreement.

As the new batsman walked out, a voice Rhona couldn't recognise, distorted as it was by the megaphone, said, 'Buckets are coming round, ladies and gentlemen. Please give generously to the theatre fund.' It was a timely reminder. In her concern for Matt, Rhona had almost forgotten about the reason for the match.

The two now in the middle settled down and proceeded to score steadily, much to Gary Oldfield's public dismay, as he saw his efforts go for what from his point of view were far too many runs. It was another bowler, however, who made the break-through, removing both batsmen in the same over.

Eventually, the score stood at sixty-nine for six, and Terry, now padded up, said, 'Stay here, Matt. I'm going in your place.' Before Matt could object, he was walking out to the wicket.

Rhona watched what for her was an incomprehensible game, simply hoping the Amateurs' fortunes would improve. She had started the day disinterested in the result, but now she was desperate for an upturn. She hated to admit it, even to herself, but her attitude had changed the moment Gary had gloated so sickeningly about Matt's absence.

Her aspirations were dealt a blow when Percy Whittaker was clean bowled with the score at eighty-one, and she was wondering who was going to take his place, when, out of the corner of her eye, she saw Matt fastening the last strap on his pads. 'No, Matt,' she said, 'you can't.' Bev was shaking her head fatalistically. 'You don't know what he's like,' she said.

'I'm beginning to get the picture.' She watched him walk out to join Terry at the wicket. There was a brief conference before Matt took guard to see out the over. She watched the next three deliveries take place without incident, and asked Bev, 'What's happening?

'Terry will have told him to block.'

'What does that mean?'

'He'll have told him not to try to score. He just has to hold on to his wicket while Terry does the scoring.'

Rhona was beginning to understand what Matt had meant when he spoke about Terry's ability as a captain. She'd also learned something else about the girl who'd spent her school career being written off by those who should have known better. She said, 'You know a lot about cricket, don't you, Bev?'

'Not really. I used to come here to watch Matt play when he was in the Club.' She said modestly, 'That's all, really.'

They watched Terry add nineteen to the total before he was clean-bowled by Gary, who had been brought back into the attack, according to Bev, 'to mop up the tail'. As that tail included poor, beleaguered Matt, Rhona was naturally anxious.

Greg Whitfield went in at number nine and returned two runs later, to be replaced by David Warburton, who had to wait while Matt faced Gary in the next over, repeatedly blocking his deliveries without scoring. Gary's frustration at being unable to turn the tables on his past nemesis was obvious to those who watched him and, particularly, those close enough to hear his often-obscene observations. Rhona had exceptionally keen hearing.

'Listen to him,' she said, 'cursin' like a drunk at closin' time.' Then, remembering Bev's tender years, she corrected herself. 'Don't listen to him, Bev.'

'I'm used to it,' she said, 'but you don't expect a teacher to eff an' blind like that, do you?'

'No, bonny lass, you have to make allowances for them that knows no better.'

'I bet you're glad, now, you're not goin' out with him anymore.'

'I was glad of that the moment I chucked him.'

'Rhona,' said Bev, 'does everybody talk like you where you come from?'

'No, some of them are so broad, you'd struggle to understand them.' She smiled at a stray thought. 'My granny and grandad would be an education for you, and so would me mam. I'll tell you what.' She'd been thinking about this lately. 'If you like, I'll take you up there when I go again, an' you can find out for yourself what it's like.'

'It's a long way, isn't it?'

It probably seemed so to someone who'd never been anywhere. 'It's less than a hundred miles to Newcastle. It usually takes me about two hours.'

Bev's response was lost when the last wicket fell at 105 runs, with Matt the not-out batsman on no score.

'Howay, Bev, an' we'll get some food for Matt when he comes off.'

They busied themselves in the pavilion, and were carrying three plates and drinks out to the bench when Gary came off the field grinning and as contentious as ever.

'What did I tell you, Goldilocks? Your side doesn't stand a chance, now.' Jerking his head in Matt's direction, he said, 'He can hardly stay on his feet, so you can forget about him bowling.'

'Gary Oldfield,' said Rhona with great feeling, 'you're despicable.' She might have said more, but there were too many people around, although that didn't stop Bev adding her contribution.

'You still can't bowl him out,' she said, 'even when he's poorly!'

Rhona put a protective arm around her, but Gary merely scowled and moved on.

'I never liked him at school,' said Bev, an' I didn't have him for anything.' She got up to make room for Matt, who subsided gratefully on to the bench. He looked at the plate of food Rhona had brought him and shook his head apologetically.

'You can't play all day with an empty stomach,' Rhona told him. 'Have a sandwich, at least.'

'Thanks, Rhona, but my throat's so raw, I can't eat anything.'

'Here's some iced water,' said Bev, mopping his forehead again with the condensation.

'Don't get too close, either of you,' he warned. 'I'm probably infectious.'

'Matt,' said Rhona in a final appeal to his good sense, 'for my money, you've got tonsillitis or something of that kind, and you're in no fit state to be playing cricket or anything else.'

'I had a rest while I was out there,' he insisted. 'Terry told me not to do any running.'

'I know, but Bev and I are going through torment for you while you're out there. I wish you'd see sense.'

He looked as surprised as his condition allowed. 'I don't deserve you two,' he said.

'No, you don't, not when you behave like this. I know you've got a grudge going on with Gary Oldfield, and I know what an exasperating sod he can be, but this is just plain daft.'

'I hear what you're saying, and I appreciate your concern, Rhona. Bev, will you pass me that water, please?' He took it from her gratefully, removing a cube of ice and holding it in his mouth. Clearly, his mind was made up.

After tea, the Amateurs walked out to take the field, followed by the Club's opening pair.

'Matt's got the ball,' said Bev. 'He's going to open the bowling.'

'Now I know how Alice must have felt,' said Rhona despairingly, 'when she ran down the rabbit hole. I don't believe any of this is happening.

The on-strike batsman took guard, and Matt walked back to his mark. As he ran up, Bev said, 'He's taking it easy.'

'You could have fooled me.'

'He'll be saving his pace for Bunny Oldfield,' said Bev confidently.

Even at a reduced pace, Matt's second ball was caught behind, and the umpire raised his finger accordingly.

Things settled down in the second over, which was a maiden, and then Matt took over the strike again. Once more, he ran in at a gentle medium pace, worrying the batsman with his first three deliveries before clean-bowling him.

Bev was as animated as Rhona had ever seen her. 'That's two wickets for two runs,' she exulted. Rhona retreated further into disbelief.

There was an early bowling change, which Bev explained to Rhona. 'Terry knows Matt can't go on bowling like he usually does, so he's saving him for later.'

'I'm glad Terry's being sensible,' said Rhona. 'Somebody has to be.'

Matt had only been at what Bev told her was first slip for one over, when there was a shout of 'How's that?' Matt threw the ball triumphantly into the air and caught it again. The umpire raised his finger for the third time, and the Amateurs' total of 105 no longer seemed quite as paltry as it had a short time earlier.

There was a period of consolidation, during which the Club increased its score slowly but without further loss until Terry made another bowling change and brought Matt back into the attack. It seemed that two overs were all the captain would allow him in each spell, but they were sufficient for him to claim another wicket.

'Three for seven,' sang Bev, the child who was deemed to struggle with the basic subjects. In keeping score for her hero, she found that arithmetic posed no challenge.

A run-out brought the number of wickets to five. It also brought Gary Oldfield, now looking rather less ebullient, to the crease. Terry waited for the current over, and the next, to be completed before recalling Matt to bowl from his original end.

'He won't ask Matt to bowl uphill while he's poorly,' explained Bev.

'But why has he brought him back so soon?'

'He's giving him a chance to bowl Bunny Oldfield out,' said Bev with a chuckle. 'He won't keep him bowling for long.'

Now running in at an increased pace, Matt made his first delivery, causing a gasp from the crowd as Gary played and missed at a ball that cleared the off stump by a fraction. Matt stopped to give Gary a long look before returning to his mark.

'That's just to let Bunny Oldfield know he's on his case,' said Bev, now quite assured in her role as Rhona's personal commentator.

They watched Matt run in fast again to unleash his second delivery, which removed Gary's off stump and bails to the Amateurs' raucous delight.

He reverted to his former, gentler pace for the remainder of the over, after which, Terry sent him back to first slip.

'Four for eight,' chanted Bev, still enjoying the memory of Gary, who had been clearly furious as he headed for the sanctuary of a bench as far from theirs as he could find.

Matt took one more wicket before the Amateurs bowled out the Club for ninety-one.

'Well bowled, Matt,' said Bev as she and Rhona helped him into the passenger seat of his car.

'Well,' he said, closing his eyes wearily, 'I had to get on with the job while I still could.'

Rhona asked, 'Who's your doctor, Matt?'

He considered the question and then gave up. 'I can't remember his name,' he said. 'It's the surgery beside the library.'

'Okay, I'll wait for Bev to get you home, and then I'll phone them.' After further thought, she said, 'I'll come round later with something for dinner.' Yet another surprise, she reflected as the car left the cricket ground, was that Bev had a driving licence. She'd learned more in working for Matt than she'd ever learned at school.

15

Kindness is a Way of Life

When Bev opened the door, Rhona said, 'Let me put this in the kitchen, bonny lass. It's soup for Matt. I'll get fish and chips for you and me when I've given him this.' She carried the soup through into the kitchen and put it on the worktop. 'Has the doctor been?'

'Yes.'

'What did he say?'

'He's got… tonsil viralitis.'

'Do you think he meant viral tonsillitis?' It was the likeliest possibility.

Bev nodded. 'That was it. He'll be okay in three or four days, but he has to take headache tablets and something to sooth his throat.'

'Right. Paracetamol and something like honey and lemon. I've got all those things at home.'

'He has to do something with salt and water.' The mechanics of it seemed to have deserted her.

'Gargle, I expect.'

'How did you know?'

'There's a limit to what you can get up to with salt water when you have tonsillitis, Bev, and it's very good for sore throats.' Gesturing upstairs, she asked, 'Is he in bed?'

'Yes.'

'I'll go up and see him. Which room is he in?'

'Go that way,' she said, pointing with her left hand, 'at the top of the stairs, and it's before you get to the bathroom.'

'Thanks, Bev. I'll see you in a minute,' she said, reminding herself that lots of people confused left with right without necessarily being slow learners.

On reaching the door before the bathroom, she tapped and waited. 'Matt,' she said, 'are you decent?'

The answer was a groan, so she took that as an affirmative and pushed the door open to find him, as she expected, in bed, but unclad, at least as far as she could see. 'Matt, have you no pyjamas?'

'No.'

'You can't go wandering around in the bare buff with a young girl in the house. You'll frighten the life out of her.'

He pointed weakly to the foot of the bed, where his dressing gown hung ready.

'Your dressing gown, right. Listen, I've brought you some soup, as you're struggling with solids, and I'll cook properly tomorrow. I'll bring some honey and lemon as well, and you have to gargle with salt water. Can you manage that?'

'Yes.'

'Now, don't worry about anything. I'll look after Bev, and she'll answer the phone. All right?'

He swallowed with difficulty and said, Thanks, Rhona.'

'It's nothing compared with what you did for the Amateurs this afternoon. Everybody went away feeling that they'd had value for their money. As far as I know, the only person who was upset was Gary Oldfield, and I'm sure you won't lose any sleep over that.'

In spite of his discomfort, he managed a smile.

'Anyway, I'll be back in a few minutes with some soup.'

It was fortunate that the weekend of the cricket match was followed by Spring Bank Holiday and the school half-term break, because it enabled Rhona to spend as much time as she needed in helping Bev look after Matt, and in keeping house for him. Bev was naturally ill-prepared for the domestic role, but it was surprising how quickly she began to pick up cooking, as well as generally running the place, confirming, as Rhona suspected, that her past difficulties stemmed not from her inability to learn, but from the shortcomings of at least some of those responsible for her education. The week was also an opportunity for Rhona to start Bev on some of the reading she'd prepared for her.

After three days, Matt recovered from the infection, as the doctor had prophesied, and his temperature returned to normal. His recovery coincided with the news that the cricket match had earned even more than expected, which meant that construction of the theatre ceiling and sandblasting of the seats could go ahead. The next job would be the stage, which would have to be constructed from scratch, and then the curtain operating gear could be installed. At the same time, work could begin on the plumbing and heating. Rhona's prime concern, however, was Matt's health.

'Are you sure you're going to be all right, looking after yourself while I go up home?'

'As right as rain,' he assured her.

'And can you manage without Bev, just until Sunday night?'

'Of course I can, and it'll do her a power of good. I don't think she's ever been outside the dale.'

'All right.' After recent events, it seemed natural for her to offer a hug as well as the customary kiss on the cheek. 'Look after yourself, Matt, and I'll see you when we get back.'

The journey to Newcastle was easy, as well as a continuous source of wonder for Bev, who remarked on each new excitement and was finally rendered speechless on encountering the celebrated Tyne Bridge.

'I hesitate to admit it,' said Rhona, 'but it was built by a Yorkshire firm.' On reflection, she said, 'Well, Middlesborough was in Yorkshire when they built it.'

The country girl's excitement at seeing a big city for the first time continued undiminished until Rhona pulled up outside her Granny and Grandad Headley's house.

As usual, the house door was open before they were out of the car, and Mrs Headley greeted Rhona in her usual unreserved way before turning to Bev. 'So you're the lass we've been hearing about,' she said.

'Howay inside, hinny. This is my husband. He looks frightenin', but diven't be fooled, he's a big softie, really.'

'Who are you callin' frightenin', woman?' Enclosing Bev's hand gently between his huge, leathery palms, he said, 'Welcome to Newcastle, bonny lass.'

Bev whispered uncomfortably in Rhona's ear.

'Why aye, it's been a long journey. It's upstairs and the first on your right.' While she was out of the room, Rhona said, 'You'll find her shy to begin with. She was brought up by a mam that's not fit to have bairns, and she struggled at school, but she's really come on since she started working for Matt.'

'Poor little scrap,' said Mrs Headley. 'I'll put the kettle on for a cup of tea.'

Mr Headley asked, 'What's goin' on between you and this Matt fella, Rhona?'

'Nothing, Grandad. We're friends, and he and Bev did my kitchen. They made a good job of it an' all.'

'That's the sort of friends to have, right enough.'

Returning from the kitchen, Mrs Headley said, 'Your mam tells us you've stopped seein' that games teacher, Rhona.'

'That was ages ago, Granny. I told her when I was up here in… February half-term, I think it was.' Memories of the cricket match prompted her to say, 'Good riddance an' all.'

Before either of them could react, Bev came back into the room, and Mr Headley said, 'Rhona tells us you're a builder, Bev. Howay and tell us what sort of things you do.' Seeing that she was struggling to overcome her shyness, he asked her, 'Do you do bricklaying?'

'Yeah.'

'Plasterin'?'

'Yeah.'

'What about electrics?'

'Matt does the electrics. I help him.'

'You sound like a handy sort of lass to have around.' Standing up, he said, 'Howay and let's show you somethin'.' Taking her by the hand, he led her outside.

'He's goin' to show her next door's pointin',' said Mrs Headley, shaking her head at her husband's silliness. 'He'll upset Mr and Mrs Wood if he's not careful.'

'What's wrong with it?'

'They got a one of them fly-by-night jerry-builders to do it, an' it's a right mess, but that doesn't make it right for your grandad to show it to everybody who comes to the house.'

Rhona couldn't help smiling. 'He's probably doing Rhona a power of good. He'll bring her out of herself.'

Mrs Headley put the teapot down on the table and left it to brew. 'You said her mam should never have had bairns. Why's that?'

'She's completely irresponsible and she takes on the worst kind of men. One of them tried it on with Bev. That's why she ran away, and Matt took her in.'

'No. That's awful, Rhona.'

'Matt went round there to pick up Bev's stuff. I'm glad I wasn't there. I can't abide women of that sort.'

'Was that man there?'

'Yes, and he got stroppy, but Matt dealt with him.'

'I hope he gave him a good hidin'.'

'I believe he did.' Again, Rhona had to smile, this time at her granny's reaction. She was the gentlest of people, but there were things that angered her, usually when children were involved.

'Bev has a little brother,' she told her. 'He's just coming up to eleven, so there's nothing Matt can do for him.'

Mrs Headley was shaking her head. 'Why, it's a tragedy,' she said.

The door opened, and Mr Headley returned with Bev. Clearly, the ice was now broken, because she was chattering happily. 'The easiest way is to use a finger trowel,' she was telling him.

'Is that so? Not a pointing trowel, then?'

'No, a pointing trowel's no good, and Matt uses an old kitchen knife for putty and mastic. He says if you use the right tools, you never get the job done.'

Rhona felt a warm glow. Her grandad had come up trumps, as he always would.

'This is Bev's first visit to Northumberland,' said Rhona, having introduced her to her parents. 'I threw her in at the deep end with me granny and grandad, but she managed to understand broad Geordie.'

'Poor lass,' said her mother. 'I hope you prepared her for it.'

Bev seemed fascinated by the fact that Rhona and her mother shared the same unusual hair colouring.

'You wouldn't notice it as much with me granny,' said Rhona, 'because hers is nearly all grey now, but it was the same.'

'It was the first thing I noticed about Mrs Loveday,' said Rhona's father, 'that and her cheeky smile.'

'Haddaway,' said his wife.

'I caught her and a few more Wrens having a tea party on board my ship, didn't I, darling?'

'An' it was love at first sight. He was so taken with me, he gave me a tin of plum jam. There's just no arguin' with that, is there?'

Bev stared at them, possibly wondering how a man and a woman of their great age could still talk about love. Her eyes then went to their wedding photograph, which she'd already seen at Rhona's house.

'You see,' said Rhona, 'me mam wasn't wearing her uniform that day, because it was a special day.'

'We didn't have to wear uniform when we went ashore,' said her mother, taking a photo album from a bookcase. 'Howay and look at this, Bev.' She turned the pages of grey, recycled card until she came to a picture taken in a Fort William pub. 'There I was, in my uniform, and there's Rhona's dad looking stern. All gunnery officers have to look stern, you understand. It's part of the job.'

At last, Bev spoke. 'When was that?'

'Nineteen forty-three,' said Mrs Loveday confidently. 'Mr Loveday came to Scotland looking for me, 'cause he couldn't bear to be parted from me a moment longer.'

Bev risked a glance at Mr Loveday, who was grinning broadly. 'It's basically true,' he said. 'I was lucky to get that posting, because it brought us together again. We got married in nineteen-forty-five, and Rhona was born two years later.'

'I'll be twenty-six later this year,' said Rhona, guessing at the confused arithmetic going on in Bev's head, although she knew that the greatest source of wonder was a relationship that had survived at least thirty years. It was still wonderful for Rhona, but it must have seemed incredible to Bev, whose experience of adult relationships had been fleeting and chaotic. Rhona was saving the news that her grandparents were to celebrate their sixtieth wedding anniversary later that year.

Later, when Rhona had shown her to Steve's bedroom, she remarked on the pictures on the walls, one of which was a painting of a nude, actually a copy of a Jan Steen.

'Steve painted that,' Rhona told her, 'when he was an art student.'

'Is he an art student now?'

'No, he dropped out, and he's done lots of things since then.'

After some thought, Bev said, 'Your mum and dad are really nice, and your granny and grandad are, too.'

'I'm glad you think so, Bev. They like you.' It was important for her to know that.

Later, at dinner, Bev managed to overcome her shyness enough to take part in the general conversation, during which Rhona told the story of the cricket match.

'Not that I know the first thing about it,' she said. 'Bev explained everything to me.'

'It was a good match,' said Bev, 'even though Matt was poorly.'

'He had tonsillitis,' explained Rhona, 'but he insisted on playing, which was just as well, really.'

Her mother had been following the conversation with, as usual, one thought in mind. She asked, 'How do you come to know Matt?'

'He's Bev's boss, they built my kitchen, and we're good friends,' she told her pointedly.

Tactfully, her father changed the subject, asking Bev, 'What do you think of this place so far, Bev?'

'Everybody's really nice.' She delivered her verdict with total conviction.

'That's right,' he said. 'Kindness is a way of life up here.'

Rhona had to agree.

16

GOWNS, HOODS AND HISTORY

Rhona arrived at school the following Monday morning, less than surprised to find that little had changed. As expected, her pigeon hole contained a rehearsal schedule for *Annie Get Your Gun*, and also on cue, a reminder of the annual School Fête, or 'Fête Worse than Death', as Rhona preferred to call it, and a peremptory decree that reports must be handed to Ian Crawley, the Curriculum Deputy, by Friday, the 29th of June. The only feature of the final half term that caused her to raise an eyebrow was the notice alerting everyone to a 'plenary' staff meeting that day at 4:30.

'I've attended a few staff meetings in my short career,' she told Ian Crawley, 'but I cannot remember a "plenary" one. As you're a member of the inner brotherhood, will you please translate?'

' "Plenary" means "entire", Rhona,' he said, as if the meaning should have been obvious.

'So it's a full staff meeting?'

'In essence, yes.'

'Then why the hell don't they say so?'

Whether Mr Crawley had no idea, or had been instructed to draw a veil over management decisions generally, remained a mystery, because he gave no reply, but continued to pin his substitution list to the notice board, leaving Rhona in ignorance. On reflection, though, she could see that the term made sense. The Latin word *plenus* meant 'full' or 'entire', and a French farm animal that was *pleine* was in calf, foal, lamb, whelp or farrow, not unlike a staffroom filled with grudging staff, all waiting to emerge, blinking in the sunlight, from the carpark exit. The adoption of the new terminology she attributed to anal retention on the part of the Headmaster.

She was coaxing the last of the hot water into her coffee mug when a familiar voice said, ''Morning, Goldilocks.'

'Good morning, Bunny.'

'Don't call me that in here.' It was a plea rather than a demand, and that made Gary seem more pathetic than ever.

'In that case, don't call me "Goldilocks".'

'It's only Matt Brocklehurst who calls me "Bunny",' he told her in a low voice.

'I'm not surprised. He was running a temperature of a hundred-and-four and feeling like death-warmed-up when he bowled you out.' Her laughter caused her to spill a drop of coffee on the staffroom carpet, not that anyone would notice it among the other spillages.

'It was a freak dismissal.'

'In that he dismissed a freak? I'll agree with that. The fact remains,' she said, feeling that someone should take a grown-up line, 'that the match raised more than any of us expected for the theatre fund.'

'Big deal.' The hurt would be slow to ebb. 'What use is a theatre, anyway?'

'It's very useful as a place where intelligent people go for entertainment, Gary, so I suppose your conundrum's quite understandable.'

He placed his mug under the tap and turned the lever, only to find that the boiler was empty. 'You were never like this when you were going out with me.'

'No, I put up with an awful lot, didn't I?'

Her riposte was lost on him, because he asked, 'Is there nothing you miss, now that you're not going out with me, Rhona?'

Rhona narrowed her eyes in an attitude of thought, and then pursed her lips, after which she bit her lower lip in studied concentration. Finally, she said, 'No, I can't think of anything.'

'Nothing at all?'

Feigning memory searching once more, she stroked her chin briefly before holding up one finger for a moment and then allowing it to fall. 'No,' she confirmed, 'nothing at all.'

The bell rang for registration, bringing the conversation mercifully, at least from Gary's point of view, to a close.

The day went quite smoothly. Rhona had always maintained that the best part of the job came with being in the classroom with the kids. It was the rest that was irritating, although, as she kept reminding herself, no job could be rewarding all the time.

She dismissed Lower Sixth German at 4:15 and went to the staffroom to find a seat for the meeting, thereby proceeding from the sublime in the shape of Müller's poetry to the stupefyingly ridiculous.

In due course, the Senior Management Team entered the staffroom, and the pantomime commenced. The first item was Speech Day, which would take place early in November to allow for the arrival of GCE and CSE certificates, but which had to be planned well in advance. Rhona had no idea why that was: she simply accepted it as law.

Mr Purbright, the Headmaster announced, 'Academic dress will, of course, be worn.'

'Oh, bloody hell,' said Norman Davis, Head of Art. He was sitting three places away from Rhona, so he had to whisper loudly, 'Can I borrow your BA gown and hood again, Rhona?'

'Of course you can, bonny lad. You're welcome to 'em anytime.' In accordance with convention, she would be wearing her MA robes, which meant she could be generous with her lesser trappings.

'A discussion appears to be taking place at the back,' observed Mr Purbright. 'Is it something important, Miss Loveday?'

'Vitally important, Mr Purbright. It was about academic dress, but it's all settled, now.'

'I take it I may continue?'

'Be my guest, bonny— Mr Purbright.'

'To continue,' he said, looking meaningfully at Rhona, 'hopefully with one meeting at the front. We have yet to secure the services of a guest speaker.'

It seemed to Rhona that he might manage better if he tried not to be such a sarcastic bugger, but she naturally kept that thought to herself.

The meeting ground on, with the usual suspects lengthening the proceedings for no better reason than for the pleasure of hearing their own voices. Eventually, Mr Purbright announced item number nine on the agenda, which was the Annual Fête. The date was decided and noted, and responsibility was to be shared, unsurprisingly, between those who had participated in past years. Once ensnared, there was no escape.

'Miss Loveday, may we rely on you again to mastermind the Baking Competition?'

'Consider it masterminded, Mr Purbright.'

With the lopsided grin that usually accompanied his awkward attempts at humour, he asked, 'Will you be making your characteristically droll appeal in plenary assembly?'

That word again, thought Rhona. 'Yes, Mr Purbright, *in plenus et in partim facetiae.*'

'What? Oh, I see, yes, "wit in entirety and in part". Very good, Miss Loveday.' Gathering his sober wits, he said, 'You will try to keep it non-controversial, this year, won't you?'

'I haven't decided yet what I'm going to say, Mr Purbright, but I'll do my best.'

'Good. Mrs Wray, will you be favouring us by operating your husband's badge-making apparatus?'

'Of course, Mr Purbright.'

As Head of Home Economics, Mrs Wray should have been getting her hands floury with the Baking Competition, but life was too short for pettiness. It also occurred to Rhona that it was also too short for interminable meetings, but that was beyond her control. She listened happily as Gary Oldfield consented, reluctantly as ever, to sit in the stocks and be pelted with wet sponges, and hoped the meeting would end before the supermarket closed.

As arranged, Rhona went to the theatre, after dinner, to lend a hand with the sweeping up, the seating having been removed for sand blasting. Matt had thoughtfully provided a bag of sand to keep the dust down, so the experience wasn't too unpleasant, and the place quickly began to look respectable. Rhona also noticed that the stench of insecticide was no longer as noisome as it had been in recent weeks. When all was swept and ready for the next development, she went home for a bath and to prepare a recipe for a Victoria sponge cake.

The next morning, feeling unusually virtuous at being at school a whole hour before the bell, she rolled off a generous number of Banda copies of the recipe before treating herself to a leisurely mug of coffee in the almost-deserted staffroom.

At the bell for assembly, she ushered her tutor group to the hall and took her place at the piano, the music department being very much in evidence, though showing no appreciable sign of shame.

'O Jesus, I Have Promised' to the modern, convulsive tune, went reasonably well, particularly with the more hyperactive pupils, and Rhona was aware of the sound of hymn books making contact with heads, as members of staff fought to restore an appropriate level of decorum.

L. M. Purbright's address was largely ignored, and the time came for 'messages' from individual members of staff. In due course, the Headmaster's glance fell on Rhona.

'Ah,' he said, like a botanist discovering a rare and welcome species, 'Miss Loveday has something to tell us.'

'Put your hand up,' Rhona told the assembled pupils, 'anyone who knows anything about King Alfred.' She wasn't at all surprised when not a single hand moved. 'King Alfred,' she informed them, 'was King of the West Saxons – that was down in the south-west of England, somewhere – in the ninth century AD, and during that time, England was being attacked regularly by the Danes, who burned, pillaged, destroyed things and… and made free… with… anything that took their fancy.' She could see that she had their full attention, which was something of a bonus at morning assembly. 'One day,' she continued, 'the Saxon army were in full retreat, and King Alfred himself was running for his life. Well, he came upon a cottage, where he threw himself on the mercy of the woman that lived there and begged her to let him hide. She said, "Why aye, bonny lad, but you'll have to make yoursel' useful, mind. I've just put some cakes in the oven, and I want you to watch 'em while I go to the shops. Just make sure they diven't burn. Okay?" He couldn't very well refuse, so he sat himself down in front of the oven to watch the cakes baking. He was very tired after running so far, and the heat from the oven made him sleepy. Before long, he was fast asleep. Anyway, the woman came home from the shops to find him snorin' his head off and the cakes burnt to a cinder, so she took a broom and gave him a good whacking, telling him what she thought of him, 'cause she didn't know he was the King. She probably apologised to him when she found out, 'cause you would, wouldn't you?' She was rewarded by a chorus of agreement, which proved they'd been listening. 'Well, don't run away with the idea he was a softie all the time, though, because he organised a fleet of boats to meet the Danes at sea and send them on their way back to Legoland with a few bruises and black eyes as souvenirs.' She let that sink in, before coming to the point. 'You're probably wondering why a teacher of languages is giving you a history lesson,' she said, 'so I'll tell you. Believe it or not, the original recipe for those cakes survived the Danish wars and everythin' else that's happened since then, and I happen to have it... yes, in my possession. Now, I'm not a selfish person, as you know, and I'm prepared to give a copy to anybody who brings me ten pence. That's one shilling, for those who are still struggling with the new money, bless you. Bring me ten new pence and I'll give you a one of these copies of the recipe.' She held them up so that they could see them. 'Look,' she said, 'they're printed in the purple ink they used in Saxon times. Buy one of these, go home and bake a cake, enter it in the Baking Competition on the day of the Fête, and the winner will get a book of fabulous recipes.' While that was sinking in, she said, 'By the way, the entries will be judged by members of my tutor group, not by me.' She shook her head to dispel any lingering misunderstanding. 'You know what I'm like,' she said. 'I'd want to give you all a prize, and that would never do, even if I could afford it.'

The Headmaster caught her as she was leaving the hall. 'Miss Loveday,' he said, 'thank you for getting the Baking Competition off to your usual, creative start. I do have one reservation, however, and that is regarding your reference to Legoland. We don't want anyone to run away with the idea that Lego had been invented in Saxon times.'

'I think they'll have worked that out for themselves, Mr Purbright,' she said. 'That's if they gave it a second thought.' Rhona's thoughts were on the day ahead and, after that, the state of progress at the theatre.

17

ECSTASY POSTPONED

Rhona arrived at the theatre to find that a quantity of timber, galvanised nails and plasterboard had been delivered, so that Arthur Bentley and his assistant could make a start on the false ceiling, and Matt and Bev could begin building the stage. She found Matt examining his working drawing.

'All right, Matt?'

'Hi, Rhona. All right?'

'Not bad.' She peered at the drawing and said, 'I didn't know it was going to have a trapdoor.'

'It might as well. It's easier than putting one in afterwards.' He rolled up the drawing and gave her his full attention. 'Bev's never stopped talking about visiting your family in Newcastle,' he said. 'It did her a power of good.'

'I'm glad. They were all pleased to see her.'

'She says she liked everybody, but most of all, she liked your grandad. She was a bit wary of him at first, but she soon got to know him.'

'Aye, he's like that.' Looking at the stack of timber, she asked, 'When are you thinking of making a start?'

'As soon as the stuff arrives. We haven't much on, this week.' He noticed her look of puzzlement, and explained, 'That lot's for the ceiling joists. Ours is on its way.' Looking at his watch, he asked, 'Do you fancy a drink?'

'I thought you'd never ask. Is Bev coming?'

'No, she's got a date.'

'Oh? The same lad as before?'

'No.' He picked up the drawing. 'He got a bit too friendly, so she showed him the door.'

'Good for her.'

'Yes, it's the strangest thing. She's had the worst kind of example, but she still manages to live by her own rules.'

'Does she talk to you about that kind of thing?'

'In a roundabout way.' He laughed. 'It doesn't help that I'm a fella.' Then, perhaps feeling that he should explain, he said, 'Her exact words were, "Lads are all the same, but he tried it on from the start." '

'Right enough,' she said, 'it's always up to the girl to say, "no". I'm glad she's got that much about her.'

As they crossed the street, he asked, 'Have you seen Gary Oldfield since the match?'

'Yes, and he's still sulking.'

'Is he?'

'Not just about the match. He still hasn't been able to accept that it's all over between him and me. It was short-lived, anyway, but anyone would think I was the love of his life.' She followed Matt into the Pack Horse.

'I know. What'll you have?'

'A glass of red wine, please. What do you mean by, "I know"?'

Matt ordered the drinks and paid for them. 'I know it still bothers him that you broke up with him. I think you really were the biggest thing in his life – not that there's anything strange about that – but he can't get used to the idea that he's no longer a part of yours.'

'How do you know?' It surprised her that anyone else knew about it.

'Well....'

'Tell me, Matt. I've got a right to know.'

'Of course you have. It's just that he asked me if there was anything going on between you and me, and that was when he told me how hard it had hit him when you gave him the push.' He took the drinks and handed Rhona hers.

'Thanks, Matt. You know, I feel uneasy, now. I mean, you hear things about people being obsessed and... not wanting to let go. It's uncanny.'

'He shouldn't be a problem, but let me know if he starts being a nuisance.'

'I can probably handle him, Matt, but thanks for the offer.' Just talking to Matt was reassuring, but she was happier still when he changed the subject.

He asked, 'Are you going to the recital at Metcalfe Hall?'

It was news to Rhona. 'It must have passed me by. Who's doing what and when?'

'Damien Franklin again, on Friday. He's playing a general programme from Scarlatti to… Prokofiev, I believe.'

'Wonderful. I don't know how I missed that.'

'You've had a lot of excitement lately, but I'm going into town tomorrow, if that helps.'

'If you can get two tickets, Matt, I'll pay you for them. I think we're agreed that these things are enjoyed better in company.' She added quickly, 'That's if you fancy it, of course.'

'Of course, but it's my turn to pay.'

That Friday, Rhona was tidying her desk prior to leaving, when Gary came into the room.

'Hello, Gary,' she said, a little surprised. 'No rugby practice today?'

'The rugby season's over 'til September, Goldilocks.'

'Commiserations, Baby Bear. That must leave a big hole in your life.'

'You left a bigger one,' he said, sitting on one of the class chairs in front of Rhona's desk, 'and do you have to call me that?'

'I'll do a deal with you, Gary. Stop calling me "Goldilocks" and I'll stop calling you "Baby Bear" or "Bunny". How's that?'

'I only call you that out of affection,' he said, like a child pleading his miserable case, which, in effect, he was.

'The time for affection is over, Gary. Let's just regard each other as… colleagues.' She'd been about to say, "professional colleagues", but she realised it was a lot to ask.

'If you come out with me for a drink, I'm sure we can iron out any differences.'

'And I'm equally sure we can't.' She was about to say more, but the door opened, and Nigel Ellis put a stack of blue-covered books on the nearest desk, saying, 'First-Year French reports, Rhona. Pass them on to the History Department when you've done them.'

'Thanks, Nigel. Now, Gary, say after me, "*Um die Ecke, kann Mann immer besser finden*".'

When Nigel was gone, Gary asked, 'What was all that about?'

'I was pretending to help you with your German, so that Nigel didn't get the wrong idea. He's not the quickest to form a conclusion, but you never know.' By way of further explanation, she said, 'It was actually a translation of, "There's always something better round the corner", and there is. You need to find someone who shares your interests.' Even as she said it, she realised she'd set him an impossible task, but she continued nevertheless. 'I play and listen to music, I go to concerts and the theatre, and I read a lot. Be honest, Gary, if only with yourself, and admit that none of those things interests you. The only appeal I've ever had, as far as you're concerned, is the physical kind, and that's not enough for me.'

'You never complained when we were doing it.'

'You misunderstand. I resented being seen as something to round off an evening of drinking and rugby talk with your mates. You might just as well keep an inflatable sex doll in your bedroom, and that's not how I see myself, believe me.'

Like someone grasping a lifeline, he said eagerly, 'We could go somewhere different. I don't have to talk about rugby.'

'You're missing the point, Gary. You and I are poles apart.'

Still, with the unquenchable spirit that no doubt enabled him to score tries in the face of fearful odds, he persisted. 'I still think we can find... what's it called?'

'You tell me. You're the one who's looking for it.' She put two textbooks on the shelf behind her desk, hoping she could bring the conversation to a close.

Inspiration finally came to him, and he said, 'Common ground, that's the word I was looking for.'

'Two words, Gary, and I'm afraid we have no common ground. I'm sorry, because I never intended to hurt you, but you're wasting your time.'

Almost sullenly, he said, 'Maybe you should have thought about that sooner.'

'Thought about what?'

'That you didn't want to hurt me.'

Now he was trying to make her feel guilty, as if that was going to win her back. 'Listen, Gary, she told him wearily, 'As I recall, you and I lasted four weeks—'

'And three days.'

'Four weeks and three days, give or take a minute or two,' she conceded, 'and for two of those weeks, not to mention the three days, I tried to think of some way of letting you down gently. Now, subtlety was always a non-starter with you, and that was why I had to—'

'You're just not listening.'

'*I'm* not listening? Gary, I told you at February half-term that we were finished. You've had four months to get used to the idea. Why can't you just accept it and move on?'

'You don't understand, Rhona.' He was shaking his head, presumably in disbelief that she should fail to understand something as basic as his inability to accept that his cause was lost.

'On that key point, I have to agree. I don't understand what is so incomprehensible about the word "finished".'

The classroom door opened again, and Nigel leaned inwards to ask, 'Are you all right, Rhona? I thought I heard raised voices.'

'I'm fine, thank you, Nigel. As a matter of fact,' she said, picking up her bag, 'I'm just leaving. Goodbye, Gary.' Nigel would never know how grateful she was for his interruption.

···

On the way to Metcalfe Hall, she told Matt, 'I had a visit from Gary, just as I was leaving. Believe it or not, he wanted me to join him for a drink to smooth things over. What do I have to do to persuade him that he's blown it and he's not getting a second chance?'

'Leave him to me, Rhona. I'll probably see him tomorrow or Sunday.'

'No rough stuff, please, Matt.'

'No, I'll just explain things to him,' he said, adding with a smile, 'man to man.'

'I hope you can be more persuasive than I've been. Three months have gone by since I finished with him.'

'He's a funny bloke, like a kid in some respects.'

Rhona parked and switched off the engine. 'You can say that again.'

'When I say that,' said Matt, paying for a parking ticket and handing it to Rhona, 'I mean that he was most likely brought up learning that if he asked for something often enough, he got it. I think, as well, that he was never taught to cope with disappointment.'

'I've seen him after his team has lost a match. He's inconsolable.'

'Let's go and enjoy ourselves,' said Matt. 'Forget about Gary, if you can.'

They took their places in the auditorium, where Rhona found the familiar surroundings soothing in themselves, as if Matt's company weren't enough.

On the stroke of seven-thirty, Damien Franklin appeared on the platform to welcoming applause, and the recital began with two of Scarlatti's sonatas. They were brilliant little pieces, but Rhona was still trying to close out the problem of Gary. It must have been somehow obvious to Matt, because he leaned towards her and took her hand, whispering, 'Leave him to me.'

The combination of those few words and his hand enclosing hers provided the warmth and comfort she needed, and she was able to banish Gary from her thoughts and enjoy the music.

The Beethoven, Chopin and Liszt items were superb, but the highlight of the programme for Rhona came with Prokofiev's *Third Piano Sonata*, which was possibly as startling for her as the programme notes said it had been for the critics of the time. She was so enthused by its electrifying force and its contrasting moods, dazzling and plaintive by turn, that she had to make herself concentrate on the two encores.

As they left the hall, she said, 'I'm going to get a copy of that Prokofiev sonata and learn it.'

'Don't tell me Schumann's got competition.'

'Of course not. It's only a fling, but an exciting one for all that.'

'It's probably worth celebrating. Do you like Italian food? There's a very good restaurant just off Town Hall Square.'

It did seem like a good idea. 'I think I know the one you mean. Shall we see if we can get a table?'

'There's one reserved for us. This time, I thought we'd have something a bit more sophisticated than fish and chips.'

'Don't be a snob, Matt.' She took his arm, nevertheless, and walked with him to Town Hall Square. The easy way he'd taken her hand in the concert hall and whispered reassurance was all part of the relaxed relationship theirs had become. She could do most things in Matt's company in total confidence.

When they reached the restaurant, the waiter struggled with the name 'Brocklehurst' at first, but the problem was overcome, and he showed them to a corner table, giving them each a menu and assuring them that everything on it was available.

'I always think Italian restaurants are warm and welcoming,' said Rhona, 'and I'm really glad you booked this one. I just hope you'll let me do the honours.'

'I wouldn't hear of it.'

'I was afraid of that.' Resigning herself to the fact that she was never going to change his mind, she changed the subject instead, and asked, 'What's Bev doing tonight?'

'Boyfriending.'

'That same one?'

'No, a new one.'

In the light of recent events, she asked, 'Do you feel easier about it, now?'

'A lot easier, yes. She has a good head on her shoulders.'

'She has, and all that time she was at school, they thought she was backward.'

He surprised her by saying, 'I think a lot of kids start their education after they leave school. A certain kind of learner does well at school and goes on to flourish academically, but there are those who struggle in the classroom and then find a sense of purpose in the workplace.'

'I'm sure you're right, Matt. Bev's living proof of that. She really came into her own as my personal commentator at the cricket match. She seems to have a good grasp of the game, and she taught me a lot as well.'

The waiter came, so they gave him their order, and Matt asked for a bottle of Montepulciano.

'That wasn't bad,' said Rhona when the waiter had gone.

'What wasn't?'

'Your Italian pronunciation. It's not one of my languages, so I'm impressed.'

'I've spent a lot of time in Italian restaurants,' he told her. 'It was a part of my education that began after I left school.'

'Well, you can't expect school to teach you everything.'

They chatted easily through the meal until Rhona said, 'I think we should go home and let the restaurant staff go to bed. Don't you?'

'I'm sure they'd welcome that.' He caught the attention of their waiter and asked for the bill.

Rhona tried one last plea. 'Can't we go Dutch, Matt?'

'No, I don't know the language.'

'You're incorrigible.'

'It's no use swearing at me in Dutch,' he said, putting the money on the dish. 'That's fine,' he told the waiter.

'*Grazie mille, signor.*'

'Not at all. Thank you.'

They took their leave of the waiter and walked back to the carpark.

'It's a luxury for me,' said Rhona, 'having an escort at this time of night.'

'Do you mean to say you actually feel safe with me?'

'As safe as houses.'

They drove back to Matt's house, where there was no sign of light in any of the windows, suggesting that Bev had not yet returned from her date.

Matt asked, 'Would you like to come in for coffee?'

Rhona looked at her watch and said, 'Tomorrow's Saturday. Will you be getting up early for work?'

'Not very early.'

'Go on, then. Let's spoil ourselves.' She followed him into the house and waited in the sitting room while he made coffee, enjoying the memory of the recital, and particularly the Prokofiev. Then, by association, her thoughts returned to her peculiar conversation with Gary. They were welcomely interrupted when Matt came in with two mugs of coffee.

'It's instant, I'm afraid. I'm completely out of ground coffee.'

'Don't worry, Matt, I'm not a proud woman.' As he sat beside her, she said, 'I'm grateful, though, for your help.'

'What help's that?'

'With Gary.'

He took her hand, as he had at the recital, and said, 'I told you, don't give him another thought. Just leave him to me.'

'What will you do?' She already had fears of the situation getting out of hand.

'I'll tell him he's wasting his time and annoying you, and that if he goes on like this, he'll make himself a laughing stock.' Giving her hand a reassuring squeeze, he said, 'I don't want you to lie awake most of the night, worrying about him.'

'I won't, Matt. Not now, anyway.' It was at such a time, she told herself, that, with the two of them in such close proximity, something was likely to happen, and she was quite right, because at that point they heard the outer door open and close. Bev was back from her date, and she came into the sitting room to find them drinking coffee, but not, to Rhona's relief, looking at all flustered.

'Hi, Bev,' said Matt. 'Everything okay?'

'Yeah, I'll get some chocolate.'

'Good for you.'

She stopped on her way to the kitchen, to ask, 'Was it good, that thing you went to?'

'It was excellent,' Rhona told her.

'That's what you said last time.'

Recalling the occasion, Rhona said, 'I think, that time, I called it "ecstasy".' As she said it, she reflected that if ecstasy were to be repeated, it would have to wait for another day, whichever day that happened to be.

18

SLURS AND SPONGES

Rhona arrived at school that Monday, not knowing quite what to expect from Gary, but assured at least that Matt had kept his promise and spoken to him, so she knew not to expect a recurrence of Friday's confrontation.

There was actually no sign of him until shortly before the first bell, when he looked around the staffroom, pointedly ignoring her before picking up his register and disappearing in the direction of his registration room. It was a pattern that would have satisfied Rhona, had there been any likelihood of his being able to keep it up, but she knew he was incapable of maintaining a stance, pose or pretence any longer than his impetuous nature allowed, so she put him out of her mind until she saw him at morning break.

He would have found it impossible to ignore her again, at least without appearing totally loutish, because he was at the hot water urn when she went to fill her mug.

''Morning,' he said, acknowledging her in the most convincingly off-hand way he could muster.

'Good morning, Gary.'

He closed the tap and stood aside for her. 'Have a good time, did you, on Friday night?'

'Yes, thank you. It was excellent.' She'd no idea what he knew about Friday night, but that didn't matter. She poured hot water on to her coffee and moved to the table next to the refrigerator, where the milk was kept.

'Huh!' It was his only response, and possibly the wittiest he could manage.

She asked, 'Are you all set for the Fête?' She thought one of them ought to be polite.

'I suppose so. Are you?'

'I've taken quite a lot of entries this morning, and I should get more as the week goes on, so yes, it's looking promising.'

With a lop-sided and oafish grin, he changed the subject to the one that was doubtless at the forefront of his mind, and said, 'You're a bit old for Matt Brocklehurst, aren't you? I thought he preferred 'em half his age.'

'I don't know what you mean, and I really don't want to know. Excuse me, will you?' She left the staffroom and returned to her classroom to be ready for her RoSLA Spanish class, giving no more thought to Gary's jealous utterance, because that was what she imagined it to be. His insulting remark was presumably a reference to Matt's relationship with Bev, in which case, Gary had only succeeded in cutting himself down to size, as he so often did.

The next hour was fairly uneventful; even Lee Gregory and his partner in disruption were docile, at least by their own standards, and Rhona could only deduce that they were still wary of upsetting the teacher who knew all about their thwarted assignation in Brittany. The rest of the class worked as conscientiously as usual.

At lunch-time, instead of joining the kids in the dining hall, she drove to the nearby bakery and bought an egg-salad roll, which she took to her favourite riverside spot so that she could have a time of peace and solitude with her own thoughts.

On the face of it, Gary's remark had been the kind of petulant and childish jeer she'd learned to expect from him. He was lashing out because he couldn't have his own way, and Matt's relationship with Bev was beyond his understanding. He'd evidently formed the conclusion, albeit quite erroneously, that she and Matt were now an item, and his reaction was reminiscent of the shouts of the street kids she'd known years earlier in Newcastle, when a disagreement about anything at all, from clothes to ice lollies, might end in, 'Anyway, you haven't even got a decent telly!' She'd worried about that TV set until things improved, her dad's books became popular, and they'd moved further north, where kids didn't make rude remarks about fourteen-inch screens. In any case, they'd got a seventeen-inch screen, and that was only until they got an even bigger one. She'd missed that development, because it took place while she was still at university, during her MA year.

She bit into the roll, relishing the crisp iceberg lettuce leaves and the more delicate crunch of the cucumber, still thinking about what had passed for a conversation that morning in the staffroom.

Okay, she'd dismissed Gary's puerile remark for what it had seemed at the time, but could there have been just an element of truth in his ignorant slander? She didn't believe for one minute that Matt was one of those monsters that preyed on children. That was unthinkable, and the fact that Bev had her own room and went out with lads her own age gave the lie to Gary's insult, but could it be that Matt's assumed responsibility for Bev's wellbeing, itself not only healthy, but laudable in the extreme, left room for no one else in his life and that the exclusion she felt was driven by altruism and innocence?

She knew why it bothered her. She'd already admitted to herself that Matt had come to mean something more to her than the friendly builder and co-visionary he'd been at first. She'd begun to realise it at the cricket match, when she'd surprised herself with the extent of her concern for his health and, whilst she'd dismissed his stubbornness as bravado, she couldn't ignore a retrospective glow at the way he'd managed, in spite of a raging fever and a burning throat, to put Gary in his place.

Unfortunately, the signs were that the attraction was one-sided, and that she held no appeal for him, a state of affairs she found unflattering as well as frustrating. As she ate the last of the roll and crumpled the empty paper bag, she resolved to dismiss him from her... well, at least from *those* thoughts, romantic thoughts. She told herself that carnal thoughts were the province of men, although it had crossed her mind that sex had been missing from her life for a full three months. She half-wondered if, given time, she might become a born-again virgin, healed, like a piercing might become when the item of jewellery that had first prompted it had fallen out of favour. That would keep her dad quiet about her goings-on, if anything would.

Sex with Gary had been 'less than fulfilling', to borrow an expression from Cosmopolitan or, to use her own terminology, downright naff. Now, that was something Gary wouldn't want to hear. Fortunately for him, he was unlikely ever to hear it, unless he found one of those awful, self-empowering women who saw it as their mission to de-ball every man they could find, simply because it was the next step after burning every bra in their possession. No, she decided, that kind of woman wouldn't consider him for a moment and, in that one isolated sense, she was in sympathy with them.

Her wristwatch told her she'd left herself ten minutes to get back to school and register her tutor group. It also told her it was high time to turn her back on rumination and introspection, and return to common sense. It could be just as cruel, but at least she didn't feel quite so daft.

Unusually, the day of the Fête dawned fair and, at least, fairly bright. It would be pleasant to hold it on the playing field, rather than in the assembly hall and the gym, as they'd been obliged to for the past few years, and the revellers would remain dry while they pelted Gary Oldfield with wet sponges as, clad in his wetsuit, he languished in what was a fair representation of the stocks that were once a feature of every medieval town. Pupils would pay five pence for the privilege of bombarding one of the least popular teachers in the school. It promised to be a lucrative attraction. Rhona was setting up the cake stall when Gary paused on his way to the stocks to speak to her.

'Morning, Rhona.'

'Good morning, Gary.'

'Is Matt coming today?'

'I doubt it. He'll be working.'

'Aren't we all?' He sniffed at the cakes already on display, and said in his usual charmless way, 'Save some for me.'

'Bugger off.'

As he took her advice, three of Rhona's fifth-year girls, the cake judges, turned up, soon followed by the other two, so she set about briefing them. 'You're going to judge each cake according to three *criteria*,' she told them. 'If that's a new word for you, you can work out what it means when I tell you that the criteria are texture, appearance and taste. "Texture" means whether they're too heavy and stodgy or just right, "appearance" means whether or not they look appealing, and I don't really have to explain "taste", do I?'

They assured her she did not.

More competition entries arrived, and Rhona put them with the others on a long table that did alternate duty at school jumble sales.

Two third-year lads came to ask, 'Can we have some cake, Miss?'

'No, you can't,' she said, taking a 10p piece from her purse and giving it to the nearest, 'but you can chuck a couple of sponges at Mr Oldfield.'

Her suggestion had immediate appeal. 'Thanks, Miss.' They tore off to enjoy the treat.

'That was a bit tight, Miss,' said one of the girls.

'What did you expect me to give 'em, Amanda? A five-pound note? I'm not made of money, you know.'

'No, Miss. I meant gettin' 'em to chuck sponges at Mr Oldfield.'

'It's just a bit of harmless fun, bonny lass. That's all.'

There was more evidence of fun when an ex-pupil, a girl who'd left at the end of the previous year, came to see Rhona, but it soon became evident that the fun had been of a very different kind, and it had certainly not been harmless.

'Hello, Miss.'

'Hello, Dawn. How are you getting on, these days?'

'Look, Miss.' She opened her gabardine raincoat to draw attention to her condition. 'I'm pregnant. Seven monfs, now.' As if the prognosis were less than complete, she added, 'Only two more monfs to go.'

'I can see you've been busy since you left school, Dawn, and you can't have been sixteen all that long. Who's the proud dad?'

'Eiver Philip Dawes or Brian Davies.'

'Maybe they'll have to toss for it.'

A voice behind her said *sotto voce*, 'It's a pity they didn't do that seven months ago, instead of putting her in the club.'

Rhona let that pass, asking, 'Has either of them owned up to it, Dawn?'

'No. Miss.'

'You need a dad with a shotgun.'

'No, he legged it when me mum told 'im he'd got her pregnant, an' I were on t' way.'

'I'm sorry, Dawn. I forgot.'

'That's all right, Miss. Anyway, nice seein' you.'

'And lovely to see you, Dawn. All the best with the baby.'

128

'Fanks.' Dawn wandered off to share her news with someone else.

'Such a pity, and a waste of a young life,' said Rhona, watching her go. Then, turning to her judges, she said, 'Don't get caught out like that, will you, girls?'

'No, Miss.' The assurance was repeated four times, and Rhona hoped for their sakes, they wouldn't. One of them said, 'She was daft not to take precautions.'

'Ah well, there are times when urgency overrides caution, but you can spend a long time regretting the mistake, so it's always best either to remember the n-word or be more careful.'

'What's the n-word, Miss?'

' "No".'

The girls nodded sagely.

As she reflected on that, some more boys came, lured by the sight, if not the smell, of cakes and looking as hungry as youngsters of their age unfailingly were.

'Let's have a bit, Miss,' pleaded one of them, 'pleeease.'

'No, lads, these are waiting to be judged. How many of you are there?' She had a quick look. 'Half a dozen. Here,' she said, delving into her purse and counting out 30p, 'go and throw some wet sponges at Mr Oldfield.' She put a finger to her lips to dissuade the girls from betraying her.

'Thanks, Miss!'

'You're welcome, but mind you throw straight. You only get a chance to do this once a year, mind.'

They assured her they would be deadly accurate.

'It is nice to be popular,' Rhona told the girls. 'I'm sure Mr Oldfield will appreciate the attention he's getting.'

'I wonder what this lot want,' said one of them, looking at the three girls approaching the table.

'Maybe they're looking for MacBeth,' said Rhona, knowing as she did the newcomers' reputation for gratuitous unpleasantness.

'Miss,' said one of them, 'what's "German cow" in German?'

'I've no doubt you want to use it as an insult, so I'm not going to tell you.'

The girl who'd asked the question said, 'Them cakes look all right. Are you givin' 'em away?'

'No, I'm not.'

She tossed her hair and walked away, followed by the others.

'They only want to know swear-words in German to bully that lass in the third year, the one that was born in Germany 'cause her dad was in the Army,' said one of the judges.

'I know, Belinda. That's why I wouldn't tell her. I'm afraid there's some wrong 'uns about.'

'Yes, there are, Miss.'

'Mind you, these two are okay.' She smiled broadly as Bev approached the table with a young, fair-haired boy at her side. 'Hello, Bev.'

'Hello, Rhona. This is Troy.'

'Hello, Troy. I'm pleased to meet you, bonny lad. You'll be coming to this school in September, I reckon?'

'Yes, Miss.' He was plainly distracted by the cakes behind Rhona, but after a nudge from Bev, he said, 'Fanks for that....'

'You're welcome, bonny lad.' Surrounded as he was by girls, he was obviously reluctant to mention the teddy bear. 'I got a one for Bev, and I didn't want to leave you out. It was very nice to get your note, as well. Thank you for that.' Picking up a kitchen knife, she said, 'Just wait there a minute.' She selected the most appealing of the cakes and cut two wedges, which she wrapped in paper napkins and put into a plastic bag that had contained one of the entries. 'There you are. Don't unwrap these until you're away from the school, or everybody'll be wanting some.' Turning to the judges, she said, 'Your turn will come, girls. Don't think you've been forgotten.'

Bev took the bag readily and said, 'Thanks, Rhona.' She nudged Troy, who said, 'Fanks, Miss.'

'You're welcome. Keep it a secret, mind.' When they were gone, she said to the judges, 'Poor little scrap. He looks neglected.' Taking in their nods of agreement, she said, 'When I see a bairn like him, I want to take him home and feed him.'

'Not everybody's like you, Miss,' said Belinda.

'Aye, but never mind.' She looked at her watch and said, 'It's officially judging time, girls. Let's start with entry number one. It seems logical. Now, write the number on the left of your pad and then, in the next column, give it marks out of five for texture. It's just like the Generation Game, isn't it?'

Her observation surprised them, but they agreed with her that it was very much like the TV show.

'Okay. Now, marks out of five for appearance.' They continued, with Rhona doing the complicated arithmetic at the end, although she told them that it wasn't all that complicated, or she wouldn't be able to do it. Finally, it came as no surprise to anyone that the winning cake was the one Rhona had cut into for Bev and Troy. It was so good that she cut another five pieces and gave them to the judges. She suspected very strongly that the cake had been baked by the entrant's mother, but she'd no way of knowing that, and it was all in fun, anyway. It seemed, also, that the fun wasn't over, as two of the boys Rhona had treated earlier to a shy at Gary came to tell her with great glee, 'Mr Oldfield's soaked to t' skin, Miss! He isn't right chuffed about it, neither.'

'Are you surprised?' She saw the evidence when Gary was finally released from the stocks and he sludged his way to his dressing room via the cake stall.

'Just look at me,' he said, dripping from every fold and crease.

'That's the price of popularity, Mr Oldfield,' said Rhona. 'You're such a good sport, the kids can't help themselves.'

'I reckon somebody's been encouraging them,' he said, wretchedly using one of Rhona's paper napkins to dry his face.

'Now, who would do a thing like that?'

The judges were helpless with laughter, but they made no attempt to enlighten him, such was the measure of their loyalty to Rhona.

Rhona asked him, 'Would you like a piece of cake?' She laughed and said, 'Maybe not. You've probably seen enough sponges today.'

19

Fun in the Pool

It was a popular fact at Banfield High School that, when called upon to sign a document, the Headmaster, L. M. Purbright, M.A. (Cantab), would only take the trouble to read it if money were involved. Otherwise, he would give it a less-than-cursory scan and append his signature. In the case of school reports, he would add either, 'Keep up the good work', or 'More work required,' the two comments representing his entire repertoire. The practice naturally provoked some amusement in the staffroom, and it was decided, on this occasion, that a report would be written for a boy who'd left the previous year, just to see if Mr Purbright noticed anything untoward. Rhona regarded it as a schoolboy prank, but she went along with it and wrote her comment.

French: His idea of the past tense is, at present, futuristic.

Other comments followed.

German: When, in the morning, the lesson commences itself, is-he always the last to arrive.

Latin: He is remembered in absentia.

Mathematics: His mistakes continue to multiply.

Geography: He behaves as if his future is already mapped out for him.

History: He insists on living in the past.

English: His spelyng is atroshus and his gramer is even wurserer then what his spelyng is.

Chemistry: $ZN+H^2SO^4 = ZNSO^4+H^2$. *Need I say more?*

Physics: He hasn't a clue about Newton's Fourth Law.

Biology: Seems not to know his anus from his cubitus.

Art: Needs to get his ideas in perspective.

Woodwork: His nails are always dirty. So are his screws.

Metalwork: He spends all his time forging, but never makes notes.

Technical Drawing: His efforts are two-dimensional.

Music: He thinks 'ensemble' means taking girls into a practice room.

Religious Education: The Romans would have thrown him to the lions.

Physical Education: He's in a different ball game from everybody else.

When L. M. Purbright returned the reports to the staffroom, it became clear that he'd excelled himself, with the comment, *More work required, especially in Chemistry. L.M. Purbright.*

With the Fête and reports out of the way, the next excitements were Sports Day and the Swimming Gala, both opportunities for the not-so-academic to distinguish themselves, for Gary to complain about the work involved, and for other members of staff to remind him that it was only once a year and that it was easier than proper teaching.

For some reason, possibly to avoid violent exercise immediately after a full meal, the Swimming Gala, unlike Sports Day was held during the morning, and Rhona and her tutor group arrived at the swimming pool for the event. Competitors headed for the changing cubicles whilst spectators filled the balcony and competed with each other to make the most noise, their efforts being amplified rewardingly by the expanse of water and the hard surfaces that surrounded it.

One of Rhona's group noticed that she was carrying a sport bag, and he asked her what was in it.

'It's me towel and cozzie, bonny lad. I thought I might fancy a bit swim later on.'

'Great!' He set about informing the other lads on the balcony. It was only natural that they should be keen to see her in a swimsuit; they were teenage lads, after all, but it would have been better if they could have been more discreet with their excitement. Still, the whole idea of staff involvement at the end of the gala, a recent innovation by Gary in one of his more grown-up moments, was to give the kids a laugh and remind them that teachers were only human.

With everyone assembled, the gala got under way, with spectators bellowing and shrieking their support or derision, depending on their relationship to a particular contestant, because sporting behaviour could never be guaranteed. Meanwhile, the PE Department worked its way through the programme.

When they reached the Under-18 100 Metres Front Crawl, Rhona went downstairs to change into her swimming costume and the baggy overalls the school caretaker had lent her for the event. She listened for the final item on the programme and waited for her cue.

Eventually, there was a lull in the shouting and shrieking, and she heard Gail Harding, one of the girls' PE staff say, 'There's a bloke out here, Mr Oldfield. He says he's come to do some work.'

Overacting outrageously, Gary said, 'I wasn't expecting anybody. What's he come here to do, anyway?'

'I don't know,' said Gail, but here he comes.'

It was Rhona's cue to leave her cubicle and walk up to the two tracksuited members of staff.

Gary asked, 'What do you want?'

In the gruffest and deepest voice she could manage, Rhona said, 'I've come to mend the leak.'

Some of the kids were already beginning to latch on. In her white cap, Rhona was almost anonymous, but plumbers didn't have women's voices, and neither, in their limited experience, did they wear swimming caps. Rhona pressed on, nevertheless, and when Gary demanded to know where the leak was supposed to be, she said, 'Over here,' pointing into the deep end of the pool.

'I can't see a leak.' He bent over to look for it, and Rhona looked up questioningly at the spectators, at the same time miming the threat of pushing Gary into the pool. Naturally, they lent raucous encouragement. Rhona pushed, and Gary went flying into the water amid helpless laughter from the spectators.

'Hey,' said Gail, 'you can't do that.'

'What can't I do?'

'This.' Gail pushed her into the pool as well. Then, flailing with her arms and pretending to lose her balance, she joined the other two in the water, where they had a free-for-all, chasing and ducking each other, to the unbounded delight of the pupils watching.

As lunchtime loomed, they made their way out of the pool, and Rhona stepped out of her overalls and removed her swimming cap. Her strawberry blonde hair tumbled free, and the children recognised her and set up a loud cheer that all-but drowned out the wolf whistles from the unmannerly minority. Rhona took a bow and retired to her cubicle.

On the way back to school, one of the girls in her group said shyly, 'You don't 'alf look nice in a cozzie, Miss.'

'Thanks, Julie. It's kind of you to say so.'

'I wish I looked like you.'

Rhona looked at the slender teenager and smiled. 'You've a while to go yet, before you fill out, bonny lass. Give yourself time.' It was one of the perks of the job, being able to reassure kids like Julie, and knowing she was doing a useful job into the bargain. It made up for the wolf-whistles. While it was on her mind, though, she intended to have words with Lee Gregory and his mate, because she was pretty sure they were the wolves doing the whistling. They would soon be left school, but a few stern words wouldn't go amiss in their last couple of weeks.

On her way home from an *Annie Get Your Gun* rehearsal, she noticed that the door of the theatre was open, so she called in and found that the ceiling joists and some of the boards were now in place. There were signs of progress everywhere, although the only person in the auditorium was Matt, who was working on the almost-complete stage. He held the loose trapdoor, and he was working on it.

'Hello, Rhona,' he said.

'Hi, Matt. No Bev?'

'No, she's taken Troy shopping. I believe there's a second-hand clothing sale at your school. They've gone to get him a blazer and some bits and pieces, rugby kit and stuff.'

'Aye, and I suppose his mam can't be bothered to take him there herself.'

'Not only that, she gave Bev little enough to spend on him,' he said, taking a chisel and cutting a recess for a hinge. 'I reckon she might have been able to get him a shirt and tie with what she had.'

'So you made it up, eh?'

'Somebody had to.' He offered up the hinge and found the recess a little shallow, so he went on paring. 'I've said little Troy can work with us this summer,' he said. 'It'll get him away from home during the day, at least, and I can always find him plenty to do.' He tried the hinge again and found that it was a perfect fit.

'You've a heart of gold, Matt.'

'I don't know about that. I'm just sorry for kids who get dealt a rotten hand. Troy's eleven now, and unless somebody gives him a leg up and a bit of guidance, there's no hope for the poor little sod.'

Almost tearful, Rhona said, 'Matt, I could kiss you for that.'

'I don't recommend it, Rhona. I'm covered in sawdust, and you should be wearing a particle mask, by the way.'

'I suppose so.' She was conscious of a cruel kind of symbolism in that advice, not that Matt would ever be deliberately cruel, and she had to admit that a mask would be more useful than a chastity belt. 'I'd put a one on, but I've a lot of marking to do, so I'll leave you to your work instead.'

The marking took until almost eleven, when Rhona was ready to turn in. Before that, however, she spent some time thinking about her grandparents' wedding anniversary, which was less than two weeks away. In the end, she decided to give them a special rose tree, something that would please them both. Relieved at having made the decision, she considered the next day, when she would see Lee Gregory and Keith Bentley for a Spanish lesson, followed by one in manners.

20

PRURIENCE, AGONY AND SISTERLY ADVICE

It was the final Spanish lesson of the year for the reluctant Fifth Year, but most of them had made the best of their extended school career, and they now had a means of communicating with their hosts and hostesses, should they decide to follow the current fashion and take their holidays in Spain.

'Before you dismiss,' said Rhona, I'd like to say "Goodbye" and wish you all well, although perhaps I should say, '*Adiós, mis amigas y amigos. Buena suerte.*'

Most of them managed to respond by saying, '*Adiós*, Señora Loveday,' giving Rhona the impression that she'd made a small but useful contribution to their lives.

'Off you go, everyone. Lee and Keith, will you stay behind for a minute, please?' She waited until the rest of the class had gone, before confronting the disrespectful duo, who were trying hard to look mystified as to the reason for their summons.

'Lee and Keith, do you know why I've asked you to come and see me?'

As usual, Lee spoke for them both. 'No, Miss.'

'Yesterday, at the end of the Swimming Gala, I took part in a bit of horse-play, if you remember, with Mr Oldfield and Miss Harding for the innocent entertainment of those present, and I felt very disappointed and, in fact, insulted, by wolf-whistles coming from the balcony.'

Keith asked, 'How did you know it was—'

Lee said quickly, 'It wasn't us, Miss.'

'There seems to be some disagreement here. What were you trying to say, Keith?'

He shuffled awkwardly. 'It wasn't us, Miss.'

'But you asked me how I knew it was you.'

Now blushing, he managed to say, 'We didn't mean nowt by it, Miss.'

Lee said angrily, 'I told you to keep quiet.'

'Well, now that he's let the cat out of the bag,' said Rhona, 'you may as well admit that it was you two, the Giggling Gigolos of Akengarth.' Before they could deny it, she asked, 'Why did you wolf-whistle at me?'

Keith said again, 'We didn't mean nowt by it, Miss.'

'It were just a way of sayin'….'

'Saying what, Lee?'

'We….'

'Go on. What were you trying to say?'

'We thought you looked… fit, Miss.' The last two words were barely audible.

'Fit? When you say "fit", you don't really mean "healthy, strong, sturdy" or anything as innocent as that, do you?'

'No, Miss.' Again, it was no more than a whisper.

'I know exactly what you meant. Even when it's intended as a compliment, however coarse, wolf-whistling is insulting, condescending and in the worst possible taste. Do you both understand that?'

'Yes, Miss.'

'Yes, Miss.'

'Good.' She looked up at the wall clock and said, 'It looks as if you've missed First Sitting, although that's no worse than you deserve. When you do go to the dining hall, remember not to wolf-whistle at the dinner ladies. They might not be as lenient as I am. Go on, off you go.'

'Yes, Miss.'

Keith said, 'Sorry, Miss.'

'Yes, Keith, I do believe you are, at least, for now.'

'We weren't the only ones, Miss.'

'I don't suppose you were, Keith. You just happened to be found out.'

It seemed that it was a day for juvenile prurience, as Rhona discovered when she returned to her classroom with her group that afternoon, having coaxed one of the other leavers into photographing her with them on the grass verge outside her room. On hearing their surprised laughter, she followed them into the room and found that someone had drawn male genitalia somewhat haphazardly on her blackboard. Taking the board rubber to erase it, she said to the group, 'Anybody who looks like that needs to see his doctor urgently.'

Her tutor group were amused, but when she'd seen them out, she re-entered the classroom and found a similar, but larger, drawing, which she also erased. She had to allow the perpetrator a degree of credit for his ability to sneak back into the room and do it while she was dismissing the group, but that didn't make the misdeed any funnier than it had been the first time. However, she returned at the end of the day, having discharged her school bus duty, to find an even larger penis on her board, just as badly drawn, and with the scrawled message, *The more you rud it the digger it gets!* Presumably, the perpetrator had tried to write, *The more you rub it, the bigger it gets.* Whatever his intentions were, however, her first reaction was to remove it, but then she remembered her camera. Working on the adage that, by contrast, grot served to highlight the good things in life, she recorded the graffiti as a full-stop at the end of RoSLA's first, faltering year.

After the expense of the kitchen extension, a holiday was out of the question, but there was plenty to be done at home. To begin with, the little bit of garden she had needed attention, and there was no shortage of sunshine, so she would get to work tidying the flowerbeds and giving the neighbours less to complain about. She could almost hear them. *That garden's a disgrace, and she's a schoolteacher, so it's not as if she's too busy with work.* Well, she would show them. It was her birthday, as well, and what better way was there to celebrate her birthday than by communing with nature? Well, there were probably much better ways, but none of them was immediately possible, so out came the hand fork, trowel and bucket, on went the most disreputable pair of jeans she owned, and into the garden she went. Hi-ho, hi-ho.

Her enthusiasm lasted almost fifteen minutes, after which she decided it was time for a brew. Anyway, she reckoned, fifteen minutes' worth of weeding was pretty good for someone who wasn't in training for that kind of thing.

She levered herself up, suddenly aware of the unaccustomed stiffness in her knees, and turned to go into the house. As she did, she slipped off the flagstone and went over on to her left ankle, which buckled immediately so that she found herself sprawling over the flowerbed she'd been working on. It was a ludicrous situation to be in. To begin with, she was relieved that there didn't seem to be anyone around to see her in that predicament, and then she realised she was going to need someone to help her up. The injured ankle was very painful; even if she could roll over and get to her knees, she doubted her ability to reach the house without making the pain even worse, and with nothing to hold on to, hopping on her good foot would be impossible. It seemed that all she could do was wait for some passer-by to appear so that she could enrol that person's assistance. She looked one way and then the other, but the street was dishearteningly empty, and the pain in her ankle whenever she moved was now excruciating.

After what seemed a long time, she heard footsteps along the street and she raised herself into a sitting position, which was as much as she could manage, to look for the person she hoped would be her rescuer. It turned out to be a young woman with a dog, and Rhona waited for her to come closer.

Incredibly, the dog was wearing a sunhat with cut-outs for its ears, but Rhona didn't care. Even a woman who dressed dogs in silly clothes would be welcome if she would only help her to the door. She was on the other side of the street, but she was close enough to hear Rhona call out to her. 'Hello! Will you help me, please?' The woman wasn't even looking her way. She had those earphones that looked like hearing aids, and she was obviously glued to whatever rubbish her transistor radio was pouring out. Rhona tried again. 'Hello! Help me, please! I've sprained my ankle!' The dog gave her a bored look, but the woman's thoughts were elsewhere. Rhona waved vigorously, hoping desperately to find a corner of the woman's peripheral vision, but Led Zeppelin or whoever was violating the airwaves continued to hold the woman's attention, and she walked on. Rhona sank down again, thoroughly dejected, and she was about to grit her teeth against the pain and crawl to the door, when she heard an approaching vehicle. At least, she thought it was approaching. She levered herself up again and, sure enough, the pick-up was coming her way. She began waving immediately and shouted, although there was little chance of the driver hearing her above the noise of the engine, but the pick-up was actually slowing down. As it approached, she almost wept with relief when she read the name *Matthew Brocklehurst, Joiner and Builder*.

The pick-up came to a halt, and Matt jumped out. 'When I saw you were fully clothed,' he said, 'I knew you weren't sun-bathing. What's happened?'

'I've sprained my ankle or something. Thank goodness you came. I've been lying here for ages.' She blinked when she felt tears starting.

Matt signalled to Bev, who opened the cab door. 'Bring the first-aid kit, Bev,' he said. 'Right,' he said to Rhona, 'it's as well you're not wearing wellies. Let's get your shoe off.'

Rhona was also glad she was wearing her new, trendy training shoes, with lots of eyelets. It would be a painful process, but leather shoes would have made it more painful still. Now she thought about it, wellies would have been impossible.

Bev, and then Troy, arrived with the first-aid kit, and Matt took out a crepe bandage. 'Go inside and soak this in cold water,' he told Bev.' Then, unlacing the shoe carefully, he eased it off.

'Aah!'

'I knew you'd say that.' He put the shoe down and asked, 'Are these socks precious?'

'No.' She spoke the word through gritted teeth.

'Good, because I'm going to perform surgery on this one.' Taking a pair of scissors, he cut the sock so that he could remove it painlessly. Meanwhile, Bev and Troy returned with the bandage liberally soaked in cold water.

'Have you got any frozen vegetables in the house?'

'In the— ah! In the freezer, yes. Frozen peas.'

'Go and find them, will you, Bev?' He handed the sock to her.

'Chuck that in the bin while you're about it. We'll have to take Rhona to the hospital to have her ankle looked at properly.'

'I'm sorry to be a nuisance, Matt,' said Rhona.

'You're not a nuisance.'

'I will be in a minute. I need a wee.' It had been creeping up on her since before the accident, and it was now quite pressing.

'All right. I'll help you to the bathroom. Then you'll be on your own.'

'Yes, I'll be able to manage that.'

He slipped one arm around her shoulders and the other behind her knees, and lifted her. 'It'll be quicker than hopping,' he explained.

Rhona kept quiet, knowing she was in expert hands, as he carried her indoors past Bev and Troy, who were equally surprised, and continued upstairs to the bathroom, where he left her on her good foot, propped against the washbasin. 'Let me know when you're ready,' he said.

'I will.' When Matt had closed the door and gone downstairs, she unfastened herself gratefully and experienced relief for the second time in ten minutes.

As Matt carried her downstairs, he asked, 'What's the insurance on your car?'

'Owner-driver only, I'm afraid.'

'We'll have to go in the pick-up.'

It sounded impossible. 'I don't think I can climb up there,' she said.

'There's always the tail-lift.'

She hoped he was joking.

In the event, he opened the cab door on the passenger side and lifted her into the seat. 'Right, Bev,' he said, 'let's have those frozen peas.' He placed them over Rhona's foot. 'Now, Bev and Troy, you'll have to ride on the back, but keep your heads down.'

The diagnosis was a sprain, but it was as well to be certain, and Rhona was sent home with a dressing, pain-relieving tablets, a pair of forearm crutches, and the knowledge that Matt had forgone half a day's work.

'It would have been different,' he said, 'if I'd just had wet concrete delivered. I'd have had to leave you in your garden and come back for you later.'

'You've been too kind, Matt,' she said.

'Are you sure you'll be all right, tonight?'

'Perfectly, thank you.' She kissed him on the cheek, and he climbed into the pick-up to take Troy home. She realised then that she'd forgotten all about her birthday, and no one else was any the wiser, but what the heck?

That evening, with a glass of wine and her teddy bear for company, she sat, half-listening to a performance of Verdi's *La Traviata* on Radio Three, thankful that the accident had happened when it had, and not in a week's time, when she had to drive to Newcastle. She was thinking about that when the phone rang. Happily, she'd moved it so that it was within easy reach. She turned down the radio.

'Hello?'

'Rhona. it's me.'

'Now, which of the many people I know that are called "me" can that be?'

'Don't be daft, Rhona.'

'No, that's your department, bonny lad. How are things with you?' It was good to hear from her brother, whether it was once a year or, more often, when he wanted something. If it was the latter, she hoped it wasn't money, because she wasn't particularly in funds, and it was unlikely that he wanted to wish her a happy birthday, because he never remembered it.

'I'm okay. How about you?'

'I sprained my ankle this morning, but I'm all right apart from that. How's the job at the removal firm going?'

There was an awkward silence, and then he said, 'It's not. That's why I'm phoning you. That and Granny and Grandad's diamond wedding, really.'

'Speak on, little brother, but before you ask me for the usual, let me tell you that I've just had my kitchen extended at considerable expense, and my bank account is now in intensive care.'

Again, there was a pause. 'I was really phoning to ask you what you're giving them for their wedding anniversary.'

'Oh, that's not difficult. I'm giving them a special potted rose tree, as Granny loves roses and Grandad gets so much pleasure out of growing them.'

'That's a good idea.'

'Thank you, Steve. I'm glad I've been able to help you with that one.'

'The thing is, I'm a bit skint, just now, and I don't know what to do about a present.'

It seemed perfectly obvious to Rhona, although Steve was usually the last to see what was immediately beneath his nose. 'Why don't you give them one of your paintings?'

There was an unusually long silence, which told Rhona he was giving her suggestion some thought. Then, he said, 'What kind of painting do you think they'd like?'

'Anything to do with old Newcastle. You painted the Tyne Bridge a while ago, didn't you? Have you still got it?'

'It's at Mam and Dad's.'

'Of course it is.' She remembered seeing it, now. 'They'd love that.'

'Do you really think so?'

'I'm positive. It's something meaningful to them, something they'll enjoy, and the fact that it was their grandson who painted it will give them something to show everybody who comes to the house.'

Again, he was silent. When he did speak, it was with genuine appreciation. 'That's a brilliant idea, Rhona.'

'I thought it was staring you in the face, meself.'

'No, I'd never have thought of it.' Then, as if in a much-delayed double-take, he asked, 'Did you say earlier that you'd done something to your ankle?'

'I've only sprained it, but it's painful enough. I was weeding my bit of garden, and I went over on my ankle. I'm told it'll be all right in a week or so.'

Steve surprised her, then, by responding without the usual pause for thought. 'If I lived nearer, I could do your gardening,' he suggested, and there the surprise faded. It had the classic signs of an attempted cadge, after all, and they were second nature to him.

'You've forgotten that my garden's little more than an outsize window box, Steve. I'll soon have it done when I come back from Newcastle. Anyway, I can't afford to pay union rates.'

'No, but if you were to put me up, I could do it in exchange for my keep.'

Memories of the last time she'd given him board and lodging flashed before her inward eye. She recalled the bedroom floor littered with dirty washing, the numerous empty and part-empty coffee mugs by his bed, and the empty cereal packets and spent toilet rolls left without a word, for her to discover and replace in a hurry. 'No, Steve,' she said. 'Thanks for the offer, but I'll manage.'

He seemed in no hurry to end the conversation, but it was, after all, their first for probably seven months. He asked, 'How's your love life? Mam said you'd finished with the PE teacher.'

'The answer to your question is that it's in the doldrums, and I finished with Gary five months ago. How about you?'

'Oh, they come and they go.'

'Those two again, eh?' They were also features of the time he'd stayed with her; at least, she'd been aware of the former, which was usually and clearly audible through the adjoining bedroom wall. It had caused her some embarrassment at the time, mainly because it was her brother who was causing it, although, in retrospect, she felt he could have given Gary more than a few pointers.

'I think I'm losing my touch, Rhona. They don't hang around very long, nowadays.'

'Be honest, Steve. They never did, but I'm going to have to ring off. I need to visit the loo, and I mustn't leave it too long, because it means hanging on to the banister rail and hopping on one foot.'

'Okay. Thanks for the advice.'

'It's what I'm here for, Steve. 'Bye. See you at the anniversary.'

'Yeah. 'Bye, Rhona.'

As she made her ungainly ascent, she reflected that, passing as she had from the unsatisfactory to the non-existent was still preferable to the hectic, revolving-door promiscuity that characterised her brother's sex life. Beyond that, she was incapable of further thought, as the urgency of her immediate situation called for her full concentration.

21

CELEBRATION, CULTIVATION AND DESECRATION

Loyal as ever to their roots, Rhona's grandparents had hired the function room of the Riveter's Arms to welcome the biggest family gathering since their golden wedding ten years earlier. Rhona's Uncle Jack and Auntie Marigold were there with their two sons, their wives and, between them, three very tiny Headleys, one of whom, Rhona was delighted to see, had inherited the strawberry-blonde gene. The feature was not lost on Rhona's granny or her mother, whilst Grandad Headley's observation was, 'She'll break a few hearts when she's a bit older.'

Steve had brought with him the girlfriend of the moment, a pleasant and self-possessed girl with dark, well-groomed looks, called Caroline. She was a cutter with Gowns and Trains, the bridal outfitters, and Rhona found herself wondering, without being judgemental, quite what she saw in Steve. They seemed surprisingly at ease in each other's company, so it would be both insensitive to ask and interesting to see how long their relationship survived.

After a typically dry and mischievous two-minute speech from Rhona's grandad, Uncle Jack insisted, as the elder of the offspring, on following it with his bland, self-important version, which seemed set to go on for a very long time, until Auntie Marigold persuaded him that he'd made his point, possibly more than once.

'It's ever since they made him an officer in the Army,' said Rhona's mother. 'He suddenly realised how important he was, and then he multiplied it by the date, just so folk would know.' Looking fondly at her husband, she said, 'I'm glad you never got like that, Ivor.'

'There was never any fear of that,' he said. 'I was always too busy doing everything you told me to do, when, where, how and however many times you wanted it done.'

'That's right.' Looking around the gathering, she asked, 'Have you met Caroline, Rhona?'

'Yes, she seems very nice. What's the story with her?' She knew that by that time her mother would have found out everything it was possible to learn about her son's new girlfriend.

'She's bored with the job she's got now. I get the impression she fancies going into business on her own. She certainly seems to know her own mind.'

'I mean, what's the situation between her and our Steve?'

Her mother leaned forward confidentially, causing her father to smile. 'She thinks he's lovely, and before you say anything, she's right. No child of mine can be less than lovely.'

'Quite right, Mam. Are you thinking of having more?'

'No, it's your turn now, so don't keep us waiting too long. I feel upstaged with all these great-nephews and nieces, here.'

'I'll do my best. Do you mind if I leave it until I'm married?'

'Not as long as you don't take forever finding a fella.'

Rhona returned to Akengarth to find that she wasn't alone in spending the summer at home. Terry Cooper had ordered the plumbing and heating goods, and Matt was hard at work on the curtain gear.

One member of the team was mystified, and that member was Troy, who'd studied the stage from every angle, seemingly without arriving at a satisfactory conclusion. His curiosity was very evident, because Rhona took him aside to ask, 'What's bothering you, Troy?'

Recognising a genuine query after all the leg-pulling he'd undergone, he asked, 'Where are they going to show the movies?'

'What movies, bonny lad?' She told herself it was only natural for a lad of his age to have picked up the American terminology.

'On the telly, people go to one of these places and see movies at the front.'

'Ah.' Now she understood. 'This place used to be a cinema,' she explained. 'It was a long time ago, and they stopped showing films here… way back, I should think, maybe twenty-five years ago. What they're doing now is turning it into a theatre.'

Her answer prompted another question. 'What's a theatre?'

'It's a place where people come on to the stage and sometimes they act, and sometimes they sing. When this theatre's finished, there'll be orchestras as well, that'll go in front of the stage and play music so that the actors can sing.' As she spoke, it was like explaining gender to a first-year French class, and that really was a foreign language. Something else he'd mentioned, as well, was troubling her. 'You said you'd seen people on the telly watching films in a cinema, Troy. Have you never been to a cinema?'

He appeared to search his memory, and then he said, 'No.'

'You poor little scrap.' It was something that had to be put right. She knew Bev and Troy had been denied an awful lot, but there were things she'd always taken for granted that were alien to them. She looked around for Matt and found him plastering the walls in the toilets. 'Matt,' she said, 'if I can persuade Troy's mam, could you and I take Bev and him to the cinema?' She thought it would be better if two adults were present.

'Yes, why not? She won't object.'

'Right, I'll go and see her.'

He dipped his float in a bucket of water and asked, 'What's on?'

'*Live and Let Die* has just come out, and they're showing it in Bradford.'

'I don't think either of them's been to a cinema before, so it's long overdue.'

As Matt had prophesied, Troy's mother had no objection, but neither did she offer to pay for her son's and daughter's tickets. It was no problem for Rhona, but it said much about the interest the woman took in the lives of her children.

They arrived at the Odeon Cinema in time for the first part of the treat, which consisted of hot dogs from the foyer booth, and from that moment, the magic began.

The film was an exciting and entertaining nonsense, and James Bond's obligatory pun was naturally lost on Bev and Troy, but the film was the greatest treat of all. Rhona knew that because they said so repeatedly and in their different ways on the way home.

She dropped Troy at home first, taking him to the door.

'Fanks, Miss. It were fantastic.'

'You're welcome, Troy. I'll see you soon.' She watched him let himself into the house with his own latchkey, and then returned to her car.

When they arrived at Matt's house, Bev, who was usually so quiet and reserved, was still chattering excitedly about the film, and Rhona wondered a little about Troy, who would have no one with whom to share his new excitement.

Eventually, however, tiredness asserted itself, and Bev went up to bed, leaving Rhona and Matt to review the evening's events.

'I couldn't believe it,' said Rhona, 'when Troy told me he'd never been to a cinema.'

'Well, you've met his mother, and you saw what she was like.'

'Aye, as far as she's concerned, bairns are what happens if she's unlucky or, at least, if she's not careful. Mind you, even then, it'll be some other bugger's fault, just as it's up to somebody else to take care of them.' As she spoke, she had the impression that his thoughts were elsewhere, and she asked, 'What's on your mind, Matt?'

'I was thinking about what you just said. I imagine you'd like to have children, wouldn't you?'

'What a strange question to ask. Actually, me mam was dropping more than heavy hints when I saw her last week, although it wasn't surprising, as there were four generations in the room at the time. I expect she was feeling left out of things.' Smiling, she added, 'One of her great-nieces is a two-year-old with strawberry-blonde hair.'

'Seriously,' he asked, 'wouldn't you like to have children?'

She thought before answering his question. 'It's not the thought uppermost in my mind when the alarm goes off each morning, but I'd be happy enough if I did have children, although I get a lot of reward working with other people's bairns. Why do you ask?'

'It was seeing you with Bev and Troy. You just seem so natural with them.'

'I should hope so. I've been working with them for… three years, now,' she said, counting her years at Banfield High.

'That would be enough to put a lot of people off,' he said, topping up her glass.

'Aye, that's why some folks call 'em "contraceptive" schools, but it hasn't affected me that way.' She smiled mischievously. 'At least, not yet.'

'I'm glad.' Changing the subject, he asked, 'How's your ankle, now?'

'It's a lot better, Matt, thanks to your prompt attention. I should be able to finish weeding my patch of garden, now.'

'Well, be careful.'

'I will, believe me.'

Evidently reassured, he asked, 'How was Gary Oldfield after I spoke to him?'

'Good as gold. Thank you for doing that, Matt.' She thought it better not to tell him about Gary's reference to Bev. There was already enough ill-feeling.

'It was no trouble.'

'He was actually quite pleasant at the swimming gala.'

'Oh? What happened there?'

'We had a bit of fun at the end. Just Gary, another member of the PE Department and me.' She told him about the silliness in the pool. 'It was just to round off the morning for the kids,' she explained.

'There's evidently more to teaching than I thought.'

'For some of us, there is. There was only us three. I think the others were too shy to take part, but it worked well.'

'I imagine the kids would love it.'

'They did. Most of them enjoyed it in the most innocent way. Only a handful spoiled the party.' She told him about the wolf-whistling.

'You can't really blame them. You've got a lovely figure, and there must be a lot of kids who don't know a more acceptable way of expressing their admiration.'

'I know. That's why I dealt with them as leniently as I did. That and the fact that it was their last day at school.' Looking at her watch, she said, 'It's time I left you. Thanks for your help tonight.' As an afterthought, she added, 'And thanks for the compliment.'

Being careful, this time, where she put her feet, Rhona pulled out the last of the weeds and stood back to admire the result. If she knew more about gardening, she would buy some more plants to fill up some of the spaces left by the weeds. That would set the neighbours talking, and if she sent a few photos to her grandparents, they'd be impressed, as well. On second thoughts, though, her grandad could be very critical of other people's efforts. He seemed to forget that the rest of the world was only human.

She resolved to visit the new garden centre. Surely, the plants would have labels telling shoppers where, when and how to plant them. She couldn't be the only clueless gardener around. Then, having made that decision, she went indoors to run a bath.

The combination of satisfaction and warm suds was most relaxing, and she was almost asleep when she heard the phone downstairs. It was actually quite difficult to hear the ringing itself. What she actually heard was the vibration against the windowsill on which the phone usually stood. Somehow, the bathroom windowsill picked up the vibration and acted as an extension of the phone bell. At all events, it succeeded in rousing her to wakefulness. She had no intention of going downstairs wet and half-naked to answer it; it would probably have stopped ringing by the time she was halfway there, but the intrusion was sufficient to persuade her to dry herself and get on with the rest of the day.

She was drying her hair when the phone rang again, so she went downstairs to answer it.

'Hello?'

'Rhona, it's Matt.' He sounded more serious than usual.

'Hello, Matt. What's up?'

'I tried phoning you earlier. You must have been out.'

'The phone rang when I was in the bath. What's the problem?'

'The theatre's been vandalised. I'm there now, waiting for the police to arrive.'

22

SHOCK AND A SURPRISE

The shock was slowly dawning on her. All the hard work and expense…. 'What's the damage, Matt?'

'They forced the lock to get in. I'll have to fit a new door. Apart from that, though, it seems to be mainly paint. We left ten litres of non-reflective paint here, and someone's had a merry old time with it. I should warn you, there are some things you won't find at all pleasant.'

'I don't care. I'll come down now.'

With her hair still damp, she drove to the theatre. Vandalism suggested kids, most likely local kids, and for them to have forced the door open, they weren't likely to be primary kids, either. She would no doubt find out more when she got there.

Parking beside the police panda car that stood outside the theatre, she went in and found Matt talking with a policewoman. Everywhere she looked, paint had been hurled and, in some cases, daubed.

'This is Miss Loveday,' said Matt, 'the prime mover and fundraiser in this venture.'

'How do you do, Miss Loveday?' The WPC pointed to one wall that had been liberally besmirched, and said, 'Whoever did this evidently knows you.'

There was no denying it. A life-size representation of a woman had been painted on the wall with certain features crudely drawn and the words, *Ma Lovebay* beneath it.

'Presumably, this was done by someone who knew you were connected with the theatre.'

'That narrows it down to most of the population of Banfield High School.'

'Have you any idea who might have done it?'

Rhona studied the graffiti. Her first suspicion had been Lee Gregory and Keith Bentley, but then something else occurred to her. 'I may be able to narrow it down to about fifteen lads,' she said.

'Oh, how's that?'

'They may have been in my tutor group. I have a photograph at home,' she told the WPC, 'of some graffiti I found at school on the last day of term. If you like, I'll drop it off at the police station. Whoever was responsible for that has difficulty in getting "d" and "b" the right way round, and so had the kid who did this.'

The WPC made a note and asked, 'How old are those kids, Miss Loveday?'

'Sixteen, the first year to do the extra, compulsory year. They all left school at the end of term, but it'll still be possible to compare....' She laughed humourlessly. 'I was going to say, the "handwriting", but I don't think that's quite the word for it.'

'This must be very upsetting for you, Miss Loveday.'

'The vandalism is, naturally. A great many people have put a lot of effort into this project, some more than others.' She gave Matt a sympathetic nod.

'There's an eye-witness, who saw two lads lurking round here, last night. She gave me a description.'

'It probably wouldn't mean much to me,' said Rhona. 'I only saw them at registration.'

'Didn't you teach them at all?'

'No, I took a class of RoSLA kids, the compulsory stayers-on, for Spanish, but none of that group was among them.'

'Well,' said the WPC, 'if you'll drop the photo into the station, we'll take it from there.'

'Wait a minute,' said Rhona, remembering. 'The photos are still in the car. I picked them up when I returned from Newcastle, but I didn't take them into the house. In fact, I didn't even have time to look at them. Bear with me a second.' She hurried out to her car and looked in the glove compartment. As she'd remembered, they were there. She picked them up and took them back into the theatre to show the WPC. 'There's the photo of the graffiti,' she said. 'Don't ask me why I took it, but you can see how he tried to write, "rub" and "bigger"." I should explain that he'd already drawn two of them, making each one bigger than the last.' Looking further, she found a picture of herself with the group. 'That's all of them,' she said. 'Take it, by all means, if it'll help you find the culprit.'

'Thank you, Miss Loveday. I just need to take a few particulars so that we can get in touch with you if we need to. Of course, we'll let you have your photos back, as well.' She made a note of Rhona's name, address and phone number before leaving her and Matt.

'I bet she's wondering why I took a photo of the graffiti at school,' said Rhona, 'and I really couldn't say. It just seemed a good idea at the time.'

'Another good idea,' said Matt, 'might be to photograph this lot before we start work on it.'

'I've got my camera here, but it's empty.'

'There's Boots down the road. You could get a film there.'

'Yes, I will.' She stared at the picture on the wall until Matt placed his hands gently on her shoulders and said, 'Don't take it personally. The kid who did that probably only had half a brain.'

'It's not that,' she said, turning and laying her head against his chest. 'It's knowing I've brought this on us. The kids who did it knew I was connected with the theatre, and I feel as if I led them here.'

'Nonsense. If they had a grudge against you, they'd have found an easier way to hurt you. I think they just wanted to get up to mischief, and the fact that you were part of the theatre was neither here nor there.' He reinforced his words by putting his arms round her and holding her close, so that, for the moment, she felt shielded from the unpleasantness and the cruel setback that had come as such a shock.

After a while, he asked, 'What shampoo do you use?'

She had to think for a second. 'L'Oréal. Why?'

'I'm getting high on it.' He inhaled deeply. 'And, of course, you're worth it.'

'How did you know about that?' The advertising slogan hadn't been around all that long, and feminine hair products didn't exactly feature in a man's world.

'I sometimes watch ITV, and I go shopping with Bev.'

She lifted her head and looked up to see if he was smiling. He looked quite serious, although that wasn't surprising. He could be quite deadpan in any situation.

'You have beautiful hair, and it's right that you use the shampoo both of you deserve, you and your hair.' Without warning, he bent and kissed her, breaking off to say almost conversationally, 'I didn't really mean to do that.'

'You're allowed to,' she assured him, 'accidentally or on purpose. Are you going to do it again?'

Without speaking, he bent again and kissed her softly and with increasing conviction. Eventually, he said, 'I'm afraid I'm out of practice at this kind of thing.'

'But it's all coming back to you, I can tell.'

'I believe it is.' He kissed her again.

'Three cheers for L'Oréal,' she murmured, responding happily.

At the Monteverdi restaurant again, that evening, Rhona reached across the table to stroke his hand with her thumb. 'You're a dark horse,' she said. 'In the five or six months we've known each other, you've made me feel invisible until now.'

'I'm not a headstrong sort of person.'

She laughed. 'You can say that again.'

'At least,' he said thoughtfully, 'I don't think I am. I don't go in for introspection. At least, I don't think I do. I can never be all that sure.'

'Better to keep it that way,' she told him confidently. 'Introspection is an awful turn-off. People who analyse themselves are just as likely to send themselves birthday cards.'

'Is that original?' He seemed quite impressed.

'No, my dad said it. He's full of home-made proverbs, except he prefers to call them "silly speaks", because he's not full of himself, either.' She considered that assessment, having put it into words for the first time. It was something she'd always accepted as normal, like everything else she'd known from childhood. 'He could never be like that, even if he wanted to be,' she concluded, 'living with me mam.'

'You always say, "*my* dad" and "*me* mam",' he said, picking up the wine.

She shook her head. 'I have to drive home.' Then, in response to his observation, she said, 'It just feels right. If you met them, you'd understand.'

'Possessive adjectives apart, they sound very different.'

She thought about that and said, 'It was a bone of contention between them at first, but then it became a joke.'

'That sounds healthy.'

'Well, you see, when they met, he was an officer in the Navy, and she was a lowly Wren. Now, because of that, and also because she was the daughter of a fitter in the shipyard, and his dad had been manager of a labour exchange, she couldn't see a future for them.'

'I imagine he'd convince her easily enough.'

She laughed shortly. 'What gives you that idea?'

'He has no difficulty persuading me to read his novels.'

'Ah well, me mam was a tougher proposition altogether. It took a battered ship and news that he'd been seriously injured to make her think again, and even then, she took some persuading. It was a complex story, believe me.'

Looking around the restaurant, he said, 'I'd love to hear it, but we seem to be in danger of overstaying our welcome again. I think these people are waiting for us to go home.'

Matt paid the bill, and they returned to the car.

'I should buy a better car,' he said, getting into the passenger seat of Rhona's Avenger.

'What's the hurry, when you can always cadge a lift in mine? You could get rid of yours, anyway. Being without a car is the stamp of an individual, these days. I mean to say, how many people can say they've been taken to hospital in a builder's pick-up?'

'Not a great many. You were certainly the first casualty to christen mine.'

'I should hope so, too.'

After a while, Rhona sensed a degree of preoccupation on Matt's part, so she said, 'A penny for 'em.'

'I think I should warn you that Bev's likely to be back when we arrive, and I think she's managed to detect, somehow or other, that there's something going on between us.'

'What has she said?'

'She asked me if you were going to stay over. Goodness knows how she caught on.'

Rhona said confidently, 'Female intuition.'

156

'I didn't know she had any.'

'You do now. Is she okay about it?'

'She seems to be.' He shook his head, seemingly at a loss to understand what was happening around him.

'We're better than fellas at reading signs,' she told him. 'It compensates for an awful lot.'

'I'll never understand these things.'

'That's because you're a fella. It all goes back to prehistoric times, when the woman stayed in the cave and looked after the bairns while the man went hunting. When he came home, she could tell at a glance whether he'd been hunting for food all day, or fitting in a crafty bit of pleasure as well.'

'Is that what it was called?'

'It still is, if we're very lucky.' She turned into the yard and switched off the engine.

'Coffee?'

'Why not?' She followed him into the house, where Bev sat, watching television.

'Hello, you two,' she said with a look that confirmed Matt's suspicion immediately. 'Have you had a nice time?'

'Very nice, thank you,' said Rhona. 'What are you watching?'

'Just an old film.' Remembering something, she said, 'David Warburton from the Amateurs phoned. I said you'd phone him back tomorrow.'

'Thanks, Bev,' said Matt. 'Did he say what it was about?'

'Yeah, he said he'd been talking to the police, and they'd said something about a witness.'

'Good. I'm going to make some coffee. What are you going to have, Bev?'

She appeared to consider the question momentarily, and said, 'I won't bother. I'm going to bed now, anyway.' With another knowing look, she said, 'Goodnight.'

'Goodnight, Bev.'

'Goodnight, Bev.' Matt cringed as soon as she was out of sight. 'I'll put the kettle on,' he said, looking like a child who'd been found out and given a gentle telling off.

'When you consider her mam's track record,' said Rhona, reaching down the coffee for him, 'the only novelty is that we're her friends. Thank goodness she's not possessive.'

Matt poured hot water on to the coffee and stirred it. 'She's not easy to fathom,' he said. 'Sometimes, there's an awful lot going on beneath the surface, and then at other times, I'll be convinced she's struggling with something inside, and it turns out to be nothing at all.' Pouring milk into the coffee, he said, 'Having said all that, I've absolutely no regrets about taking her in.'

'You're the stabilising influence in her life, Matt.'

'I hope so.'

The coffee stood forgotten on the worktop as they kissed, still savouring the frisson of novelty, but feeling none of the hesitation they'd known that morning. He asked, 'You don't really want to go home tonight, do you?'

'Not desperately. I did come prepared.' In answer to a look of surprise, she said, 'I took the precaution when I bought the film, this morning.'

By unspoken agreement, they kissed again and crept quietly upstairs.

23

THE SAME IN ANY LANGUAGE

Rhona struggled for a moment to open her eyes, cosy beneath the continental quilt, but encouraged by the sound of something being placed on the table beside her. Her vision began to clear, and she made out a mug, a wisp of vapour and then Matt, now fully-clothed. 'Good morning,' she said as he bent to kiss her. 'You're up and about early.'

'Life goes on,' he reminded her, 'and I've just spoken to David Warburton on the phone.'

'Good heavens!' She looked around the room for a clock and her eye fell on the alarm radio on the other table. 'It's nearly half-past nine. No wonder you're up and dressed.'

'Take your time. The bathroom's all yours. Bev and I were up some time ago.' Smiling at her discomfiture, he said, 'I thought I'd let you sleep on.'

'You spoil me, Matt.'

'I'm afraid I'm a bit out of practice.'

'I've no complaints. Anyway, what did David have to say?'

'Nothing we didn't already know. He wanted to do a rant in *The Netherdale Reporter*, denouncing the vandals for what they are, but I talked him out of it.'

'Good.' She sat up, carelessly letting the quilt fall away, and said, 'I'd have done the same.'

'That's what I thought.'

'I know, Matt. You're a man after my own heart.' More urgently, she asked, 'Have you something I can put on to go to the bathroom?'

He took his dressing gown from the hook behind the door and handed it to her. 'Bev's gone into Skipton. I sent her to get more paint.'

159

'Thanks, Matt. I couldn't fault you, even if I tried.' She kissed him gratefully before hurrying to the bathroom.

Gazing again at the paint-splashed interior of the theatre, Rhona said, 'If it'll help at all, I'm happy to lend a hand with the painting.'

'Thanks, Rhona, but I think we'll manage.'

She eyed Matt suspiciously and said, 'You reckon I'd make a mess of it, 'cause I'm a woman, don't you?'

'That's right.'

'At least you're honest,' she told him resignedly. 'My grandad always said I got more paint on the brush handle than I did on what I was supposed to be painting. Mind you, he's a perfectionist.'

Laughing, Matt said, 'You can't really blame him.'

'No, he only ever let Steve do any painting. I suppose it made sense, as he was always good at it. The only problem with him was that he tried to turn every job into a work of art.'

'Did you feel left out of things?'

'No, that's something my family have never gone in for. Everybody gets treated as if they're special.' Wrinkling her nose in thought, she said, 'I try to carry it on, but I have to make the occasional exception.'

Smiling, he asked, 'Are you thinking of Gary Oldfield?'

'As a rule, I try not to, but yes.'

Putting his arms round her and hugging her from behind, he said, 'You make me feel special.'

'It's not difficult, and last night *was* special.' She wriggled around inside his arms and kissed him.

'I'm sorry I had to get up while you were still asleep.'

'If you'd waited for me… well, you saw what time I woke up. It's the latest I've slept in a long time.'

'I imagine you were relaxed. I know I was.' Looking at the damage again, he said, 'I hate to change the subject, but I really don't think this is going to be such a big operation. Those kids have done part of the job for us.'

'What do you mean?'

'They've splashed black, non-reflective paint on the floor and the seat frames, and that's where it's needed. It just has to be tidied up.'

'What about the walls and the proscenium?'

He looked around and nodded pensively. 'They'll need at least two coats of paint.'

'My portrait will,' she observed, 'and I don't think it'll ever be completely erased from my memory.'

'You mustn't take it to heart,' he told her. 'I'm sure there was no malice in it.'

Rhona was still unimpressed. 'How do you expect me to take it when they've drawn my bum as big as that?'

'Take it up with the Art Department, Rhona.'

The sound of a vehicle coming to rest outside prompted Rhona to go to the door, where Bev had parked the pick-up. She watched her jump down to open the back and, seeing several five-litre cans of paint and various substances, said, 'Bev, I don't think you should be lifting heavy things like that. You could do yourself a mischief.'

'I didn't lift 'em. The blokes at Skipton Paint put 'em on the pick-up for me.'

Matt lifted two cans off the back and grinned. 'She knows how to crack the whip and get the lads working for her,' he said. 'Some blokes are resentful of women in what they see as a man's world, but Bev usually brings out the best in them.'

'I'm glad to hear it. By the way, where's Troy today?'

'He's gone with his mum to the DHSS, in case they ask her to prove she has a dependent child.' Lowering his voice, he added, 'If you ask me, she needs all the credibility she can lay her hands on. According to Bev, they're not in a hurry to take her word for anything.'

A car drew up outside, and Rhona wasn't surprised when David Warburton walked into the theatre.

'I'm glad I've found you…' he said, breaking off when he saw Bev and Matt hard at work with rollers. 'Should they be doing that? I mean, it's evidence.'

'I took pictures of the evidence,' Rhona told him. 'I did that while the police were here.'

'I'd like to let the public know just what animals they have in this village,' he said, 'but Matt wasn't keen on the idea.'

'Neither am I, David. In my experience, vilifying kids only makes them more determined than ever to misbehave.'

'Well, if you think so.' He was evidently unconvinced.

'Give a dog a bad name, David. That's what they say, isn't it?'

'I suppose so. In any case, the police say they have a witness and further evidence to go on.'

'I gave them a class photo to narrow it down a bit, and showed them evidence of the miscreant's inability to write "b" or "d" the right way round.'

'Oh?'

'One of them drew a figure in paint and labelled it "Ma Lovebay". Needless to say, I wasn't impressed.'

David looked to where Bev was busily painting over the exaggerated bust. 'That's dreadful.'

'You can say that again, David. They've never been that size.'

He seemed about to clarify his observation, and then, realising she wasn't entirely serious, went on to say, 'How does it make you feel, Rhona, knowing that the children you teach are capable of this kind of thing?'

'Ah, but they're not. At least, most of 'em aren't.'

'But they did this.'

'Two or three of them did. There are more than fourteen hundred kids on roll, David, but I'm hopeless at maths, so I'll leave you to work out the percentage, an' I can guarantee you'll be surprised.'

...

The topic found its way into the conversation at dinner, which Rhona cooked at Matt's house.

'Why does he think all Banfield kids are bad?' asked Bev.

'I can't imagine he does think that, Bev,' said Rhona. 'He just speaks without thinking, but he's only like a lot more.'

'Times change,' said Matt, 'and for some people, any change arouses suspicion.'

Bev was looking puzzled, so Rhona explained. 'There's a generation of people who remember with great fondness a time when children who might have struggled with Latin and Physics were sent out to work when they were fourteen, while others went on to achieve great things. In case you're wondering, that's how David Warburton got to be a managing director, and maybe it's not surprising he thinks badly of Banfield High. It's a new kind of school, and he must think it's naff compared with the one he went to.'

It was another world in Bev's estimation. 'Did he do Latin an' that other thing?'

'Probably, but so did I, if I'm honest, not that I was ever any good at Physics.'

'Likewise,' said Matt.

'However,' said Rhona, 'Matt and I can still keep an open mind.'

It was a great deal for someone with Bev's limited experience to appreciate. After overt consideration, she said, 'I wish I could do proper readin'.'

'You can, bonny lass, and you're getting better at it all the time.'

Conversation became lighter after that and, several topics later, Bev asked, 'Are you going to see your granny and grandad again, Rhona?'

'Yes, very soon. Do you want to come with me?'

Instantly excited, she said, 'Oh, yes...' Then she hesitated and looked unsurely at Matt.

'I can manage on my own for a few days, Bev. You go and enjoy yourself.'

'Thanks.' Her smile showed that she was looking forward to it already.

After a while, she said, 'I think I'll go to bed.'

'I would, Bev,' said Matt. 'You've worked hard today.'

'I'll just do the washing up.'

'No,' said Rhona, 'you can leave that to us.'

'All right.' Remembering her manners, she added, 'Thanks.'

'Just a minute.' Rhona beckoned to her and kissed her on the cheek. ''Night-night.'

A little shyly, she said, 'Your mum and dad do that, don't they?'

'You poor little scrap,' said Rhona, taking her into her arms, 'you've missed out on so much.' She kissed her again and said, 'Don't forget the boss. You've got to keep in with him.'

Just as shyly, Bev walked over to Matt and received a kiss. ''Night-night,' he said.

''Night-night.' She left them and went upstairs, no doubt still coming to terms with a new and surprisingly agreeable custom.

Rhona and Matt carried the dishes out to the kitchen. 'The look on her face when you asked her if she wanted to go to Newcastle,' he said, 'was priceless.'

'Aye, I put that down to me grandad, you know. I've often thought more folks should have a family like mine.'

'It's good that you share them with her.'

'No, Matt, it gives me as much pleasure. I'll never forget hearing her chat to my grandad about building. By my reckoning, he made friends with her in two minutes flat.'

'Was he in the building trade?'

'No, he was a fitter in the shipyard, an' then later on, he got a job teaching in the local technical college. He was in his element teachin' young lads.'

Matt dried the last of the plates and stacked them in the cupboard. 'You know,' he said, 'Bev sets a good example.'

'In what way?'

'Early to bed.'

'I cannot disagree with that,' she said, putting her arms round him.

'Howay, then,' he said, kissing her.

'And who's been teaching you Geordie?'

'You have, bonny lass.'

She could think of no answer to that, so she returned his kiss and followed him upstairs.

Matt closed the bedroom door quietly behind them, whispering, 'Bev knows perfectly well what we're doing, but I still don't like to advertise the fact.'

'No,' she agreed, unbuttoning her blouse and draping it over a chair.

He drew her closer into a lingering kiss, during which he unfastened the clasp of her bra.

'What are you getting up to behind my back?' she asked as soon as she could speak.

'I don't know what you mean,' he said, unfastening the waist button of her jeans.

'Let me take my shoes off before it all gets ungainly,' she suggested. 'The penguin walk was never a turn-on.'

'I'm not so sure,' he said. 'We could try it some time. It would be good for a laugh, at least.'

'That's not what we're here for,' she said, sitting on the bed to ease off her shoes and remove her jeans.

Soon, they lay entwined beneath the quilt, kissing slowly, and carefully exploring each other's secrets after the urgency of the previous night.

Matt asked, 'What do they call this in German?'

If his question took her by surprise, she was equal to it. '*Der Geschlechtsverkehr*,' she told him breathlessly. 'If it's difficult to… pronounce, it probably… deters children from… doing it until they're… older. At least, I imagine… that's the idea.'

'I think I prefer to do in English.'

'Mm,' she agreed with growing excitement, and her murmurings increased in frequency and intensity until, eventually, she welcomed him with a blissful gasp, which was the same in any language.

24

JUSTICE

R hona had been delaying her trip to Newcastle until she knew
something more definite about the suspects. Within the next
week, though, she received a phone call from Skipton Police
Station, informing her that three boys had admitted causing wilful
damage at the theatre, and asking her if the society wanted to prefer
charges against them. Naturally, she told them she would have to speak
to David Warburton, as the decision wasn't hers to make, and she also
asked if she might be allowed to speak to the boys.

David insisted on joining her at the station. Matt went along as
company for Rhona.

They arrived to find an officer in conversation with a woman
accompanied by a dog, which appeared to be most likely a German
shepherd cross, although it was looking more sheepish than shepherd
in a flowered sunhat. It earned their joint sympathy.

David was already there, and when Matt appeared with Rhona, he
made no secret of his surprise. 'What are you doing here, Matt?' he
demanded.

'I don't know if it's escaped your notice, David, but I've been doing
the lion's share of the hard work, and I therefore have a personal interest
in this case. Would you prefer me not to be here?'

'Of course not. I only wondered.'

A sergeant asked them to follow him into another room, where
three dejected-looking boys and several tight-lipped parents waited to
learn what charges were to be brought. The policewoman who had been
at the theatre was with them.

'Michael Cook, Alan McEvoy and Jason Enright,' said the sergeant,
'I imagine you know Miss Loveday.'

'They should,' said Rhona. 'They were all in my tutor group

until a couple of weeks ago.' Addressing the three, she said, 'I don't suppose you can imagine how the members of the society must feel about what you've done. An awful lot of people have spent much time and enthusiasm raising funds so that the building can be used again as a theatre. Mr Warburton will tell you that,' she said, pointing to David. 'He's Chairman of the Society, and he knows all about it. As well as that, though, there are those who've worked extremely hard on the actual restoration.' Inclining her head towards Matt, she said, 'Mr Brocklehurst is one of them. In fact, he's worked hardest of all, and now he's seen his efforts treated with contempt.' She gave them a few moments to think about what she'd said.

One of the boys was moved to speak, and tears started as he said, 'We didn't mean no harm, Miss.'

'Pull the other one, Jason,' she told him blandly. 'You must have realised how much hurt you were causing.' She continued. 'All those people have been putting everything they have into the theatre restoration because they want to give something to the town and to the dale. They want to provide a place where people can entertain, be entertained and generally enjoy themselves. If it's ever allowed to happen, it'll be a wonderful thing for Akengarth and for the whole of the dale, but... dear, oh dear... none of them deserved this.' Aware that the parents in the room were suffering as much as the boys, she reckoned it was time to end their suspense. 'I've had to work hard to persuade the society not to prefer charges,' she told them. At this stage, all three boys and their mothers were in tears, and Rhona waited until they were more composed. 'You won't have to go to the Magistrate's Court,' she said, 'and you can think yourselves lucky that you won't have a criminal record, because that's a rotten start in life for anybody.' She could almost sense their relief, and she was grateful for a chance to turn it into something even better. 'There's something else you can do instead. You've already demonstrated how you can wreck other people's honest efforts, but we're giving you a chance to make amends, a chance to do something good and useful, and win everyone's approval instead of their resentment.' She nodded to Matt and left him to explain it to them.

'You've all seen me around the village,' he said. 'I'm Matt Brocklehurst, the joiner and builder, and I want to see all three of you at the theatre at eight o' clock on Monday morning. Don't come dressed up, because you're all going to labour for me. It'll be hard work, and you'll get mucky doing it. It's just in the theatre – I won't ask you to work for me anywhere else – but you're being given this chance to put things right and do something for the community. Do you understand?'

All three nodded readily.

'You owe your reprieve to Miss Loveday, because it was her idea, so I want you to work your boll… your socks… off, to repay her kindness.'

Turning to the parents, Rhona asked, 'Is that all right with the mams an' dads?'

There was a chorus of grateful and tearful agreement.

'Right, lads, the society members aren't the only people who've been inconvenienced. These police officers have to work hard enough as it is, without extra work being created for them, so I want you to tell them how sorry you really are. Then, you can start putting things right.'

When the boys, their parents and their tearful gratitude out of the way, the sergeant said, 'I think you made a wise decision, Miss Loveday.'

Rhona shook hands with him, saying, 'Don't you start cryin' as well, Sergeant. I couldn't cope with that.'

'No,' he said, laughing, 'it takes more than that.'

…

On the way home, Matt said, 'I give you full marks for that, Rhona. It was an excellent idea.'

'Oh, shucks. It was obvious, really. David wanted the *Reporter* to say how much people despised those lads, and nobody responds well to bein' told they're despised or hated. I simply wanted to give them a chance to redeem themselves.'

'And you did.' As one thought followed another, he said, 'I keep wondering what that woman was doing there with the shamefaced Alsatian.'

'Oh yes, the sergeant told me she was the witness who identified the lads.'

'That's a relief. I wondered if she'd been trying to get Maisie a job on the force. We wouldn't want to see her patrolling the streets in that hat she was wearing, would we?'

They turned to face each other and simultaneously shook their heads.

With Matt, Troy and the three boys hard at work on the theatre, Rhona took Bev on her second visit to Newcastle and Amble.

On this occasion, Bev met Rhona's grandparents without shyness, beaming with pleasure when her grandad said, 'Well I never. It's that buildin' inspector come to look at the pointin' again. Howay inside, hinny.'

Later, Rhona's granny watched them chatting together. 'Just look at them,' she said. 'They're like Dick an' Liddy, them two.'

'She couldn't wait to come up again,' said Rhona.

'She's welcome anytime, but hasn't she got a granny an' grandad of her own?'

'If she has, she doesn't know who they are or where they are.'

'It's a crying shame.' She nursed that thought briefly and then asked, 'Didn't you tell me there was a little lad as well?'

'Troy's eleven, now. He'll be at Banfield High in September, but he's working with Matt this holiday. It's the only way he can make the poor kid's life bearable.'

'He's only a bit bairn an' all. It's a pity something more cannot be done for 'im.'

'Matt could take Bev in because she was eighteen, Granny. There's no way he could have Troy as well, without attracting gossip, anyway.'

'Oh dear, but now we're on the subject, what's the situation with you and Matt?'

Rhona held up her hands in surrender. 'Okay, Granny, Matt and I are now an item.'

'What funny language you youngsters use. Does that mean you're courting?'

' "Courting" is maybe a bit strong. Let's just say we have a special relationship.'

'An understanding?'

Laughing at the old-fashioned language, she said, 'I suppose so.' Still smiling, she said, 'You know, the daft thing is, when I go up to Amble, me mam's bound to ask me the same thing all over again.'

'Why aye. You have to know what your bairns are getting up to.'
Rhona was glad that was all her granny knew.

There was naturally a similar welcome when they reached Amble and, just as Rhona had prophesied, her mother lost no time in enquiring into her love life.

'Have you found a nice fella yet, Rhona?'

Her father sighed. 'Come on, Bev,' he said. 'I'll show you the marina.'

Bev had no idea what a marina was, but she handed him his walking stick and followed him out to his car.

'Now we can talk,' said her mother.

'All right,' said Rhona when Bev and her father were safely outside. 'I'm going out with Bev's boss.' She laughed involuntarily. 'We have what Granny calls "an understanding".'

'Good. What's he like? I mean, I know he's a builder an' he's good at cricket, but what kind of man is he?'

'In a nutshell, he's thoughtful and considerate, and he has a generous nature.'

'He sounds okay. I hope he's not forever pestering you for you-know-what, like the other chap, the rugby player.'

'No, Mam, I can honestly say he's never pestered me for that.'

'Good, I'm glad.' Her mother was no fool, but she seemed satisfied with Rhona's answer.

'Let me tell you about something that happened the other night.'

'Go on, then.'

'We'd just had dinner at Matt's place, Matt, Bev and me, and Bev decided to go up to bed. She'd had a hard day, working at the theatre. Anyway, I called her over and kissed her goodnight. It was the first time anybody'd done that, and I could tell she found it really special.'

'Haddaway.'

'No, it's right, and then Matt did the same. Just imagine, she's eighteen, and that was the first time it had happened. Troy's still waiting, although he doesn't know it. I bought him and Bev their first teddy bears after I got back from France.'

'Oh, bless you, Rhona. Poor little scraps.' She seemed to ponder that until another thought occurred to her, and she asked, 'Have you heard from our Steve, lately?'

'Not since the anniversary. He must be in funds, because he only ever phones me when he needs a sub.'

'Oh, Rhona, that's unkind.'

'It's true, though.'

Surprisingly, her mother decided not to contest that assertion. Instead, she said, 'I was happy when he was living at your house.'

'I wasn't.'

'Well, at least, I knew you were keeping an eye on him.'

'You do ask a lot, Mam.' Returning the ball to her mother's court, she asked, 'Have you heard from him lately?'

'I spoke to him on the phone only this week.' The news was obviously good, because her mother was smiling. 'He's still seeing Caroline.' The fact evidently gave her some pleasure, but that was only to be expected, given her matchmaking zeal.

'The girl who makes wedding dresses? Amazing.'

'Yes.' With a mischievous look, she said, 'She might make a one for you yet. You never know.'

'You never give up, do you, Mam?'

'Not while I think there's still a chance of getting my daughter married off.'

'I was at the police station on Saturday,' said Rhona in a bid to change the subject.

'What on earth were you doing there?'

'Helping them with their enquiries,' she teased.

Her mother sighed. 'I suppose you'll tell me sooner or later.'

Rhona took pity on her. 'Some lads got into the theatre and splashed paint around. They made an awful mess and what's more, one of them painted a picture of me.'

'No.'

'It's true. It was a terrible picture an' all. He gave me a huge backside and bosoms like beach balls.'

'It's the only way you'll get them that big in this family. Anyway,' said her mother, returning to the original subject, 'That was an awful thing to happen. Have they caught them yet?'

'Yes, that's why we went to the police station. We decided not to press charges.'

'Why ever not?'

'We arranged for them to make good the damage.' She looked at her watch and said, 'As we speak, they'll be labouring in the theatre for Matt. It'll do them a power of good.'

'It probably will. It'll do 'em more good than putting 'em on probation. That's for sure.' It was her turn to look at the time, and she said, 'I wonder where that dad of yours has got to.'

'I think he took Bev to show her the sailing boats.'

'If I know your dad, he'll find some way of spoiling her.' The thought evidently pleased her.

'She'll take some spoiling, Mam. She's had little enough in the past.'

'Aye, it's an unfair world, Rhona. We can only try to tip the scales where we can.'

'Yes,' said Rhona, 'that's how justice works, isn't it?'

25

DISCLOSURE AND COMPOSURE

The new term began, as expected, with a plenary staff meeting. Rhona could only imagine the Headmaster was still searching for the Latin that would describe the occasion *in totum*, but she had every confidence that he would eventually find a suitably pretentious description.

'Before we move to the formal part of the meeting,' said Mr Purbright in his important way, I have to say how pleased I am that the three boys who were found to have defaced the interior of the new theatre have undergone a change of heart and made a significant contribution to its renovation.'

His announcement was greeted by a murmur of approval, largely from those who'd been unaware of the incident and, in some cases, of the theatre's existence.

Norman Davis, Head of Art, raised his hand.

'Is it important, Mr Davis? We must get on.'

'It's very important, Mr Purbright, depending on your point of view, of course. The change of heart you mentioned didn't happen by freak accident. It was the result of an inspired initiative on Miss Loveday's part, and I think she should be congratulated for it.'

Rhona squeezed Norman's hand in thanks. Mr Purbright simply said, 'Quite. Well done, Miss Loveday.'

'*Tardo remeavit cogitatio melius quam nulla cogitatio*, Mr Purbright,' said Rhona.

'What?'

'Thank you, Mr Purbright.'

Purbright looked questioningly at Arnold Baker, Head of Latin and Classical Studies, who whispered in his ear.

'What did you say, Rhona?' whispered Norman.

' "An afterthought is better than no thought at all".'

He chuckled. 'Well bowled, Rhona.'

'Now,' announced Mr Purbright, 'Item One on the Agenda concerns the allocation of graded posts.'

His use of the plural puzzled Rhona, and she continued to listen, even though she knew that the point made available by John Fieldman's departure was surely earmarked for one of the Maths, Physics or Chemistry staff.

'An unexpected change in the salary structure has resulted in the availability of no fewer than four scale points.' He paused, possibly enjoying a feeling known normally only to Santa Claus, and then only once a year. 'I've decided to give one to Mr Dawes.' It seemed that Rhona's prediction had been correct, at least so far. Dawes was a member of the Physics Department. 'The second I'm allocating to Mrs Lund.' That was the Maths Department catered for. 'I'm giving one to Mr O' Gorman.' That made three out of three. Rhona waited to hear about the fourth. 'Finally,' he said, 'I'm giving one to Miss Loveday.' With a mischievous smile, he said, 'That wasn't an afterthought, Miss Loveday. I'd had you in mind from the start.'

'I'm humbled, Mr Purbright,' said Rhona. 'Thank you very much.'

'Hoist with your own petard,' chuckled Norman Davis, 'but congratulations, Rhona. You deserve it.'

She mimed a kiss and resolved to refrain from scoring with Latin witticisms at staff meetings.

'I'm now second-in-command of the Modern Languages Department,' she told Matt, 'Captain Ahab's faithful lieutenant, you might say.'

'And richly deserved.'

In response to Bev's puzzled stare, Rhona explained, 'I've been made Number Two. That's next to Mr Ellis.'

Taking her hand in his, Matt said, 'You're still Number One with me. You always will be.'

'Always?' The question had occurred to her from time to time.

'Absolutely.'

Fortunately for Rhona, Bev broke the silence, saying, 'I was in Mr Ellis's tutor group in the fourth form. He didn't take me for anything, though.'

'Be thankful, Bev.'

'Why do you say that?' asked Matt.

'He never uses a simple word where he can insert a long, complex one. The kids must find him difficult to follow.'

'I believe Horace called it *sesquipedalia verba*,' said Matt, 'using complex words needlessly.' Self-consciously, he explained, 'It's just something I picked up during my brief spell at university.'

'I've declared a moratorium on Latin wit,' said Rhona, 'having been caught out, today.' She told him about the incident at the meeting.

'Hoist by your own petard,' suggested Matt.

'That's what Norman Davis said, and he was right.' She considered her undoing and said, 'I've wondered, sometimes, about the origin of that expression, but never enough to look into it. I know it's from *Hamlet*, but that's all I know.'

'It means that the bomb-maker was blown up by his own device,' explained Matt, 'but Shakespeare, being the rogue he was, can't have ignored the French connection.'

As usual, Bev looked lost, so Rhona explained, 'In French, "*péter*" means "to break wind".'

Puzzlement gave way to amused embarrassment.

'You see, Bev,' said Matt, 'it's surprising what you can learn when there's a French teacher in the house.'

Later, when Bev had gone to bed, Rhona asked, 'How long were you married?'

'Less than four years. It was a mistake, but a fleeting one, so I tend not to dwell on it.'

'Very sensible.' She had no intention of pursuing the subject, but Matt was in an outgoing mood.

'There were minor problems,' he said, 'but the main disagreement was about children.'

'What was her name?' asked Rhona. 'Just so we know who we're talking about, and then I'll stop interrupting.'

'Patricia.'

Rhona nodded. She'd known a few Patricias, the name having evidently been popular in the late nineteen-forties.

'Pat was keen to have children, and I wasn't averse to it, but I wasn't in a hurry, either. I was still trying to get the joinery established as an independent business, so it wasn't financially the best time to start a family, but I gave in, being the accommodating soul I am.'

Rhona waited, reluctant to probe, but still keen to hear his story.

'The trouble was, nothing happened. It was a sensitive time.'

It was also a sensitive subject, so Rhona hesitated before asking, 'Did you have tests?'

He gave an embarrassed smile. 'Yes, and I was found wanting, although we were told we might be successful if we kept trying. Apparently, I produce lazy sperm.'

'And the irony is that you're such a hard-working man. I can see, obviously, how it can be a huge obstacle if you're really keen to have children, but it's not the be-all and end-all for everybody.'

'No,' he agreed, 'but it was my attitude, rather than my malfunction, that brought our marriage to its end. I wasn't sufficiently committed, you see.'

'At the risk of sounding frivolous, I should think it takes more than commitment to propel the little buggers with sufficient force.'

Smiling at her description, he said, 'It's what happens after the gun's fired that's crucial. They have to swim, literally, for their lives.'

She put her glass down and said, 'What a strange conversation we're having.'

He topped up her glass. 'It's that kind of topic.'

'You once asked me if I was keen to have children,' she reminded him.

'Did I? It was just idle curiosity, I imagine.'

'Look, I hope I haven't re-opened an old wound. I'd hate to do that.'

176

'You've cut me to the quick,' he told her, taking her hand to lead her upstairs, 'but I was never one to bear a grudge.'

'Ten weeks, *ten weeks!* That's all we've got,' said Jane Baxendale despairingly, 'and you still don't know your words!'

'Just a minute, Jane,' said Helen Porter, appropriately in a stage whisper, 'this is a *floor* rehearsal. You've had a whole term of music rehearsals.'

'But they've forgotten the bloody words!'

Helen looked helplessly around her, no doubt divided between the need to get on with the rehearsal and her anxiety that the cast must inevitably have been affected by Jane's emotional outburst. Some kind of intervention was urgently necessary.

'Mrs Baxendale,' said Rhona, holding up her copy of the score, 'may I have a word?'

Jane hurried over, still distraught, and Rhona nodded to Helen, who retrieved the reins and continued with the rehearsal.

'Jane,' said Rhona, 'come out here a minute.' She opened the nearest door and held it for Jane to join her. 'Listen,' she said, 'you know how these things go. As soon as the kids start floor rehearsals and they're given something else to think about, the words and music fly out of the window, but only for a short time. They'll get it together by the next rehearsal. It won't be perfect, but it'll be a heck of a lot better.'

'I know that.' She sniffed wretchedly.

'Good, but don't start cryin', for goodness' sake, or the kids'll have a field day.'

'I'm all right.'

'Remember, as well, that they've had six weeks' holiday since the last rehearsal, and distractions don't come much bigger than that.'

'Yes, of course. I was… I reacted.'

'No, you overreacted. How do you expect the kids to perform with any confidence when you're panicking and telling them they're hopeless? They need a confident grown-up out there, somebody they can look up to.' She peered through the glass pane and said, 'They've got one grown-up, but they need two more, so let's go in there and behave like professionals.'

Instead of waiting for a response, she opened the door again and walked over to the piano. Helen nodded gratefully and said, 'Okay, everybody, "Colonel Buffalo Bill", from the top, please, Miss Loveday.'

Rhona started the number and smiled to herself. The kids were completely at sea with the words and music, but she knew they'd get it together, just as she'd told Jane Baxendale. Jane wasn't a bad teacher, but she was just a little too emotional at times, so that she needed a reminder from a hard-headed Geordie. Jane had collected herself, and was now singing along with the cast, which was what she should have been doing from the start.

'Good,' said Helen as the number ended, 'we'll come back to that, but let's go on, for now, and set the next number. Frank and the girls' chorus, let's do "I'm a Bad, Bad Man". From the top, please, Miss Loveday. Frank, come swaggering on stage.'

They made several false starts, but eventually, Frank Butler stated his case. It was the girls' turn, but they missed their cue. Helen stopped the number. 'Miss Loveday, will you give us the intro to the chorus, please?'

Rhona played the two bars' intro and sang the opening line. ' "You are making too much fuss." ' The girls picked up the line and continued with the chorus.

After the rehearsal, Jane came to Rhona to say, 'Thanks for what you did, Rhona. I knew better than that, but I let it all get on top of me.'

'Well, you'll remember that another time, bonny lass. You'll be okay, and remember. You have ten whole weeks before the show goes on stage.'

As she left the hall, she reflected that with the likes of Mrs Caukwell objecting to what she saw as a waste of time and resources the show had to be a success for the annual production to survive. Everyone had a duty to perform and, as she'd reminded Jane Baxendale, composure was essential.

26

OCTOBER

FLOWERS IN WINTER

After spending so much time with Matt at his house, it felt almost strange for Rhona to be back at hers, doing the normal things she did there. Neither she nor Matt wanted to rush into a decision about moving in; she would naturally be the one doing the moving, as he had to live over the shop, but they were both inclined to wait and see how things worked out between them.

She was marking a Second-Year French homework exercise when the phone rang. Still with her mind focused on the perfect indicative, she picked up the receiver with her non-marking hand. 'Hello.'

'Rhona, it's Matt.'

'Hello, Matt. This is a surprise.' They'd parted less than an hour or so earlier.

'I'm sorry if I've disturbed you. There's a couple of things, actually. Do you remember coming back from visiting your family, and telling me about an idea your mother had for covering the theatre seats?'

'Yes, she suggested the kind of moquette they use to cover bus seats.'

'Did she tell you where the stuff is made?'

'Aye, but I'll have to ask her again. It's a firm she used to deal with quite a lot. I'll find out for you.'

'Thanks, Rhona.'

'You said there was something else.' She didn't want to rush him, but she had another set of books waiting to be marked.

'Have you heard the news tonight?'

'Nothing that really caught my attention. What have you heard?'

179

'It's about the Arab-Israeli war.'

'Go on.' She couldn't imagine what a war between Middle-Eastern states had to do with either Matt or her.

'As a reprisal against the USA for backing Israel, the Saudis have imposed an embargo on selling oil to them.'

'I still don't get it.'

'The shortage of oil will inevitably affect its price, so that, even though we're not involved in the argument, prices at our petrol pumps are likely to soar and make work on the theatre impossible.'

'How's that?' She realised she was being impossibly obtuse, but it was still beyond her.

'We do all our work by the light provided by my generator,' he reminded her.

'Of course.' Now she understood.

'I can finish the electrical installation, but we need someone to apply to the electricity board for a supply. It needs to be done pretty quickly, because they'll have to inspect the installation and install three meters before they can connect the supply. Can you speak to David Warburton and get things moving?'

'Okay, I'll phone him now.' Belatedly, she asked, 'Why do we need three meters? My house only has one.'

'Because of the heavy-duty curtain machinery, it needs a three-phase supply. I'd explain it to you, but I'm a bit short of time just now.'

'That's all right, Matt. I probably wouldn't understand it anyway. Don't worry, I'll phone David.' It would be less interesting than the perfect tense, but life couldn't be all fun and merriment.

A week later, motorists and business people watched with growing anxiety as prices at filling stations rose daily. Elsewhere, dealers removed the price labels from their used cars, as values were tumbling in inverse proportion to fuel prices. Anyone wishing to sell a car with a cubic capacity of more than one litre had to regard it as an impossibility, at least until the crisis could be resolved, and that was not in the foreseeable future.

There was good news, however, at the theatre, which soon had an electricity supply. Work could go ahead without Matt's petrol generator. Furthermore, the moquette manufacturers, who were based in the West Riding, were inclined to be helpful. They had suffered a cancellation that had left a large volume of fabric on their hands, and they agreed to let the society have the requisite quantity at a much-reduced price. There had to be some good news among the rest, and Matt and Bev took the pick-up, filled with precious petrol, to collect the material. For the rest of the week, they concentrated on normal business.

That Friday, Rhona discovered expertise in an unexpected quarter. She had just returned her register to the office prior to a marking period, when one of the administrators asked her how the work on the theatre was proceeding.

'Pretty well, up to now,' she told her. 'Of course, the tradesmen involved are affected by the petrol crisis, so that's slowed things down.'

'Who isn't affected by it?'

'Right enough.' Jokingly, she asked, do you know of an upholsterer, by any chance?'

'Yes, I do. Mind you, he'll be retired by now, but he might be inclined to help. I used to go to his adult education class, oh, a couple of years ago. I've still got the tools I bought to cover an ottoman and a stool I found. I'll get you his number in a minute.' She picked up the phone book and thumbed through it. Arriving at the entry, she said, 'Just a minute. I'll give him a call.'

'That's ever so good of you, Beryl.'

'No, it's no bother.' She dialled the number and, after a few rings, someone answered. Beryl said, 'Hello, Mrs Thurman, it's Beryl Simpson calling. I came to one of your husband's evening classes a while ago. If he's around, do you think I could have a word with him, please?' Whatever Mrs Thurman's response was, it made Beryl grimace slightly. Cupping her hand over the mouthpiece, she said, 'She's sounds as friendly as him. I meant to say to you, he's not the life and soul of the party at the best of times. He's inclined to— Hello, Mr Thurman. I'm sorry to interrupt whatever you were doing. It's Beryl Simpson. I was in your evening class at Banfield High School.' She hesitated, presumably when he said something, and then said, 'I have with me Miss Loveday, who's involved in the restoration of Akengarth Savoy, and she's looking for an upholsterer, who—' She listened with her eyes firmly closed, a gesture that seemed not to bode well. Finally, she said, 'I'm sorry I've troubled you. Goodbye.' Putting the phone down, she said, 'The miserable old so-and-so.'

'I take it he's not interested, Beryl.'

'I'm afraid not. He's says he never did owt for nowt when he was working, and he's not about to start now he's retired.'

'Oh well, thanks for trying, Beryl. It was good of you. We'll just have to look further afield.' She pushed her register into its slot and was about to leave the office, when Beryl said, 'What am I thinking of? What do you want upholstered, Rhona?'

'Theatre seats. They're just panels that are let into iron frames, but they'll need to be tensioned properly and fixed.'

Beryl shook her head. 'There's nothing to it. Listen, if I come and show one of your people how it's done, they'll be able to do it themselves.'

Rhona relayed the information to Matt on the phone.

'Excellent. I'll volunteer to be her pupil. I don't suppose there's an awful lot to it, but there must be tricks of the trade that are worth knowing.'

'Have you got everything you need?'

'Plywood, wadding, webbing and fabric. I'm sure we can get any other bits and pieces that are needed.'

'That's fine, then.'

'Before we hang up, would you like to come over this evening?'

'Seeing as it's Friday, I think I can allow myself that indulgence. Why don't we all eat at the Pack Horse? Before you agree, let's call it a Dutch treat.'

Rhona was making her way back to her classroom when she met one of the Metalwork Department. He was dragging Troy by his collar, and it was obvious that there was something gravely amiss.

'What's the matter, Mr Bennett?' she asked, barring his path.

'I'm takin' this 'un to one o' t' deputies, if I can find one. He hasn't been 'ere two minutes, an' I caught 'im knockin' 'ell out of another lad. Happen somebody'll warm his backside wi' 'is cane.'

'Have you left a class unattended to do this?' It was difficult to believe it.

'I left 'em wi' Mr Harris.'

'Something's not right. Put him down a minute and let me talk to him.'

'You're welcome to t' little….' With an ill grace, he released Troy, who buried his face in Rhona's jumper, sobbing.

'Take your time, Troy, and tell me what happened.'

Eventually, he managed to say, 'Keith Skinner said… me mum's… a prozzy.'

'Did he, now?' Turning to the clueless member of staff, she asked, 'How would you feel if someone said that about your mum? I bet you'd want to hit him with your blacksmith's tongs, wouldn't you?' Receiving no answer, she said, 'I think you'd better leave this lad with me. Then you can carry on bullying the rest of the class.'

'You don't know what it's like down there, Miss Loveday.'

'No, but I'm learning fast. I'm going to speak to the Head of Year about this, and I think Master Skinner will be in for a surprise.' Taking Troy gently by the arm, she said, 'Come into my classroom, pet lamb, an' you can dry your eyes an' tell me what happened.' She knew the official line about physical contact with pupils but, as she saw it, no one else was going to give the poor little scrap a cuddle.

…

Rhona waited until Bev was out of the way before she told Matt about the incident. 'He was dragging the poor little thing by his shirt collar. He wanted one of the deputies to cane him.'

'For sticking up for his mum?' Matt sighed. 'I know she's a poor excuse for a mother, but no lad wants to hear that.'

'It was a poor excuse for a teacher that was frog marching him to the deputies' office.'

'Did you say it was Malcolm Bennett?'

'Yes,' she said, surprised, 'do you know him?'

'He joined the cricket club shortly before I left. He used to boast about the way he treated kids. What he seems to forget is that little lads grow into big lads, and they've all got long memories.'

Rhona winced. 'I'm not keen on violence, Matt, but he invites it simply by wielding it.'

'Not that it would have been a good thing, but why didn't he deal with Troy himself?'

'He would have, last term, but there's a new directive that physical punishment can only be administered by members of the Senior Management Team.'

'I see, although, from what I remember, Bennett has nasty little ways that wouldn't be viewed as corporal punishment.' After a little more thought he asked, 'How did you leave it with Troy?'

'I've spoken to his year tutor, who's going to see the Skinner character. Basically, Troy knows he can go to his year tutor if he needs to talk, but I think he's more likely to come to me. He knows me, and he knows I'm sympathetic. I'm happy for him to do that, but I don't want him to be seen by the other kids as a teacher's pet.' She mused about that for a minute or so and said, 'It's Parents' Evening for New Pupils next month.'

'How does that work?'

'It's for parents and staff to talk about how the new intake are settling in. I don't suppose Troy's mam will be there.'

'No, all bets are off. I don't suppose she's ever been to a parents' evening, but we could deputise for her.'

Rhona laughed. 'I'm sure she'd agree to that, but don't forget I'll have parents to see as well.'

'Leave it to me, Rhona. I'll take Bev with me to show me around, and while I'm there I'll have a few little words with Malcolm Bennett, just to leave him in no doubt about how Troy hasn't to be treated.'

She smiled broadly. 'You're incorrigible, Matt, but listen. Now we've discussed the horrible side of life, let's do something nice.'

'Have you anything in particular in mind?'

'I thought you might suggest something.'

He adopted a thinking pose. 'There's Scrabble,' he said, 'or—'

'Let's just go to bed,' she suggested.

'Good idea. Can we do it with the light on?'

'If we can find a spotlight, you can be the star of the show.'

'Yippee! Still, it is Friday night, after all.' He switched off the sitting room lights and they went upstairs together.

Rhona closed the bedroom door and said softly, 'I still feel that I have to whisper because of Bev, and that's laughable, considering her upbringing.'

While she unbuttoned her blouse, she told him how she'd been given the third degree by her mother. 'She even asked me if you pestered me for sex,' she said.

'I wouldn't know where to start, honestly. No, I'm more the kind of chap who waits until he's invited.'

'I've noticed.'

'What did you tell her?' he asked, helpfully unhooking her bra as he spoke.

'I said you were more the kind of chap who waits to be asked.' She stroked his hair while he draped her bra across a chair. 'Actually, I didn't let on that we get at all physical. Me mam's okay, but my dad's a bit old-fashioned. He likes to think I'm still pure.'

'You're pure delight,' he said, kneeling to ring her navel with a garland of gentle kisses.

'Come on, get undressed or I'll think I'm in this on me own.'

'Whatever happened to poetry?' He undressed while she shed the last of her clothes and climbed into bed.

'I left it with the Sixth Form.'

'What?'

'Poetry. They're studying Müller's *Die Winterreise*, but I've left it with them for the weekend.'

After a long and heartfelt kiss, he said, 'I've never thought of German as a poetic language.'

'It's very poetic.' Placing a finger over his lips, she recited:

'Doch an den Fensterscheiben
Wer malte die Blätter da?
Ihr lacht wohl über den Träumer,
Der Blümen in Winter sah?'

'You make it sound good,' he admitted. 'What does it mean?'

' "But on the windowpanes,
Who painted the leaves there?
Do you laugh at the dreamer,
Who saw flowers in winter?" '

'Is it about someone who dreams of something others see as an impossibility?'

'Right in one, Matt. Go to the top of the class and give the pencils out.' She kissed him as an added reward.

'What do the Sixth Form think about it?'

'Most of the girls and, secretly, a couple of the boys love it. The rest of the girls can't understand why Led Zeppelin haven't yet set it to alleged music, and the rest of the boys prefer to talk about cricket and rugby, but don't worry, I'll get them all through A Level, you'll... see.' She faltered as he traced a line of kisses, working downward from her lips. 'Now that's... poetry, Matt,' she gasped. 'Stick... with it.'

27

NOVEMBER

UNDER THE SPOTLIGHT

If the whole world were a stage, Banfield High School was a microcosm of that metaphor. At least, it was for most staff and pupils. The less artistically-inclined as well as the confirmed non-believers, practised passive non-cooperation, only complaining loudly when preparations became impossible to ignore. Others went assiduously, and sometimes warily, about their specialist tasks. The Physics Department had not forgotten how, three years earlier, the Fire Service had made its usual last-minute inspection of the performance area and auditorium, and complained that the orchestra lighting constituted a fire hazard. The cast had been obliged to delay the start by a further ten minutes while the deficiency was dealt with to the inspecting Sub-Officer's satisfaction, although it was agreed by most concerned that the interruption was regrettably necessary.

During this period of intense preparation, Rhona took the skeleton orchestra to various forgotten spaces – in fact, wherever she could find a piano and seclusion – to rehearse its members. The confusion of disciplines was not lost on one pupil, a clarinettist, who asked, 'Why do they get you to do this, Miss, when you teach languages?'

'I don't know if you've noticed, Wayne, but musical terms are usually couched in Italian. How can you expect anyone else to understand them?'

'Can you speak Italian, Miss?'

'No, but I can play it. Okay, everybody, the Overture, from the top.' Languages teacher or no, she drilled them until they were supremely confident, which was how things had to be by the next stage, which was the Dress Rehearsal.

At the due time, she found Jane Baxendale in a state of nerves, and was obliged once again to brace her up. It seemed there was no limit to what a linguist could be required to do. She was earning her scale point many times over.

Eventually, everyone was ready, however, and the band played the Overture. There was no applause because there was no audience, but they received Rhona's encouraging praise before *segue*-ing into Scene One and, in encountering that word, learned at first-hand the need for a linguist.

After two brief numbers, the chorus came on stage to sing 'Colonel Buffalo Bill'. There were two hitches involving props, but they performed the number quite well. Even Jane was beginning to calm down.

When the girls came on stage for the number 'I'm a Bad, Bad Man', the boy playing Frank Butler looked nothing like the *roué* he claimed to be. After swaggering through several rehearsals as if he'd been born in the theatre, he looked terrified. With the greatest difficulty, he delivered his cue line, 'He's not that lonesome', and the band began the introduction. Fearfully, he looked towards Rhona, who smiled encouragement and gave him a thumb-up with her free hand. It seemed to brace him, because he launched himself into his song, gaining confidence as he progressed.

There was a dance sequence, and then Annie Oakley's song 'Doin' What Comes Natur'ly', which went superbly well. The girl was a born performer; in fact, the title of the number said everything.

The dress rehearsal came to its close, prompting Helen and Jane to give some last-minute advice, finally making sure everyone knew when to arrive for changing, make-up and so on.

A surprise, casual observer during the last numbers of the rehearsal was Sue Womersley, the naïvely scrupulous member of the Modern Languages Department. She hung around to speak to Rhona after the rest of the band had gone.

'Rhona,' she asked, 'do you remember telling me in France about a limerick? Something to do with your name?'

'Not my name, Sue. It was "Rhoda", as edudciated by Johd Fieldbad, dow workid at the Educatiod Office.' If Sue wanted to be holier-than-thou, it was up to her. It had been a busy day, and Rhona was disinclined to be lectured on that subject or any other.

Surprisingly, she made no criticism, but asked, 'Just what is that limerick?'

'You don't want to know, Sue.'

'I'm not as prim as you like to make out, Rhona, and it's been tantalising me.'

'No, Sue, you're far too demure to hear it.'

'You're just teasing.'

'That's right,' said Rhona, closing her score and picking up her bag, 'but wouldn't you rather be teased than offended? Goodbye, Sue.' She smiled politely and left the hall. It had been a gruelling afternoon.

The evening performance went extremely well, with a capacity audience. Because of the youthful cast, Saturday would see the second, and final, performance, when Matt, Bev and Troy would be there. Troy's mother had declined Matt's offer of a ticket, but neither he nor Rhona was surprised.

Once again, the school hall was filled to capacity. Looking around the auditorium, Rhona suspected that some of the pupils in the audience were there for a second time, but it meant they were keen, and that could only be good.

Matt, Bev and Troy were on the first row of the balcony, and she waved discreetly when she saw them. Not surprisingly, they waved back excitedly.

She thought about the recent parents' evening, when she'd been busy the whole time with anxious parents of the new intake, but Matt had been to see all Troy's teachers, including his old team-mates Malcolm Bennett and Gary Oldfield, both of whom agreed readily that Troy would be treated fairly and without even a suspicion of heavy-handedness. She smiled at the thought.

Soon, the house lights came down, and Jane gave the downbeat for the Overture, with its enticing promises of 'They Say it's Wonderful', 'No Business Like Show Business' and 'I Got the Sun in the Morning', all of which captivated the audience to the extent that most of them forgot to talk through most of it. At all events, prompted by the more theatre-savvy among them, they applauded enthusiastically, and Jane started the music for Scene One. The curtains opened, drawing further applause as Norman Davis's sets earned the audience's much-deserved appreciation, and the show was under way.

The cast, buoyed up by a successful first night, gave another excellent performance, with a couple of members of the band faltering only minutely, and Rhona rescuing them adroitly, so that the audience were doubtless unaware of any momentary wobble.

Applause at the final curtain was more exuberant than ever, resulting in a cast of happy and fulfilled pupils, which was, after all, the main object of the enterprise. Rhona thought it was just a shame that Mrs Caukwell wasn't there to see the good the show had done, but concluded that she would never have acknowledged it, anyway. By contrast, however, three senior members of the cast appeared with bouquets for the hardworking and deserving adults. First, two girls made their presentations to Helen and then Jane, and finally, one of Rhona's Upper Sixth German class, alias Colonel Buffalo Bill, presented his with a flourish. Knowing how important the occasion was for him, she inclined her cheek to receive a surprised kiss and an ebullient cheer from the audience.

It was necessary for as many staff as possible to oversee the after-show party, when spirits were higher than ever, but Rhona was eventually free to leave and make her own way to Matt's house.

When she arrived, Bev was about to go up to bed, but she lingered long enough to tell Rhona how wonderful the entertainment had been. It was the first stage show she'd ever seen. Rhona kissed her goodnight and accepted a welcome drink from Matt.

'Troy chatted about the show all the way home,' he said. 'When I dropped him at the door, his mother didn't even ask him if he'd enjoyed it. There was no word of thanks for us, either.'

'It was the same after *Live and Let Die*,' said Rhona. 'She just wasn't interested.'

'I'm not sure whether she really is a witch without a broomstick,' said Matt, looking into his glass as if it might offer the solution to the mystery, 'or just a disagreeable ignoramus.'

'My money's on the latter, with an added helping of unashamed, selfish slag.'

Suddenly, his expression brightened. 'On a pleasanter note,' he said, 'I felt terribly proud, tonight, when I saw you holding the band together and making sure the cast got their cues. I realised just how important you were to the production, and it meant a lot to me.'

'Oh Matt, that's a lovely thing to say.' She put her glass down to join him in a long, indulgent kiss.

After some time, they broke apart, and Rhona said, 'The only fly in the ointment now is that the Amateurs are getting excited about the opening of the theatre, which means yet more work.'

'I think that calls for an early night,' said Matt.

'Any excuse, but howay, anyway.' Their relationship had developed naturally into the easiest kind. Following a few that had been rather less rewarding, it was particularly welcome for Rhona, and she was aware of none of the niggles and suspicions of the past.

They went upstairs as quietly as usual, avoiding the creaking step and closing the bedroom door gently behind them, whispering as they undressed, and finally sinking into bed in a ready embrace.

28

December

No Holding Santa

As well as the excitement of a new relationship, there were still practical matters to be addressed, the most pressing of which was that of Christmas arrangements. Rhona, had always gone to her parents' home for Christmas Day, along with her grandparents and Steve, supposing communication with the latter were possible, which was sadly not always the case. She discussed the matter with Matt.

'If your mum's catering for half-a-dozen already, it wouldn't be fair to burden her with more,' he said.

'Agreed, but I'm determined to see that Bev and Troy don't get the usual treatment this time.' She added hurriedly, 'I know Bev wouldn't while she's living here, but....'

'I know what you mean.'

Rhona pondered the problem a little longer until a solution emerged. 'I have a suggestion to make, Matt.'

'Trot out your suggestion.'

'Okay. My suggestion is that you and I give Bev and Troy a proper Christmas Day. I'm sure Troy's mam won't mind. In fact, it'll surprise me if she gives a bugger one way or the other, and I'm sure Troy would far rather come here or to my house than stay at home.'

'What about your family?' As ever, Matt was reluctant to see the worthy innocents disappointed.

'They know me well enough, Matt. They'll understand, and I'll go up to them shortly after Christmas. It'll be as if I've never been away.'

'In that case, I'm happy to fall in with your plans. We need to make the most of Christmas, this year.'

'Why this year, particularly?'

He tapped the folded copy of *The Times* that lay on the small table beside him. 'You know the miners are operating an overtime ban, don't you?'

'Yes, but they voted against an all-out strike.'

'That could change quickly. The miners' leaders are spoiling for a fight. Last year's strike failed because the power stations had huge stocks of coal. This time, for my money, they're running them down, either to put pressure on the Government that way, or to ensure that a strike will be successful. Either way, when the power stations run low on coal, that's when the lights will go out. There'll be misery at home and at work, and the theatre will just have to go into limbo until things return to normal.'

Rhona had to admit, albeit to herself, that she hadn't studied the problem to anything like that extent. She was also surprised by Matt's attitude. 'You sound very anti,' she said.

'Oh, I've a degree of sympathy for the miners. Like everyone else, they're finding life difficult with inflation as it is, and it's true that the conditions they have to work in make them a special case, but a forty-two percent increase is ridiculous. The Government won't agree to it, and that can only lead to one thing.'

Rhona nodded sadly. 'Coming from the north-east, I have to say I usually tend to side with them, but I'm inclined to agree about their pay claim.'

As Rhona had prophesied, her family understood her decision and looked forward to seeing her after Christmas. She was also right about Troy's mother, who had recently embarked on a new relationship and who would doubtless value the privacy and freedom of movement Troy's absence would afford.

After the usual tumult associated with the end of term, Rhona was able to apply herself to her new role, preparing the Christmas meal and it's peripheral delights. Bev watched, fascinated, as mince pies left the oven to be placed enticingly on a cooling tray. A teacher by inclination as well as by profession, Rhona quickly recruited her, teaching her yet more skills.

Greater excitement occurred on the day itself when Matt donned a hired Santa suit to carry out the present-giving ritual. Bev and Troy were still recovering from it when Rhona carried the turkey into the dining room and placed it on the table.

'What is it?' asked Troy, torn between curiosity, suspicion and the appetising aroma emanating from it.

'It's a turkey,' Rhona told him.

Both he and Bev stared in wonder, because neither of them had seen one until that moment, having only ever eaten processed turkey roll when the school served Christmas lunch.

They watched Matt carve it and were further surprised when he gave them each a leg as well as a quantity of breast meat. 'The best meat is on the legs,' he told them, and they believed him, because the whole experience was so new.

'Veggies,' said Rhona, indicating the tureens on the table, 'Roast potatoes, Brussels sprouts and carrots. There's chestnut and sausage-meat stuffing as well.'

Troy eyed the sprouts doubtfully, but Bev was quick to reassure him. 'They're not like the ones you get at school, Troy,' she said. 'Rhona cooks 'em properly.'

'I'm going to be in trouble,' said Rhona, 'for putting the school cooks in the shade.'

Having poured wine for Rhona and himself, lager for Bev and something innocuous for Troy, Matt held up his glass to say, 'Before we begin, let's express our thanks to Rhona for preparing this wonderful meal. Thank you, Rhona!'

'It was nothing.' Even so, it was evident that she appreciated the compliment, echoed as it was by Bev and Troy.

The main course was a triumph, but Rhona still had a surprise in store, and its effect was instantly rewarding when she carried in the pudding, now wreathed in flames thanks to a modest application of Matt's precious cognac.

'We'll just wait for the flames to go out,' said Rhona, and then we'll see what you two can find in it, but mind how you dig. You have to be careful with buried treasure. With the flames now extinguished, she cut into the pudding carefully, dividing the secretly-marked portion between them, as her mother and her grandmother had done on many occasions.

The first to detect something unusual in the pudding was Troy, who lifted his greaseproof-wrapped discovery carefully on to the side of his dish, scraping custard and pudding from it with the earnest excitement of an archaeologist unearthing Roman remains. Finally, he removed the wrapping to expose a new coin. 'It's fifty pence,' he said in genuine surprise. Almost immediately, Bev found the same in her portion.

'There's no holding that Santa fella,' said Rhona. 'He just doesn't know when to stop.'

'And neither does his helper,' observed Matt quietly.

Sooner than any of them would have liked, the time came for Troy to go home.

'We're not working 'til the New Year,' Matt told him as Rhona prepared to drive him home, 'but you're welcome to come back tomorrow, if you like, just to be sociable.'

Troy was quiet on the way home, and Rhona found it easy to imagine why. After a day of newly-discovered fun and outgoing company, he was returning to a house in which his mother lived solely for her own pleasure.

'I'll take you to the door,' Rhona told him, letting him out of the passenger side. She held out her arms to him, and he clung to her. 'Come back and see us tomorrow if your mam'll let you.' She had no doubt she would. Meanwhile, he was reluctant to let her go, and she held him a little longer. 'All right, pet lamb, you'd better go inside now, and we'll see you soon.' She kissed him goodnight.

Without a word, he turned his key in the front door and let himself in.

She returned to find Matt and Bev watching the Morecambe and Wise Show. She joined Matt on the sofa.

'Was he all right when you left him?' asked Matt quietly.

Rhona closed her eyes and said, 'I can't talk about it just yet, Matt.'

He squeezed her hand understandingly.

After a while, as much to avoid the subject of Troy as for any other reason, she said, 'The Amateurs are going to find it cold, rehearsing in the theatre.' It had been decided that the opening, when the current situation allowed, would include a concert.

'They have to suffer for their art, Rhona.'

She could only agree. Meanwhile she was concerned about the work on the interior. 'Is there much more to do?' she asked.

'Just a few finishing touches and the boiler will have to be commissioned, but that's impossible without oil.'

She nodded. 'All the same, it's a huge achievement.' She added, 'Mainly yours.'

'Oh, I don't know. Others have made their contribution.'

'But you've done more than anybody, and you've masterminded the whole operation.'

He smiled. 'Like Noel Coward and Michael Caine in *The Italian Job*?'

'Yes, but more quietly and without leaving anything dangling over a cliff.'

Bev stirred from her place in front of the TV and said, 'I'm knackered. I think I'll go to bed.' Getting up, she said, 'It's been a brilliant Christmas. Thank you.'

'Good girl,' said Rhona. 'You're welcome.'

'It was a pity Troy had to go home.'

'Yes, it was.' There wasn't much else she could say except, ''Night-'night, Bev.'

''Night-'night, Rhona.' She bent for a kiss and, because it was becoming a habit, she bent quite naturally to kiss Matt as well.

When Bev had gone up to bed, Matt put his arm round Rhona and said, 'You made today as special as it was.'

'Not just me, Matt.'

'But mainly you.'

She didn't take the argument any further, being preoccupied with something else. 'It was awful,' she said, 'having to leave Troy at his mam's.'

'I got that impression, and I'm not surprised. All the same, though, we gave him a Christmas Day he's never going to forget.'

'It just seemed so awful after such a lovely day.'

'I know,' he said, drawing her closer, 'but consider this. He's used to it, and he can cope with life at home much better than you can cope with the thought of it.' He considered what he'd just said, and asked, 'Does that make sense?'

'It makes perfect sense.' After a little more thought, she said, 'I'm in the wrong job.'

'There's a lot of people who'd disagree with that. I'm thinking of all those people who saw you hold *Annie Get Your Gun* together.'

'Oh, that was nothing. When I say I'm in the wrong job, I mean that I'm supposed to teach those kids without ever getting involved in their troubles and, sometimes I just want to take them home.'

'But only once in a while.'

'Once in a while is enough, Matt.'

'It means you're not in the wrong job but, like every other earth mother, you are only human.' He looked into her eyes to check that his words had registered, and said, 'It's just as well, because I can feel bedtime coming on.'

Suddenly, she brightened and asked, 'Are you going to wear your Father Christmas outfit?'

'I suppose I could be persuaded. I was thinking of hanging it up neatly in the wardrobe, leaving my wellies in the porch, and shaving my whiskers off until next Christmas.'

'You wouldn't be such a rotten spoilsport, would you? Tell me you wouldn't.'

He thought for a moment and said, 'I was tempted but, seeing your little face just now, I couldn't bring myself to disappoint you.'

'I know. There's no holding Santa, is there?' She stood up and beckoned to him. 'Howay, then.'

29

FEBRUARY 1974

CELEBRATION BY CANDLELIGHT

With Britain officially on a three-day week and the price of oil showing no sign of returning to a sane level the misery seemed endless.

'I'd been thinking of getting a smaller car,' said Rhona, 'and when I went looking, I was told that my car, which was recently valued at seven-hundred-and-fifty is now worth four-hundred-and-fifty. It's because it has a fifteen-hundred cc engine, and I certainly don't call that big.'

'Be gentle on the accelerator,' Matt advised her. 'It's the only way to save petrol, and prices will return to normal one day.'

'What a prospect. Meanwhile, I've been playing the piano at rehearsals in woollen gloves. The results are extraordinary as well as discordant, and even in gloves I have to stop occasionally, sometimes in mid-song, to restart my circulation.'

'They should be thankful for small verses.'

'Don't you mean "small mercies"?'

'Yes, it was a sort of play on words.'

'Even my brain's iced up,' said Rhona miserably. 'I don't even know when you're making a feeble joke.' Forcing herself to think of other things, she asked, 'Do you think the election will make a scrap of difference?'

'Who can say? We don't yet know who's going to win. Both sides say that if they win they'll get the miners back to work. They'll just go about it a different way.'

The General Election seemed to be in everyone's thoughts. At school, a pupil would ask apropos of nothing, 'Who do you want to win the election, Miss?'

Rhona would say, 'Mike Yarwood. He can replace all three party leaders and probably talk more sense than any of them.' Yarwood was such a popular impressionist, even the less-able kids had seen him on television and knew who he was.

Some would press her further. 'No, seriously, Miss, who do you think is right, Heath or Wilson?'

'I'm much more interested in teaching you about the dative case. In any case, teachers don't discuss politics with pupils.'

'Mr Bennett does, Miss. He says if was up to him he'd ban trade unions and make going on strike illegal. Mr Oldfield agrees with him.'

It was basically what she might have expected of the Metalwork and PE Departments, although she had to wonder how popular Gary Oldfield's Jordanesque views would be in his native colliery town of Barnsley. Still, she had to maintain a non-political stance. 'I don't care what they say. I'm not going to discuss the election, but I am waiting to start this lesson, or would you rather fail O level miserably? That's what you'll do if you insist on talking politics in lesson time.'

Meanwhile, the staffroom was a place of intense political argument, with Labour and Conservative sympathisers seemingly in equal numbers. There were some, as well, who erred towards either the lunatic left or the risible right, one extreme advocated inviting Leonid Brezhnev to occupy Buckingham Palace, whilst the other earnestly suggested that a military junta with unlimited powers offered the logical answer to the nation's woes. Rhona found it pleasanter to avoid the staffroom altogether. At times, she even envied the furry, woodland creatures who opted to hibernate. The twenty-first of March would be an excellent time to re-emerge, yawning and stretching, with birds singing, all disputes settled and life much as it had been in earlier, saner times. With no such option available to her, however, she continued to live with increasingly gritted teeth and whitening knuckles, hoping for an end to the fevered polarisation that gripped the population.

Marking had become a welcome distraction. Also, very occasionally, she would take time to talk to her mother on the mutual understanding that they would discuss anything but politics. On one occasion, they found themselves discussing Rhona's brother Steve and his girlfriend Caroline, and Rhona learned that, incredibly, they were still together.

'I don't believe it, Mam. What special quality has she got, or is it a revolutionary kind of glue she's found?'

'Don't be like that, Rhona. She's a very nice girl, and our Steve's obviously decided to buck his ideas up an' all.'

'Has he got a job yet?'

'Apparently, but I've only got half a story so far. It seems that Steve and Caroline have joined forces. She's somehow found a way of channelling his artistic talent, although that's as much as I know.'

'I'm intrigued, Mam. You will let me know when you find out more, won't you?'

'Of course I will, and on that subject....' She was going to ask about Matt. Rhona knew the signs, and surely enough, her mother went on to ask, 'How are things between you and Matt?'

'Things between us are very nice, thank you. The theatre is almost finished. Did I tell you?'

'In a minute, bonny lass. Last time we saw you, you and Matt had been playing happy families at his house.'

'We had Christmas Day with Bev and her brother Troy, Mam, that's all.'

'What a strange name. Is his mam keen on Thomas Hardy?'

'I can't imagine she's ever heard of him. In fact, I'd be surprised if she's ever opened a book. Her first choice of name for him was Dart, after the character in *Space Patrol*, but she changed it to Troy two years later, after the main character in *Stingray*.'

Even over the telephone, her mother's disbelief was tangible. 'No, you're making it up. Poor little bairn, havin' his name changed when he was two, and such a silly name an' all.'

'No one could make it up, Mam. When she's not entertaining her boyfriends, she watches kiddies' television, and you can gauge the level of her interest in the other when I tell you that she doesn't see a lot of television nowadays.'

'Well, at least you managed to give the poor bairns a proper Christmas Day.'

'That's right, Mam. By the way, what's me dad working on now?'

It was a crude stroke, but any way of distracting her mother from the subject of Matt and her was worth trying.

'Oh, he's gone back to the kind of thing he was doing when he met me. His latest story is about a thing called a Q-ship. It's based on HMS *Hosta*, which was his ship at the time.'

'What's a Q-ship?'

'It was a warship disguised as a merchant ship, a sort of wolf in sheep's clothing that suddenly revealed itself in its true colours when a U-boat surfaced.'

'It sounds sneaky to me.' It was also keeping her mother from introducing the topic of matchmaking, which was good.

'Well, all's fair in love and war, and the U-boats didn't exactly play according to the rules, did they?'

'Ah, I see. It was one underhand trick to combat another.'

'That's right. Anyway, just what is the situation between you and Matt?'

Rhona had to admit defeat.

Matt's phone call brought welcome news. 'We've had a delivery of oil,' he told her, 'so now Terry and I can get on with commissioning the boiler. We just need an end to this blasted three-day week, and then we can set a date for the opening and the concert.'

'It seems so cruel,' said Rhona, 'that the thing we've been looking forward to for so long has to be overshadowed by harshness and unpleasantness.'

'Maybe you're looking at it the wrong way round,' suggested Matt.

'Do you mean that the opening will be like the Festival of Britain, an occasion for celebration and enjoyment during an otherwise bleak and dismal episode?'

'Not in so many words, but that's the sort of thing I had in mind.'

After an extremely lacklustre committee meeting of the Amateurs, Rhona drove Matt back to his house. When they arrived, she saw for the first time a notice in his kitchen window. It read:

NOTICE TO POLITICAL CANVASSERS
HOW I VOTE IS MY AFFAIR, SO BUGGER OFF!

'I'm inclined to agree,' she said.

They went inside, and Matt had just poured two glasses of wine when the lights went out. 'Bugger,' he said good-naturedly. 'Now we'll have to drink it by candlelight.'

'Have you still got some candles?' They had become almost impossible to find during the three-day week.

'Specially imported from France,' he confirmed. 'All I have to do is find them in the dark, and I think Bev must have taken the torch.' He hunted around in the dark until he found a torch. 'I accused the poor girl wrongly,' he said, locating the candles. 'It's Friday, it's dark and it's cold. What shall we do, Rhona?'

'It seems to me we haven't a lot of choice,' she said. 'In fact, there's only one course of action open to us.'

'You're not suggesting...?'

'I am,' she confirmed. 'Let's carry the wine and these candles upstairs, and... find somewhere warm to spend the night.'

'I know the very place.'

'So do I.'

In the next couple of weeks, they spent a great deal of time in the seclusion and warmth of that place, and with no one to blame but those who had created the problem in the first place. Like the proposed opening of the theatre, it was an agreeable, convivial activity at a time of open conflict, and they were happily aware of it. In fact, they could have been tempted to spend the remainder of the month in that special place, but for the intervention of everyday matters, such as joinery and teaching, but they agreed that it remained nevertheless a welcome retreat from those mundane interruptions.

'This seems so natural,' said Matt during a convenient interval, 'that the question of where we go from here springs to mind.'

'Are you asking me to move in with you?'

'Without wishing to appear at all forward, the fact is, yes, that's what I'm asking.'

She shook her head at his diffident manner, and then, sensing that she might have conveyed the wrong message, said, 'You had only to ask, Matt.'

It was a step forward and welcome agreement at a time of stalemate and suspense.

30

MARCH

ALL IS REVEALED

F ar from being decisive, the close outcome of the General Election kept the population in suspense for several days, until Edward Heath, the outgoing prime minister, accepted that he was unable to strike a bargain with the Liberal Party, and conceded the election. Accordingly, Harold Wilson moved into Number Ten. The National Union of Mineworkers accepted an offer of thirty-five percent, an award that one half of the population found appallingly extravagant and some regarded as absurd, whilst others were simply relieved to see an end to the three-day week. The date of the Grand Opening of Akengarth Theatre, as it was now known, could be set and, purely out of sentiment, the committee chose the twenty-first of March, the first day of spring. The *Netherdale Reporter* was ready to create a double-page feature, which, according to Matt, would be supportive, if unintentionally humorous by virtue of its inevitable mis-spellings. Thankful as ever for small mercies, he learned that the licence for the bar was already in force.

'A lot of people have been in just to nosey around instead of waiting for the concert,' observed Rhona, 'and to criticise.'

'It was ever thus,' said Matt. 'You'll always find people who won't lift a finger to help, but who'll always be ready to belittle the achievements of those who have.'

Another development was that the move was complete, and Rhona's cottage was now up for sale. Her parents accepted the news quietly, withholding judgement, at least until they could express it privately. Her grandparents were more traditionally inclined; in fact, her granny had been typically outspoken, saying, 'Well, I think that the sooner he makes an honest woman of her, the better things'll be all round.'

If Rhona and Matt were concerned about the family's reaction, they had little time to consider it, as preparations for the Grand Opening made repeated demands on them, although Rhona's contribution was in rehearsal only. For the actual concert, musicians had been hired along with what resembled a mountain of band parts for the varied programme.

On the night, Rhona and Matt along with the others involved, had to submit to being thanked publicly for their efforts. It was inevitable and, mercifully, it was over fairly quickly. After that, the programme was allowed to begin.

There were items provided by the 'usual suspects', the old stagers, who'd been with the society for years, and who wouldn't be left out, which meant that songs from *The White Horse Inn* and *The Desert Song* re-emerged, possibly for the last time. The event was extra-special for them, so the others were inclined to indulge them. There were also younger members, including juniors who Rhona knew from school, and some of them showed real ability. Rhona's attention, however, was taken by the sheer ambience of the new theatre, the realisation of her vision and the culmination of much hard work and dedication. The fact that the performers were enjoying their spell in the limelight was a bonus she found impossible to begrudge. That, after all, was the theatre's purpose. In all, the evening's celebrations were a temporary distraction from another, nagging preoccupation, for which she was grateful.

Towards the end of the concert, she became conscious that Matt was preoccupied. The signs were easy to read and, naturally, she waited until they were back at Matt's house before asking him what was on his mind. They were actually in bed by that time, so conversation should have been easy.

'I was thinking about the upstairs store room,' he began, a little mysteriously.

'As one does on a gala opening night. What on earth made you think of that?'

'It's full of junk.'

'I think you could say that about most store rooms, box rooms and the like.' He wasn't making a great deal of sense, but she was prepared to give him time.

'I was wondering about converting it into a bedroom, so that Troy doesn't have to face the prospect of going home after a day like Christmas Day, or even when we've been to the cinema.'

'Or the theatre.' Rhona was still enjoying the novelty, but she was nevertheless conscious of Matt's problem, which clearly needed to be aired. 'It's difficult for you, isn't it?'

'It is. Troy enjoys being here and working with Bev and me, but that's as far as it can go. Bev was over eighteen and legally entitled to make her own decision when I took her in.' He left the rest unsaid.

'As a single man,' she agreed, 'you're in an awkward position, even with his mother in agreement.' On reflection, she said, 'Chances are, she'd agree to anything, but yes, you're right, Matt.'

'While we're on the subject of being single....' Clearly, he'd been thinking about it.

'Yes?' she coaxed, aware that, for some reason, Matt wasn't his usual articulate self. Something was troubling him.

He managed to ask, 'Could you face the idea of spending the rest of your life with a man who consistently produces lazy sperm?'

It wasn't the kind of question Rhona was used to considering, so she had to think carefully about her answer. 'Not just *any* man with lazy sperm, I have to say. I mean, off hand, I can't think of a great many men with that characteristic, but if a long line of them were to present themselves at the door, each offering lifelong commitment, I feel I'd have to disappoint them.'

'Oh.'

'However, if the man you have in mind is yourself, I'd be more inclined to make a favourable response.' She raised herself to look into his eyes and say, 'I hope that clears things up.'

'Ah.' He sounded defensive. 'You see, I'm not asking because of the Bev and Troy situation. You mustn't think that.'

'But it would ease the problem, all the same.'

'It probably would, but that really is not why I'm asking. You must understand that.'

'You've already told me that, Matt, but the fact is, you haven't actually asked me yet. You've only posed a particularly prosaic and unusual question about a hypothetical man with lazy sperm. I think we've ascertained that you're the man in your hypothesis, but that's as far as we've come. While we're on the subject, though, if it's not because of the Bev and Troy situation, why would you be asking, supposing you ever got around to it?' His lack of directness seemed very odd, given that they were both naked and in close proximity, a situation that encouraged intimate communication if ever a situation did.

Urgency finally overcame diffidence, and he said, 'Because I love you, you soppy ha'porth.'

'That wasn't the smoothest of protestations, but it does make a difference.'

Matt stirred uncomfortably, having looked more than awkward from the moment he introduced the subject. 'What do you say?' he asked.

'My answer, you great wally, is "yes", even though your proposition should be preserved as an example of the kind to be avoided at all costs.'

'That's wonderful, Rhona. Shall we… I mean, not just live together, but get married, like your granny says?'

Rhona thought of her granny's reaction to the news of their cohabitation. 'It would be safest, at least while she can still wield a rolling pin.' Becoming more serious, she said, 'Now that we're agreed, maybe we should get a move on.'

'Why?'

She was glad he'd asked that question as well as the other, because she had something to tell him. 'I make the suggestion because I suspect… no, I know for a fact, that one contraceptive, and it does take only one, has proved itself unworthy of the description, and that one of your normally bone-idle sperm cells chose the very moment of that malfunction to break into a sprint. In other words,' she said, pointing unnecessarily to her lower abdomen, 'there's a potential joiner and builder growing in here, and I think we need to act before he finds the exit and starts hammering on the door to be let out.'

'Are you absolutely sure?'

'Positive. It's been confirmed.'

'Oh, bliss. Rhona,' he said, 'rolling over to face her, 'I love you.'

'Now, that's a lot more like it. I love you too. Shall we celebrate?'

'I think we should.'

'And we don't need to bother with protective clothing, now.'

Much later, Rhona asked, 'Could you possibly take a weekend off to come with me to Northumberland?'

'To ask formally for your hand?'

'More to apologise for helping yourself to the other bits, really, but that's the general idea.'

He thought quickly. 'I'm sure I can. Will I have to meet your granny?'

'Yes, but don't worry. You're a reformed sinner, and she usually goes easy on them. You'll be all right with my grandad, because you trained Bev, and she impressed him no end.'

'It's a complicated business.'

'It is,' she agreed. 'By the way, what's the situation with the new bedroom, now that Little Joiner's on his way?'

'I can always extend the house into the yard.'

'Poor little bairn. Would you really make your first-born sleep in an extension?'

'No, we can plan the details of who sleeps where later.' Looking thoughtful, he asked, 'When do you want to go up to Northumberland?'

'As soon as possible, really. Have you anything planned for this weekend?'

'No, give me time to pack a bag and my hard hat, and I'll be ready.'

'What do you need your hard hat for?'

'In case your granny's not so forgiving after all.'

Matt received a friendly greeting in Newcastle, although Rhona's granny couldn't resist making a reference to her unplanned pregnancy. 'You'd best be quick about organising the wedding, hinny. That's if you don't want to be embarrassed.'

'That lass down the road started in labour the moment she stepped into the weddin' car,' said Rhona's grandad. 'The chauffeur wasn't too happy about the state of his Daimler afterwards.'

'That'll do from you, Bill Headley,' said his wife. 'There's no need for coarseness.'

The old man shook his head sorrowfully. I cannot say a word in this house without gettin' wrong,' he said. 'Matt, come an' let's have a bit crack about that lass you've got in indentures. You're makin' a good job of trainin' her, I reckon.'

'Aye,' said his wife. 'You two talk about buildin' while Rhona an' me talk about the important things.'

'They've been married sixty years,' said Rhona as they left the house, 'and she still treats him like a bairn.'

'They're lovely, genuine people,' he said.

'You're just relieved because me granny wasn't waiting for you with the rolling pin.'

'There was that,' he admitted.

They left Newcastle, and Matt, who had never visited the north-east, watched through the passenger window as the unfamiliar countryside came and went. Eventually, they reached Amble and joined Ivor and Grace at their house. Before long, Matt and Ivor got into a discussion about Ivor's wartime experiences and the way he worked them into his novels. They retreated into Ivor's den, the walls of which were covered with photographs of warships and the men who'd manned them. Meanwhile, Rhona and her mother discussed more recent, as well as immediate, matters.

'Where are you going to be married?' asked her mother.

'It has to be in the parish where I live, and the vicar's a nice old soul. I know him through school.'

'Well, what about the reception?'

'There's a smashin' place in Akengarth, Mam. I know you an' me dad, me granny and grandad and Steve and Caroline have to come down, but most of the people who'll be there will be friends, so it needs to be local.'

Her mother saw her reasoning. 'We'll bring your granny and grandad,' she said, 'and Steve and Caroline can make their own way down, as they have their own transport.'

'And they're still together?' Rhona marvelled at the news, unlikely as it had seemed.

'More than that, they're business partners, but they'll tell you all about that when they arrive.'

'When are they coming?'

'This afternoon. They called at your granny's and grandad's earlier. They must have just missed you.' Inclining her head towards the door of Ivor's den, she said in a loud voice that was meant to carry, 'Hopefully your dad'll stop talking to Matt about ships long enough for him to meet 'em.'

In fact, Rhona's brother and his girlfriend arrived within the next half-hour, and Matt did get to meet them. Steve, on the other hand, lost no time in teasing Rhona.

'Hello, Sis. Mam tells me you're up the duff. It's not showing yet, is it?' He looked pointedly at the place where he expected the bulge to appear.

'Of course it isn't, you cheeky bugger. 'It won't show 'til about seven months.'

'How will this affect your surrogate family?' asked her mother, simultaneously aiming a smack at Steve.

'It won't. Bev's a fixture, anyway, and Troy needs all the love and support we can give him. Little Joiner will fit in with everybody, I'm sure.'

'Little who?' asked her father.

'We haven't thought of any names yet, so this one takes his name, at least for the time being, from his dad's line of work.'

'It makes sense,' said Steve, possibly envisaging a later addition with the given name of Arthur, or 'Art' for short.

'Talking of work,' said Rhona, who was still curious about her brother's most recent venture, 'what's this joint initiative of yours I've been hearing about?'

'We're now in the business,' said Caroline, 'of canine *couture* or, if you prefer it, what the well-dressed dog is wearing this season.'

Rhona remembered her initial impression of Caroline, with her dark, immaculate appearance and was as impressed as ever, but she couldn't help closing her eyes in disbelief at what she'd just heard.

'I know it sounds quirky,' said Caroline, 'but there's a growing market for it. Steve's designed some prints that everyone thinks are wonderful, and I have to say they are. He also designs the garments, which are basically coats and hats for all seasons.'

Rhona continued to stare in disbelief.

'That's PVC raincoats, quilted overcoats, jackets and all-in-ones and, of course, sun and rain hats.' An omission came belatedly to mind. 'Oh yes, we make wedding outfits too.' Reading the startled looks around her correctly, she explained, 'No, not wedding dresses for dogs, but special clothing for dogs to wear as guests. People want to take their pets to weddings and, let's be honest, a wedding is there for everyone to enjoy. We offer a black jacket and morning dress stripes for male dogs and something rather more glamorous for the female of the species. In the case of the ever-popular, Scottish-themed wedding, we realise that a kilt and a sporran would present practical difficulties, but we can still offer an ensemble in the appropriate tartan.' She ignored the stupefied expressions around her and said, 'I cut the patterns, and we get a machinist to turn out the finished product complete with our registered trademark. Our firm is called "Cutting a Dash", and our monogram "CAD" surmounts the image of a well-dressed Dachshund.'

'Why-yer-bugger,' said Grace, forgetting herself for the moment. 'What did your granny and grandad say when you told them about all this, Steve?'

'I cannot repeat it in mixed company, Mam, but I will say that Granny gave Grandad no end of a tellin' off about usin' language.' On reflection, he said, 'Old folks can be slow to pick up on new ideas. At least, that's what we've found.'

'In this case, so am I,' said Rhona, and it was evident from Matt's expression that he was similarly in denial. Grace and Ivor simply looked stunned.

'Well,' said Caroline, whose earnestness hadn't wavered throughout her disclosure, 'whether or not they understand it, or even approve of it, the fact remains that there's a lot of folks out there who want to dress their dogs in daft outfits, an' no one can blame us for taking advantage of it.'

Summoning a distant memory, Matt managed to say, 'I think this is where you and I came in, Rhona.'

'Why aye,' she said, recovering sufficiently from her daze to recall their first meeting, 'it's all coming back to me now.'

THE END